W9-DFN-917

WITHDRAWN

REVIVAL SEASON

REVIVAL SEASON

MONICA WEST

A Novel

THORNDIKE PRESS
A part of Gale, a Cengage Company

LIBRARY OF CONGRESS CIP DATA ON FILE.
CATALOGUING IN PUBLICATION FOR THIS BOOK
IS AVAILABLE FROM THE LIBRARY OF CONGRESS.

ISBN-13: 978-1-4328-9413-9 (hardcover alk. paper)

Published in 2022 by arrangement with Simon & Schuster, Inc.

Printed in Mexico
Print Number: 01   Print Year: 2022

To my parents, Henry and Edna West,
for roots and wings

ONE

We rumbled toward Georgia from the west, the direction from which all great and powerful things originated. "Except the sun," Caleb said, feeling particularly feisty as the novelty of another revival season settled in. Ma turned and shot him the look where her dark eyes narrowed into slits. Then she spun back around, closed her eyes, and mumbled a prayer: "Lord, watch over these Your children. Use us to do Your will. Amen."

Done praying, Ma refocused her attention to the map she was holding in the air; her finger landed on a bold black dot, far from the big star at the center of the state. We always went to smaller cities — tiny dots that surrounded the capital's star like satellites. Her stubby, unmanicured nail tracing the winding path to Americus, Georgia, was nothing like the polished nails in the magazines that I snuck glimpses of in the library.

Nails that we would never be able to have, since vanity was an unforgivable sin. I'd learned that lesson the hard way last spring when my best friend, Micah, and I had sat in the middle of her bedroom floor, an open bottle of nail polish between us. Micah lifted the wand and smoothed the shiny orb of light pink lacquer on my thumbnail. *So faint no one will notice,* she said. When I got home the next morning and linked my hand with Papa's to pray for breakfast, he forced me to remove the polish under his watchful eye before anyone could lift a fork to their mouths.

I watched Ma in the rearview mirror as the minivan merged onto the Texas highway. Papa turned up the radio as our van became one of an anonymous throng of vehicles barreling beneath an overpass. But none of the other cars had the important task that we did: driving nine hundred miles to bring the word of God to people who needed to be saved from their sins. The exhilaration before the first revival of a new season meant I could barely sit still between the cracked windows whose building pressure buffeted my ears. We'd been doing this for years — twelve, to be exact — but somehow this first moment of revival season, when everything was possible, never got old.

We pulled into our ceremonial first stop — a tacky diner 281 miles away from our house in East Mansfield, Texas. Soon, conversation flowed as we pierced straws through plastic lids and drank the syrupy sweet soda we were only allowed to have during this inaugural revival season meal. With our hands curled around sweaty paper cups, Papa dreamed out loud.

"I might break the two-thousand-soul mark this year. Wouldn't that be a blessing?"

It would be more than a blessing — it would be a miracle. The two-thousand-soul mark had been elusive for all of Papa's years of leading revivals; it was three times more than last year's soul count, and it would be even harder to accomplish this year.

"There will be lines around the tent waiting for me when I arrive. This is the year, Hortons."

My eyes searched the table's shiny surface as I took another deep sip. The caffeine made the lights extra bright as they bounced off the orange plastic tables, and it amplified the clink of ice coming from surrounding booths. The combined effect made Papa's words seem slightly forced.

"Any naysayer would tell you that's impossible, but they don't know my God," he said.

I wondered if a small part of Papa believed what those people said, especially after what happened at last year's revival, but I pushed the doubts out of my mind. Doubt was a sin.

"Back to the van, Hortons!" Papa urged. I savored the last sips of my soda and stilled the jitter in my limbs as I took my half-eaten lunch to the trash. Each rotation of the tires brought us closer to Americus, and the promise of what this revival season might have in store came into focus as we slid beneath the mournful weeping willows of Louisiana. As Louisiana passed us off to Mississippi, a thick wall of humidity smacked us in the face. By the time Georgia's plump peach welcomed us on the highway sign, the weight of this year's revival season fell on the car like a lead blanket.

Papa cracked the front windows to let in the moist air. "You smell that? That's the smell of pagan land."

My little sister, Hannah, rocked next to me; clicking sounds rose from the back of her throat, and her elbows were frozen in acute angles in front of her chest.

"Can you make her be quiet?" Papa hissed toward us in the back seat. I patted Hannah's knee and handed her the soft rubber ball that was reserved for moments like these. She reached out a clawlike hand and pulled it toward her chest, rolling the ball between her fingers and kneading it like dough. Her limbs slackened, and she loosened her jaw.

Ma and Papa never told me or my younger brother, Caleb, what was wrong with Hannah. At least not directly. Once, back in Texas, I woke up long after I thought everyone else was asleep. As I tiptoed past my parents' bedroom on my way downstairs for a glass of water, I overheard Papa say that Hannah had cerebral palsy, but his accusatory tone sounded like Hannah's disease was the result of some flaw in Ma's faith. I hurried away before I could hear her response.

Papa pulled in front of a tiny brick building with only a narrow white steeple to identify it as a church. It was much smaller than the churches we were accustomed to visiting. He took a long glance at the parking lot with only a few dozen spaces and released a sigh that sounded like it had built up over the entire ride.

"Here we are," Papa announced in a flat tone before getting out of the car.

Through the windows, we watched a large, dark-skinned man with a swollen belly that protruded over the top of his pants approach Papa. They embraced in an awkward hug; then the man looked over Papa's shoulder and pointed to the car where we all sat. As he lifted his arms to beckon us, two oblong stains darkened the armpits of his dress shirt. We tumbled out of the van: first Caleb, then my mother, then eight-year-old Hannah, then me.

We followed Reverend Davenport into the claustrophobic sanctuary of the New Rock Baptist Church, where three rows of folding chairs faced a raised pulpit. Behind the altar, an ornate gold cross was situated between two paintings of the crucifixion.

"Thanks so much for inviting us." Papa scanned his surroundings, probably comparing this sanctuary to the cavernous ones of last year's circuit. "This is my wife, Joanne; my son, Caleb; and my daughters, Miriam and Hannah."

Ma handed Hannah over to me — I folded my arms around Hannah's chest and felt her fragile rib cage like so many bowed toothpicks, her rapid heartbeat, her body's metronomic perpetual motion. Ma stepped in Papa's long shadow to meet the reverend, but he looked past her to Caleb. Ma, Hannah, and I were barely a blip on his radar.

We followed the reverend to the fellowship hall, where a platter of fried chicken, a bowl of mashed potatoes, and a plate of crisp string beans were arranged on a long table. Reverend Davenport dipped his chin ever so slightly. I couldn't even tell that he was praying until I heard his soft words. "Lord, bless these gifts that we receive for the nourishment of our bodies and the building of Your kingdom. Amen."

We sat down to eat. The food was passed in silence, first to Papa and Caleb, then to the reverend. When my mother received the platter, she carefully selected a breast — not too small, not too big. When it was finally my turn, I selected a drumstick for Hannah before reaching back on the platter for my piece.

"Don't take too much," Ma whispered as I selected a thigh. She yanked the plate from me before I could get another piece and nodded at Papa. I gnawed on the crispy skin as Reverend Davenport pulled Papa aside during the meal. They walked to the far wall and stood below an oil painting of the Last Supper. I pretended to study the Apostles as I tried to hear what they were whispering. Reverend Davenport drew invisible shapes in the air with his index finger. He shielded his mouth with his hand as they talked, but snatches of the conversation about money and revenue and how to bring the most people to Christ rode the air back to me. Reverend Davenport was saying something about healing when his gaze found my face, and I hurried to shift my stare to the translucent grease spots that the chicken had left behind on my plate. But I was too late, my eyes too slow in their sockets to change course.

"You're curious, aren't ya?" He said it like a joke, but it wasn't — the emphasis on *curious* made sure of that. I kept my eyes fixed on my plate; when I looked up, my mother's eyes were once again narrowing, this time at me.

"We've had a long drive. Do you think that you could show us to the house? Then you and my husband could have some quiet time to talk. Alone." My mother spoke up with a mouthful of partially chewed chicken. I thanked her with a sheepish glance that she didn't return.

Before Reverend Davenport could respond, a thin, light-skinned woman appeared from the kitchen adjacent to the fellowship hall. She wiped her hands on an apron and offered to walk us back to where we would be staying for the weeklong revival.

"I'm Frieda Davenport," she said when

we got outside. She shook hands with Ma. As they walked beside each other, Ma's short stride quickened to keep pace with Mrs. Davenport. With each step, Ma's knee-highs slid farther down her calves and pooled around her ankles above the scuffed flats that she always wore on long trips. Hannah and I trudged through the grass several yards behind them.

For most revivals, they put us in a mobile home or a small house attached to the church, but Mrs. Davenport opened the door to a house so new that it still smelled like plywood and drywall. Hannah broke free of my grip and dropped to her knees, her knotted hands running along the hard-wood floor in a back-and-forth motion, the corners of her mouth lifting into the closest thing to a smile she could manage.

"I'm glad someone noticed the floor we just had done," Mrs. Davenport said. "Reverend Davenport ordered it all the way from Chattanooga."

Chattanooga. The Sunday school kids back in Texas had likely never been to Chattanooga and probably couldn't even point it out on a map, but we'd driven through it last summer on our way to a weeklong revival at City of Eternal Hope Baptist Church. I remembered how the heavy air seeped into the walls of the tent, and how Papa had converted 218 souls in that seven-day period, more than any other revival in the church's history.

I unzipped my duffel bag in the room I would share with Hannah. Hannah's clothes were always easy to fit into the top drawer — small T-shirts with logos of zoo animals, long skirts in earth tones, and knee socks that covered her leg braces. I placed her stuffed tiger on top of her pillow: it was the one thing that could bring her comfort during rough nights when she thrashed herself awake under the covers.

When I finished unpacking, I changed Hannah into her pajamas and helped her into bed before climbing in beside her. Her body grew still, and I leaned closer to the curved cartilage of her right ear to tell her my favorite bedtime story: Miriam and Moses. I invented details about the way Miriam's mother's fingers bled on the papyrus reeds as she wove a basket to save her newborn son, Moses, from Pharaoh's proclamation that all baby boys should be drowned. As I spun words into the dark cove of her ear, I imagined my namesake watching over her baby brother in that basket, doing as her mother told her.

Hannah's body grew heavy as it leaned

into mine; her snoring, full and sonorous, cut off the end of my sentence. I nestled behind her with my arms around her expanding and contracting chest, playing the rest of the story out in my head, even as I kept the ending pressed behind stilled lips — about how Miriam's actions saved her brother and how her bravery was overshadowed by Moses's later success. I told Hannah the story the same way Ma had told it to me — with Miriam as the hero — even though Papa always emphasized Moses. When Hannah's breathing was slow and steady, I slid out from behind her, careful not to wake her.

The cloistered room blocked out the noise from outside. I knelt beside the patchwork spread that Ma had given me five years ago for my tenth birthday. I brought it on every revival trip — it took up the most space in the single duffel bag that each of us was allowed to shove in the back of the van. It was the only quilt I had ever prayed on, and Papa had once told me that the best thing I could do for revival was to pray every night. There was so much that we didn't have control over during these trips — summer thunderstorms, low turnout. So I took that charge seriously. When we had standing-room-only crowds that were packed inside the tent's vinyl walls, I knew I had some role in it.

I ran my finger along the jagged seams where each memory shared borders with another. In the middle of the quilt was a heart patch where I placed my elbows — close enough to each other so my hands could make a steeple with the pads of my fingers pressed together. The narrow space between my palms was the perfect size for my nose. I closed my eyes and exhaled the day. I filled my lungs with air that I liked to imagine was purified by the Holy Spirit, even though it smelled just like the old air. Back out and then in. After the third exhale, it was time.

" 'Our Father, who art in heaven,' " I began. The words of the Lord's Prayer spilled over the quilt. As I prayed, tension that I hadn't even known had built up in my shoulders and back released. I stayed on my knees until I had covered everything — healing the world, watching over my family, blessing this revival season, making me obedient. Some of those requests seemed harder to grant than others, but I had to ask anyway. God didn't ask us to limit His power, and when we only ask for things that feel achievable, we question Him. And questioning God is the root of evil.

"Amen." I ended the prayer and rose from the side of the bed. My legs felt heavy when I stretched them, but the evening's devotions had just gotten started. Climbing into bed, I opened the Bible and skimmed the chapter in Proverbs that I knew by heart before ending with a prayer of gratitude for arriving safely in Americus. I flipped open my prayer journal, past the scrawl from several years ago when I wondered if Jesus loved Baptists more since that's what we were. Papa said that even though all Christian denominations were equal in God's eyes, God looked on our family more favorably because we traveled around the South each summer, bringing the word of God like manna to the starving.

I closed my Bible and journal. For a few moments after I finished reading, a feeling of warmth settled over me. In our house, God was more than the being that people blindly worshipped on Sundays and forgot about until they needed something else. To us, God was more flesh than spirit, more being than ghost. Each morning when I thanked Him for a new day, I didn't just speak into an echo chamber. As I lay in an unfamiliar bedroom, I felt God right next to me, His breath in my ear like wind.

Even though our God saved souls and

healed bodies, He needed someone on earth to be his intermediary — that was where Papa came in. There were always doubters who shut doors in our faces as we tried to bring them into the light, but they didn't know what we knew. That the "song and dance" that they swore was a performance for money was real. All across the South, Papa had touched people and removed incurable diseases from their bodies. And those people who swore God wasn't real, who claimed that we were deluded Jesus freaks, had never set foot inside a revival tent and felt the spirit of God descend when Papa began to heal. And even though he hurt that girl last summer — something I could barely even admit to myself — that one failure didn't negate the fact that countless people who had been wheeled into the tent had walked back outside after Papa had touched them. If the naysayers had seen him when he was on fire, he would have turned them from skeptics to believers in one service.

I woke up disoriented and bleary-eyed in the unfamiliar bedroom, its paisley wallpaper making patterns in the indigo dusk. Slowly, the walls came into focus, then the prayer quilt that sat on top of the comforter, and finally Hannah, who was stirring in the bed across the room. I snapped into action as the house came alive — the whistle of a teakettle, Ma milling around with her loud footfalls on the floorboards. There were a million things to do in the few hours before we were scheduled to arrive at the revival tent.

During revival trips, long before the sun could tint the horizon with waxy crayon shades of maize and rose, my first chore was always Hannah. I stumbled out of bed and filled the bathtub with lukewarm water just high enough to cover the nubby bottom. I eased Hannah into the tub, first by swinging her knees over the edge and then lowering her into the water. Her bent knees touched each other above the water's surface, and I gently pressed them down. While I rinsed her lathered hair, I could hear Papa and Caleb through the thin walls — Papa's loud voice speaking the words of Christ, the ones that were typed in red on the tissue pages as another reminder of His sacrifice for us. Caleb's voice as he repeated Papa's words was less confident.

" 'They who wait upon the Lord,' " Caleb began. Then he paused one beat too long.

" 'Shall renew their strength. They shall mount up on wings of eagles. They shall

21

run and not be weary; they shall walk and not faint.' " I whispered in the blanks where Caleb couldn't finish Isaiah 40:31. *Isaiah* — the name of the baby Ma had two years ago. As the word *stillborn* had drifted to where I was standing, I wondered why people couldn't be straightforward and say that Isaiah was born dead. And why they had named him after my favorite book in the Bible.

For months afterward, a ragged hole had ripped through all of the verses I had known and recited, burning everything in its proximity. I knew that trials were a part of life, but rationality seemed impossible in those days, especially because my mind kept floating back to the idea that the same God who had promised us a baby — another son for Papa to groom into ministry — had snatched him away from us before he had even taken a breath.

I straightened Hannah's limbs and lifted them out of the water: first her arms and then her legs. Minuscule soapy beads formed on her skin as I glided the washcloth over one arm and then the next. She closed her eyes in delight as I cupped warm water in both hands and spilled it onto her back, so I did it a few extra times just to hear her squeal. She followed the squeal with a labored grunt — the doctors had told us that it was the closest that she would ever get to speech. When she was clean, I spread her towel on the floor by the tub and guided her out of the water — only then could I lift the lever on the drain. If I did it in the wrong order, she would shriek and only stop when I let her touch Tiger's sightless plastic eyes with her forefinger.

When she was fully dressed, I loosened the Velcro straps from her thick plastic leg braces and fitted them around her calves. Lifting her from the floor, I slipped her forearms into her crutches. As she stood, her joints preferred to stay bent rather than straightening, so I ran my palm over her elbows and then down to her knees, stopping to massage the knobby joints with my thumb and forefinger. She liked when I made a whooshing sound as I did that, like I was the one who magically helped her walk a little taller.

I brought Hannah, clean and dressed, to the kitchen. Papa always waited until we got to the new revival site to tell the host pastor about Hannah. Maybe he thought it would ruin the reputation he'd worked so hard to perfect — the flocks of people who crowded into tents would never believe that a man with healing powers could have a daughter like Hannah.

Caleb bounded down the stairs last, already wearing his suit and tie. He flopped into the chair, right in front of the stack of pancakes. During revival season, I only got to see glimpses of Caleb in passing before Papa whisked him off to meet the elders or the deacons. He was fifteen, too — younger than me by ten months — yet it felt like years divided us when I had to watch him straighten his tie and leave with Papa to do "men's work."

"Let's start breakfast with a prayer," Ma said.

I knew the revival prayer by heart — it came from Matthew 28:19. *Therefore go and make disciples of all nations, baptizing them in the name of the Father and of the Son and of the Holy Spirit. Amen.*

As Caleb scarfed down spongy triangles of pancake, I reached for the Bible in the middle of the table. It was Ma's Bible — the one she carried with her everywhere. Ma's and Papa's names and their wedding date were written in cursive inside the front cover: Joanne Renée Taylor and Samuel David Horton, July 11, 2002. It was hard to imagine that they even existed a year before I was born — when Ma was just Joanne — but I'd unearthed the wedding picture from a shoebox in the attic while packing for this revival. In it was a faded photo of an eighteen-year-old Ma, her face a carbon copy of mine. Through the sheer cream-colored veil that partially hid her strained smile, the lonely, distant look in her eyes reached back to me.

Behind the only picture of their wedding was a black-and-white local newspaper clipping whose edges had started to curl. When I flattened it, there was a small, grainy photo of Papa with bushy eyebrows and a head full of hair — his lips protruded around his mouth guard in a grimace as he held boxing gloves in front of his chiseled abs. "Samuel Horton Prepares to Defend Title," the headline read. I skimmed an article that may as well have been about someone else — someone with an 8-0-1 record with a right hook like a freight train and fast feet. I imagined Papa bouncing on the balls of his feet, moving from the ropes on one side of the ring to the other. I felt the anger that swelled in his body for his opponents before his glove made contact with their stomachs or ribs, heard the muffled sound of a glove striking flesh. I folded the article along its crease and placed it back with the other mementos — the cut hospital bracelet from Hannah's birth, a yellowed gauzy square of veil, and an old picture of Ma sandwiched between her sisters. Her smile as she squatted in front of a pickup truck with Claudia and Yolanda was such a stark contrast to the wedding photo that now sat in front of it in the shoebox that the bride and the girl might as well have been two different people, even though the scrawled date on the Polaroid revealed that the photographs had been taken only four months apart.

A horn honked in the driveway, and Caleb shoved one final bite into his mouth before running outside to join Papa. I walked to the front window and slid my finger into the narrow opening between two metallic blinds. Through the visible diamond of dusty glass, Papa gripped Caleb's shoulders in front of Reverend Davenport's silver sedan, shaking him every few seconds as though to emphasize his words. I imagined what Papa was saying — *What's mine is yours* or maybe *One day this can be yours* — as the warmth of his hand seeped through the shoulder of my dress instead of Caleb's suit jacket. Even as I pretended, my imagination couldn't wrap itself around such a frivolous fantasy.

With a piece of glass between us, it was easier to imagine Papa saying things to me that he never said when he was inches away. Whenever I had questions about the Bible after dinner, he excused himself to the study to prepare a sermon, letting me lob unanswered queries to the back of his retreating suit. When it was time for his nightly snack, I held the plate and knocked on the study door, requesting permission to come inside. The snack was always a ruse; I needed to be close enough to hear his words about disease and God's healing so they would stir the Holy Spirit in me more than they did when I was in the fourth row of a church or a revival site. But rather than asking me to come inside, he spoke to me through the door, telling me to leave the plate outside.

"Another ninety-degree scorcher," the radio announcer — Gus "Good News" Stevens on Heaven 1310 AM — broadcast from the kitchen. Then Papa's booming voice came over the airwaves and filled the room, sending a shudder through me even though the commercial had been recorded weeks ago. I released the blinds before they snapped together like lips keeping a secret. It always shocked me to hear his voice in these far-off places — "Come all of you under the sound of my voice. Come to the well that never runs dry." And with those words, revival officially began. Ma shushed me and Hannah even though we weren't making any noise, as though our breathing would overshadow Papa's voice, which could fill up any space it entered.

"Americus, this is Reverend Samuel Horton, the Faith Healer of East Mansfield. If you are hungry for a touch from the Lord, if your hearts are weary or heavy-laden, come to the big tent tonight. Take this step of faith and Jesus will be there to meet your needs and heal your bodies."

It was the same message, the same confident tone, from city to city. Though I knew the words by heart, they reformed themselves as they filtered through the pin-size holes in the speaker of the plastic transistor radio, and suddenly all the people who might have been listening to him in their kitchens vanished — it was just me and him. His words of deliverance and new life took me back to the cold shock of the lake in East Mansfield when I was seven, my adult's baptism robe getting soaked as I walked over to where he stood away from the shore with his arms stretched out from his sides. I wanted to run to him, but the lake dragged my sopping robe behind me like an anvil. When I finally stepped into his arms, he whispered the words of the Lord to me.

"Miriam Ruth, do you accept the Lord Jesus Christ as your Savior and promise to renounce the devil?" I nodded and folded my arms over my chest the way I had seen so many people do before me.

"Miriam Ruth Horton, child of God, I baptize you in the name of the Father, the Son, and the Holy Sp—" Before he could finish the sentence, his strong forearm under my back dipped me into the lake. His words sounded loud and muffled under the water, but I could hear the congregation cheer. When I was upright again, Papa gave me a soaking hug and planted a kiss on my forehead. Though I should have been happy to have eternal life, I was happier to lean into the strength of his embrace and feel the prickle of his wiry forearm hairs as he squeezed me tighter.

His voice faded into a cereal commercial, but my heart still raced the way it did that day half a lifetime ago. I couldn't wait to get to the revival tent — to see its majestic colors and watch Papa redeem himself from last summer's scandal the way I'd been praying that he would.

TWO

Two dresses hung side by side, both with what Ma called regulation-length skirts that fell at least three inches below the knee. "We can't distract the men while they're preaching," she'd once tried to explain with a straight face. I had stared at her until she seemed to hear the ridiculousness of her words coming back to her like a boomerang, and her lip twitched before she broke into throaty laughter. Soon we were giggling at the absurdity of a then nine-year-old pair of knees being a distraction for grown preachers and deacons. Nonetheless, I did as I was told from that day on.

Later that night, Ma, Hannah, and I emptied out of the house in our Sunday best, even though it was a Monday. The car ride over was silent. At each stoplight, Ma picked invisible pieces of lint from her dark gray skirt. The week before, it had just been a pattern on newsprint; this would be its revival debut. At a stop sign, I squeezed her hand. *It's going to be fine,* I wanted to tell her. But her eyes were on the road as she turned right and the revival tent appeared — first a speck that slowly swelled until it took up the whole windshield. It had the same alternating yellow and white colors of the one last August in Brownsville, Tennessee. There was no way Papa had approved this, and though we didn't believe in the superstitions or bad omens that godless people did, my stomach fell to the rubber floor mat.

I blinked the yellow-and-white pattern into a beige swirl, and suddenly the stillness in the van became the same eerie calm of the tent last summer when a family of three had stepped out of the rain and into the back of the tent. A teenage girl close to my age was sandwiched between the twin pillars of her parents, her impassive face damp from tears or rain. The girl's parents linked their arms in hers as the girl shook her head and held her stomach, protesting something that they ignored as they jerked her forward. When she finally stood in front of the crowd, her parents released their grip, and the girl's hands fell away from her lower abdomen. Exposed in front of us, she looked even younger. *Thirteen years old,*

*maybe fourteen, seven or eight months preg-
nant.* My brain made calculations as I looked away from a chubby face that hadn't shed all of its baby fat, letting my gaze land on the smiling unicorn on her dingy T-shirt instead.

Papa continued his sermon as the family stood in front of him until he couldn't ignore their unmoving presence any longer. When he glanced over the edge of the pulpit, his stoic healing face cracked when looking at a girl whose slender, birdlike body didn't seem like it was big enough to carry the weight of her stomach. Papa rushed to the ground and spoke a few quiet words to the girl's father while she strained against her father's tight grip like a chained animal.

"Young lady, what ails you?" Papa held out his hand to touch her forehead.

"Don't touch me, you fake." She backed away, leaving his hand suspended in midair. "What did you do to make them all believe in you? Or do they just give you money and you make them believe? Is that how it works?" As she spoke, the practiced calm of Papa's healing face flashed murderous. Papa took a breath, seemingly to calm himself, but his hands were shaking.

"How dare you? You come here for my

healing and insult me? Who do you think you are?" The deacons crept in from the sides of the tent to protect Papa, but Papa held out a hand to keep them back.

"Who do you think you are?" he asked again, inching closer to her and exaggerating their dramatic difference in height. "You are nothing but a sinner. You need me." As Papa placed a hand on the girl's forehead, she swatted it away. Rage swept over him again, and, seemingly as a reflex, he pushed her. She stumbled backward, almost in slow motion, landing on the grass as her parents looked on, horrified. Papa seemed horrified as well, but the look of guilt that had passed his face as the girl fell quickly morphed into more fury. He dropped to his knees beside her and pinned her shoulders to the grass with his massive hands.

"Stop," the mother yelled as she hit Papa's back, "you're hurting her."

But Papa, impervious to her screams and blows, stayed on top of the girl. The congregation fidgeted as they watched the revival preacher violently subdue this tiny pregnant child.

"I will heal her sin." Papa healed ailments, not sins, but he seemed to have forgotten that fact as he continued to shake the girl. He punctuated each of his words with a punch of his right fist into the grass next to her body.

The girl slid to the right to get away from him; as she moved, his fist drove deep into her abdomen with a sickening thud. She wailed, and her body folded on itself. Papa released her and jumped up, staring down at his hands as though he didn't know what they were capable of. Her parents rushed to her, shoving him into the front row on the way to their daughter. They picked her up from where she was curled in a fetal position on the ground, screaming. Her mother shouted at Papa before she hurried her daughter out of the tent, and her final words — *You are a monster* — were shrill in the surrounding silence.

The light at the intersection turned green, but the van didn't move. Flashes of last year must have been dancing in the windshield for Ma also. I placed my hand over hers as cars sped by us. It was the new shorthand for what we couldn't say: that the night's revival attendance would determine how far-reaching last year's news had really been or if people's attention spans were as short as we needed them to be.

The car jolted back into motion, and Ma returned her eyes to the road. As Ma pulled into a space of flattened grass, I took inventory of the other cars that were already there, covered with a sheen of dust from driving up and down these country roads. I unbuckled Hannah from her seat and slid my left arm behind her back. Her leg braces made hollow sounds as I brought her down the minivan's middle aisle, careful not to jostle her too much, even though she wasn't as delicate as she seemed. The light from inside the tent illuminated the surrounding grassy area, and heads turned as we made our way inside. Some unfamiliar faces nodded politely while others just stared, their fans flapping in front of their faces, stirring the stale scent of old perfume and cigarettes. I wondered if they were thinking about the pregnant girl the way we all were. Wondered if those up front were there because they wanted to be close to the holy man or if they wanted to be close enough to bear witness to another fall.

We walked down the plastic aisle runner to the stage, where a sheet of fake grass was being rolled out. Caleb was there, standing behind the podium like Papa, complete with his hands on his hips. Onstage, he was no longer my brother; he was a miniature preacher, ready to reach out to the audience and lay holy, healing hands on people. He was placing bottles of water in strategic

35

locations for when Papa would need them — one on the left side, and one on the right side. Papa always reached for the left one first, about twenty minutes into the sermon. The entire congregation seemed to hold its breath while he drank, waiting for his words to come out on the other side, promising people jobs, the ability to walk, the deliverance of wayward children, and everything in between.

The rugged crucifix hewn together from rough plywood boards had already been raised with cables behind the stage. Papa insisted on that type of cross rather than the fancier backlit ones. Jesus died on a simple cross, he said, and a simple cross was good enough for a preacher man like him.

We found our seats in the cordoned-off fourth row since we were never allowed to take the best seats in the house. All that was left to do was wait. An hour felt like an eternity in the still, humid air. With Hannah next to me and Ma fanning herself with the service bulletin, my lips mouthed the words to a prayer. No one else would say it, but we all wondered whether enough people would come out to see him. Papa had packed tents from Texas to Mississippi, but this revival season came with more questions than answers. I crossed my fingers and toes and prayed. It was always the same prayer, only this time it was more fervent: *Dear Lord, bring souls to this revival to be saved. Amen.*

Then, as if in answer to my prayer, more people started filing in. Mothers fresh from work in wrinkled uniform shirts with babies perched on their hips. A man whose fingers were black with grease marched down the middle aisle in probably the only suit he owned. Families, daughters my age, sons. Single people. Old people. I tilted my chin upward. *Thank you, God.*

The keyboard began a hymn, and the line of elders and deacons snaked down the middle aisle. Papa was at the end of the line, right behind Reverend Davenport. People rose when they saw him, and he took several extra moments to wave and shake the few hands that were lucky enough to be close. I watched him bask in the power that only a full tent provided, and by the time he reached the podium, he was the old Papa again. In my lap, my hands slowly released the leather cover of my Bible that I didn't realize I'd been clutching.

When we faced the front again, he was in the pulpit with his hands gripping both sides of the plexiglass podium. He raised his arms and cleared his throat — a signal for everyone to get quiet. He brought down his hands, and the volume lowered with them. "You can do this," I mouthed, even though he wasn't looking at me. He rarely did during sermons.

All heads turned toward the stage for the call to worship. I didn't know which one Papa would choose. As I looked to the pulpit, he spoke.

" 'Give thanks to the Lord, for He is good; His love endures forever.' "

I smiled when he recited Psalms 106:1. It had been the subject of my devotional the week before we hit the road for Americus. I whispered the next couple of verses, even as Papa moved on to the opening prayer. *Who can proclaim the mighty acts of the Lord or fully declare His praise? Blessed are those who act justly, who always do what is right. Remember me, Lord, when You show favor to Your people, come to my aid when You save them, that I may enjoy the prosperity of Your chosen ones, that I may share in the joy of Your nation and join Your inheritance in giving praise.*

The murmuring of people behind me interrupted Papa's prayer. I turned my neck in the slightest, fearing I'd see the unicorn T-shirt again or the light of a cell phone camera on him like last summer, but all their heads were down, and the only sound was from lips vibrating against each other as they recited their own prayers. Maybe it was all going to be fine. I caught back up to Papa as his voice waned.

"In the precious name of Jesus, our Savior and our Lord, I pray, Amen."

"Amen," came the choral reply. With each confident step back to his chair — one, two, three, four — my body tensed as the rest of us waited on a razor's edge. Then he eased his weight back like he knew the seat would be there to catch him.

A row of black-clad people rose in unison from the front row and marched to the stage in front of Papa. All of a sudden, a keyboard melody punctuated by a drumbeat filled the tent, followed by words about deliverance and salvation. Some people in the congregation jumped to their feet and raised their hands. A woman in the front row held a tambourine whose metallic rattle matched the beat of the song. Next to me, Ma was still seated, her eyes glued to where Papa was sitting. I pulled her up to standing — Papa needed us to be like the others — and she raised a reluctant arm into the sky. On my left side, Hannah stirred, clearly disturbed by all the noise and motion, and I wrapped my arm around her, bringing her closer to my chest and stilling her movements. The crowd settled and turned its attention back to the pulpit. I said a mini prayer of my own as the rest of the congregation stood.

"Brothers and sisters, are you ready for the word of the Lord?"

"Yes," the voices around me said.

"Yes," I responded a beat too late. People reached in purses for their Bibles. It was time.

"Open your Bibles to Matthew 7:13," Papa commanded.

"In Matthew 7, verses 13 and 14, the Scripture says, 'Enter through the narrow gate. For wide is the gate and broad is the road that leads to destruction, and many enter through it. But small is the gate and narrow the road that leads to life, and only a few find it.' This is the word of the Lord. May the Lord bless the reading, hearing, and doing of His word."

Papa rested his Bible on the podium and slid his glasses down the bridge of his nose. He inhaled — sniffing out sin in the congregation — and people's backs straightened where they stood. What they didn't know was that sniffing was one of Papa's tricks for figuring out if people were guilty of sin or not — it made the guilty immediately want to repent. The congregation froze, not even wanting to shift in uncomfortable high heels. Any slight motion could catch the attention of Papa's roving eyes. The electric buzz from the overhead strands of lights thundered in the silence.

"You may be seated. My message this evening is entitled: 'The Gates of Hell.'" The silence seemed to deepen. Hell was something we all believed in, had been terrified of since we first learned about it in Sunday school. It was a message that would scare people, and, for Papa, fear was as useful a tactic as any to bring people to Christ. Ma had let go of my hand and her skirt, and my heart thrummed at a normal pace for the first time that day. Just a couple more hours to go.

"Gates have very specific uses in this world. One use is for keeping things out. Some communities are surrounded by high wrought-iron gates designed to prevent strangers from entering. People live behind those gates, lured by the promise of safety that they provide. Other gates are used for keeping things in. Prisons are surrounded by miles of chain-link fencing, gates, and barbed wire precisely for keeping inmates sequestered. The rest of us rely on those gates so that we can walk our dogs or take our children to school without worrying about those walls being breached. The third type of gate is for regulating flow. When you visit a baseball game, you step through a gate one at a time so that there's no stampede. Gates allow for a controlled entry." His voice was as soft as it would get during the sermon. He took a long pause for emphasis — he had planned several of these during the message. In the seconds of silence, he scanned the crowd. By now he had already estimated its size and scoped out the fact that at least a hundred people were huddled in the back, craning their necks toward the pulpit.

Some heads nodded while other soft amens floated up from the back of the congregation. He took a deep breath, and the fabric of his dress shirt stretched around his barrel chest before he exhaled. I exhaled with him. *You can do this, Papa.*

"So, it's not a coincidence that the entryway to heaven is a gate." His voice had gotten louder, and he was starting to drag his vowel sounds. "And this heavenly gate is designed to let only certain people in. Matthew 7, verses 13 and 14, describes the type of gate that leads to heaven. Matthew uses the words *small, narrow,* and *few* to show

Christians that not everyone gets into the gates of heaven. Small sins, the ones we overlook every day, are enough to keep us from getting through the narrow gates. Take a moment to think about all the small sins that you committed today."

He got quiet again and looked around. I was writing down every word in my journal; his long pause allowed me to catch up and scribble his final sentence. But when his silence extended a few extra seconds, his words seeped into my skin. He wasn't just talking to everyone else about the sins they committed: he was talking to me about my doubt. About the fact that I kept seeing the pregnant girl's face. I spoke to God in the quiet of my heart and repented.

"I won't ask for a show of hands, but did some of you think about the lie that you told your boss to leave work early to come here? You comforted yourselves by calling it a white lie, but while you left early, someone else had to cover your shift. Did others of you think of the unkind word you said about your neighbor whose barking dog woke up your child in the middle of the night? Or about the woman who came into revival wearing a dress that was too short? I could go on all day, but I won't. You overlooked those sins because they weren't murder or adultery, but God doesn't overlook them. In His eyes, sin is sin. Sin leads you to hell: the wide gate that many will walk through. Satan wants people to enter that gate, because hell is eternal separation from God. I'm going to repeat that phrase for those of you who didn't hear it. Eternal. Separation. From. God. Darkness and hellfire." He pounded his fist against the podium on the final few words before reaching for the hand towel that Caleb had positioned on the front right corner. He wiped it across his brow, which was shimmering under the overhead lights.

"Eternal life is possible if you accept the Lord as your personal savior. You must ask Jesus to come into your heart and give your life to Him. That is the only way." His promise of salvation boomed as soft keyboard chords grew louder with each word. Amens rose from the back of the tent and increased in volume.

"Can everyone please rise?" Grateful to get back on my feet, I sprang up and seized the opportunity to stretch.

"There may be some of you under the sound of my voice who have not yet accepted Jesus Christ as your Lord and Savior. Accept the Lord Jesus Christ into your heart and start living a life that will get you through the narrow gate. The doors of the church are open."

A rustle from the nearby aisles meant that unsaved people were coming down to the front. One person got up, then another. Soon, footsteps filled the aisles surrounding us. A whoop rose from the congregation as forty or fifty people lined up in front of the stage. "Praise the Lord, saints. Praise the Lord!"

And we, the saints, shouted, hallelujahed, and played the tambourine, thanking God for deliverance. Papa stepped away from the microphone and walked down to the ground where the people were. The keyboard played the soft melody of "Come to Jesus" as Papa moved down the line and clasped his arm around each person's shoulders.

"People of God," he addressed the congregation when he had gone down the line of new believers. "Welcome these beautiful people into the kingdom."

After the sermon ended, we waited for the event that most of the people had come for: the healing. Even though the sermon had been better than I imagined it could be, my expanding chest got tight beneath my dress when Papa made the announcement.

While they came, about eighty of them, Papa wiped the sweat that had beaded on his brow. There were the typical people who came for healing — older people meandering to the front, young families whose ailments were invisible to the naked eye. My gaze drifted to a woman who slowly led a little boy down the aisle runner. Silver rings like thick bangles kept his forearms in place while his small hands gripped the handles of his crutches. His legs, even thinner than his arms, had rigid plastic braces on them, and his knees were bent as he slid his legs, one in front of the other, toward the raised altar.

Hannah's right eye fixed on him, slowly followed by her roving left eye that had been blind since birth. Her rocking stilled, and throaty grunting sounds came from the recesses of her body. I placed my arm around her shoulders where her bones jutted out from underneath her shirt's thin jersey material. Then Papa saw them. He dried his hands against his pants, his Adam's apple bobbing as he swallowed. I sucked in a breath.

Papa sprinkled holy oil in his hands and made the sign of the cross on each forehead that he passed. These were the healings that we couldn't see. Since we'd be in another city in a week, there was no way we'd be able to know if the old woman was cured of her hypertension or if the mechanic's tumor shrank. But if this boy could walk, everything that had happened last year would vanish like vapor.

Finally, at the end of the line of people, he came to the small boy. He slipped his hand underneath the boy's armpit and guided him toward the stairs. The boy's mother stayed on the ground as his crutches hit the wood of the makeshift steps — her hands worried the fabric of her long skirt as her son and Papa slowly ascended to the altar, right beneath the cross.

"Son, are you ready to walk?" Papa asked.

It was a rhetorical question, but the little boy nodded anyway.

"Congregation, are we ready for a miracle?"

A hum rose from the crowd. First soft, then louder before it floated into the tent's peaked roof. As Papa got down on one knee in his fancy suit pants, I imagined the prickly feel of the turf beneath the thin fabric as though I had slipped on his skin for a moment. He was now inches away from the boy's face — aware that any errant motion would compromise this healing that he needed. That we needed. His heart, like mine, must have been beating faster than the snare drum keeping time in the corner

47

of the room.

He said something to the little boy that no one could hear. The boy laughed, and Papa tousled his close-cropped Afro. In his right fist, Papa still had the small bottle of holy oil, and he splashed some into his hand, more than he used for regular healings. He tilted the boy's head back, and the boy stumbled on his crutches. Papa applied the holy oil in a slow sign of the cross in the middle of the boy's forehead: in the name of the Father and the Son and the Holy Spirit.

"Amen," I whispered.

Papa placed his entire palm, fingertips stretched and quivering, on the boy's head. Papa often talked about how his whole body would quake with the power of the Holy Spirit when Jesus worked through him. He said that the feeling was like getting electrocuted. The boy trembled like Papa's hand, his thin arms moving around in the crutches like hula hoops. Papa kept praying, pressing his hand on the boy's head. What he was saying was between him, God, and the boy.

When Papa finally stood up, he backed away from the boy. "Drop your crutches and walk, son."

My fingernails had bent back against the metal chair by the time Ma's warm grip landed on my hand. I reached out my other hand and grabbed Hannah's as the boy shifted his thick shoes ever so slightly. Even though Papa wasn't touching him anymore, the boy was still shaking. Then a crutch fell, and he dropped to his knees. His mother ran up to the stage in her dingy cotton dress.

"Wait," Papa said, extending his arm to still her. "Have faith. God is still working." The woman took a step back, but she was clearly torn between Papa's belief in his own power and her son, who was on his knees at the altar.

"Get up," I whispered as the boy rocked on his knees, no closer to standing even as my words chided him. I prayed that the boy's slowness wouldn't spark the same anger that had inhabited Papa last summer. Papa took one step closer to the boy, and Ma's hand became a vise on mine, squeezing out all the feeling until it was numb.

"C'mon, son," Papa said with a sweet voice that would have made anyone get up. "Rise up and walk."

Sweat rained from Papa's forehead to the turf. The hundreds of pairs of eyes in the tent were fixed on him, their expressions ranging from hope to frustration to blankness.

"Rise up and walk." Papa extended his

arms again, but this time he raised them like a puppeteer whose invisible marionette strings connected to the boy's legs. In slow motion, the boy put his hands on the ground and straightened his legs. His knees knocked together in the plastic braces.

"Rise up and walk," Papa said again, his words salve to loosen the boy's stiff joints. The boy stayed on all fours as his legs inched closer to his hands. He moved ever so slightly. Then he was on his feet, shaking, but on his feet. And I was on mine too, shouting amen. A sharp tug yanked the hem of my skirt, sending me right back to the seat. But I started something, because then everyone was cheering as the boy took one wobbly step and then another.

Papa flopped on the altar, seemingly exhausted even though he wasn't the one who'd just walked. The boy's mother rushed onto the stage, and her son collapsed into her embrace. Papa raised his arms to lead the congregation in a benediction. We all rose under the spell of his puppeteer hands as the lights from above cast an iridescent glimmer on his sweat.

Only when revival was officially over did Ma let my hand go, yet I still felt the warmth and pressure of her fingers as I flexed mine. As Ma exhaled her relief, the boy's mother shouted above the booming applause, her voice reaching all parts of the tent from the mic pinned to Papa's suit jacket.

"Glory to God and to His shepherd on earth. Thank you, Reverend Horton. Thank you."

I nudged Ma with my elbow to catch her eye, but she wouldn't look at me. Her smooth forehead had already erased the doubt of just a few minutes before as she applauded for him. I joined in, even as crowds with ravenous eyes surged the stage and swarmed Papa, their hands eager for a touch of his garment. I wanted to join them but knew that it wouldn't be proper. So my hands clapped themselves raw from the fourth row until the residue of last summer's memories was wiped clean.

Later that night, in the darkness of the bedroom, a loud groan came from Hannah's bed — a strained sound like someone was pressing on her chest and forcing air out of her lungs. Then the mattress squeaked, and I rushed to the side of her bed. Her limbs stiffened, her back arched, and her body bucked on the mattress. The blanket that had once been wrapped around her so tightly was now loose.

"Ma! Papa!" As I yelled into the darkness of the unfamiliar room, I peered at the fluorescent-green numbers on the wall clock — 11:51. The thump of my heart ricocheted in my chest and ears as I knelt next to her writhing body. I willed myself to keep my eyes open rather than closing them to mutter the first words of a prayer. Praying during seizures had become a ritual of sorts since Hannah was a baby, even though my prayers had morphed from asking God to heal her to asking Him to lessen her pain instead.

Froth bubbled around her lips and the back of her throat emitted a gurgling sound. When the gurgle receded, she opened her mouth wide and gasped like she was drowning. Her eyes fluttered open and the pupils fixated on one spot of the ceiling. Her arms flopped against the cartoon character sheets. Still 11:51.

The lights flooded on, and Ma was next to me; her body made a barrier to keep Hannah from falling off the bed. Papa rushed to Hannah's headboard, his arms and chest exposed in a scoop-neck tank top that I probably wasn't supposed to see. The gold herringbone chain, a birthday gift from Ma a few years ago, was tangled in a thicket of chest hair. I averted my eyes as he cinched his robe.

"There there, Hannah," Ma's voice soothed as Hannah bucked in the sheets. I stood silent vigil, afraid even to disturb the air. No one would say it out loud, but we were superstitious when it came to Hannah's seizures. During a seizure, Ma kneaded her hands as though to shorten the duration of each violent movement while I held my breath until my lungs burned. Papa stood by the head of her bed and extended his hands above her — a different healing motion than he had used during that night's revival. Since we weren't allowed to touch her, he moved his arms in intersecting circles above her body, almost like he was massaging the air. He lowered his head, and Ma and I lowered ours reflexively. But he didn't pray, at least not out loud.

In the silence, I peeked over at the clock — 11:54. Time stood still, interminable, dragging out every gesture into an excruciating saga. A line of watery blood mixed with saliva escaped from Hannah's mouth as her jaw clenched and her head thrashed on her pillow. A particularly powerful jolt shot her inches above the bed; her flexed body was a straight line above the sheets, and her limp neck flopped at an awkward angle as she collapsed back to the mattress.

Her limbs went slack, and her bucking slowed. Then her eyes rolled to the front of their sockets and she fixed them on us. As the haze cleared, she must have seen the three of us — Papa's closed eyes and dipped chin, Ma's kneading hands, my eyes darting from the clock back to her back to the clock.

"It's over," I pronounced the definitive words.

"It wasn't such a bad one," Ma said.

"Praise God," Papa's reply.

When Hannah's movements had finally stopped and her breathing had returned to normal, Ma sat in a nearby chair, pulling Hannah's limp body off the bed and into her chest. Hannah was finally still, except for Ma's rocking. My feet didn't want to move from where they were planted on the carpet, but I took one step toward them, and then another. Soon I was crouched next to Ma, one hand on Hannah's back. With my faded pajama sleeve, I wiped away the viscous saliva mixture: first from Hannah's mouth and then from Ma's collarbone. Ma blinked her thanks.

With Hannah in Ma's arms, Papa moved quickly, snatching the urine-soaked sheets from Hannah's bed and balling them in a messy pile. In the silence that rose when he left the room, I looked over at Ma, her body slowing its rocking motions as Hannah drifted into sleep. Ma shrugged the way she always did after one of Hannah's seizures, the only gesture that acknowledged our collective impotence. She hadn't done that all those years ago when Papa had tried to heal Hannah; she had trembled instead. She only shrugged when I was around, when Papa couldn't misinterpret her speculation about the nature of sickness as a question about his abilities.

Papa bumbled back into the room, his face hidden behind a pile of laundry, and Ma and I snapped our necks toward the door in unison. But we were safe — he hadn't seen us as he entered. His lithe hands and nimble fingers that removed disease were clumsy as they pulled a daisy-print fitted sheet over the mattress edges and rammed the fabric in the narrow space between the mattress and the rail. He grunted as the edges slipped off moments after he put them on, so I got up to fix them.

When the corners were tight and tucked and Hannah was in clean pajamas, Ma hefted Hannah to him as an offering. Hannah's weight slumped against the delicate fabric of Papa's robe, and he whispered something to her before wiping the sweat-matted tendrils of hair from her forehead —

a gesture so much like the healing he had tried years ago. He held her there for a moment before kissing her forehead and gently placing her in the freshly made bed.

"Night, honey." Ma and Papa went back to their room. The door shut behind Papa. I lay there staring at perhaps the same spot that Hannah had been looking at earlier. I pulled out my battered prayer journal from the nightstand and formed the question that had been percolating forever but had never made it to the lined pages.

Why does God let His children suffer?

THREE

We rode the wave of Papa's success all the way through that revival week. By Friday night, the crowds had spilled onto the mottled lawn. They were there to see Papa make someone else walk, but it was not to be.

The next morning, we were packed and ready to leave before sunrise. Standing in front of the open trunk, I fiddled with the zipper on my duffel in the heavy heat as sweat droplets fell from my forehead. Reverend and Mrs. Davenport walked across the lawn toward us; Mrs. Davenport held a travel mug of coffee for Ma while Reverend Davenport had a thick manila envelope tucked under his arm for Papa. Since it was vulgar to mingle money and souls, the payments for these revivals were supposed to be private. I inched into the shadow of the trunk as Papa followed Reverend Davenport to the edge of the property.

They turned their backs to the house as the manila envelope passed from Reverend Davenport's hands to Papa's. I thought about all those baskets coming down the rows — hands placing singles, fives, tens, and occasional twenties on top of the heaping mounds that only got bigger in the days after Papa healed the boy. Then there were the secretive envelopes that I imagined held checks with lots of zeroes made out to Papa: love offerings to the revival pastor. Reverend Davenport would've used some of the cash to keep the church afloat, but the bulk of the offering went to Papa. One week on the revival circuit often brought in more than we made in a month of offerings at the church at home, I'd once heard Ma say.

Money had taken down neighborhood pastors — *They forgot who their master was,* Papa had said when their new cars were towed away and they lost their expensive houses. But as their churches went under, Papa had started the building fund and moved our church from the modest chapel where I officially accepted Christ to a new sanctuary so cavernous that you couldn't hear someone speaking on the other side of it. Some families left the flock, saying that Papa was losing his way, but I knew they were wrong; he needed the extra space to make room for the expanding congregation. And as proof, we still drove the same van that they'd purchased a couple years after I was born — a van that now had 267,000 miles on it and a muffler that loudly broadcast our arrival. And Hannah and I shared a room in our cramped three-bedroom house when other pastors like Papa had built compounds on acres of land. So this money was for the kingdom, not for us.

Papa and Reverend Davenport turned around toward the house, and I snapped my attention back to the duffel's broken zipper. Caleb lugged his suitcase down the steps, the wheels bumping each piece of wood.

"What are you looking at?"

"Nothing." The zipper on my duffel was stuck on a T-shirt. Caleb sidestepped me and hefted his suitcase into the trunk.

"Here, let me get that." He zipped my duffel shut and lifted it over his shoulder with arms that had started to grow ropy muscles. His wiry build had only recently been chiseled out of the baby fat that had cleaved to his frame for the past fifteen years. Suddenly, he was beginning to look more like Papa than my younger brother.

"Since when did you become an expert at packing the trunk?"

"There's so much you don't know about me."

I wanted a witty comeback, but his words stung more than I expected them to. We'd been so close when we were younger. When Papa first pulled him into the ministry, he'd sneak in my room at night to complain about the long hours in the study and the heightened scrutiny of his behavior. But recently, as he had started having a more prominent role in each service, the visits to my room stopped as his sessions in the study with Papa got even longer. Sometimes when he was in the pulpit with the deacons, I'd try to catch his eye as he led a prayer, but he wouldn't look back at me.

We piled back into the car: next stop, Carthage, Mississippi. I hoped that the news of the boy would reach this new church before we did, and that there would be overflow crowds on the first night. The bigger the crowds, the better all our days would be. Good days were like rare coins that I stuffed into empty pockets. Days when the sun came up early without any sign of rain, when the tents were packed beyond capacity, when people were healed, when the spirit was moving. It helped to save up those coins for when we would have to use them — when only a handful of people turned out, when Papa's righteous anger about God shifted from his voice behind the pulpit to his mighty hand that struck us far away from the congregants' eyes. But I pushed those memories out of my mind as Papa turned on the car and the engine hummed to life. He shifted into reverse, and the place we had called home for the past week grew smaller. Shadows of overhanging trees crisscrossed the front window as gravel crunched beneath the tires. Reverend and Mrs. Davenport stood on the porch of their house and waved.

"Caleb, can you say our parting prayer?" Ma asked.

"Lord, watch over these Your children. Use us to do Your will. Amen."

Amen.

We stayed in Mississippi for two weeks — after Carthage, we moved to Columbus, where Papa healed run-of-the-mill ailments and was preaching to standing-room-only crowds by the final Friday service. The following week, in Pine Bluff, Arkansas, a family pushed a pallid child to the altar in a wheelchair. Papa spent a few extra minutes on the girl. As he touched her, the color came back to her cheeks. She didn't walk that night — it was not to be — but the gathered crowd seemed to be satisfied with what he could do, enough to give him a rousing round of applause.

The next afternoon, we meandered off I-64 after the green highway sign read BETHEL, NORTH CAROLINA. Ma called out directions to Christ the Redeemer Holy Church of God, where Reverend Griffith was waiting for us. It was the fifth stop of this summer's revival season — six more weeks to go. By this point last summer, I had already started to feel restless, but this summer, I was grateful for the subtle seat belt pressure on my chest and the bouncing movement of the tires beneath me. With each mile that we traveled on the highway, we outran the specter of the pregnant girl's face frozen in agony and the hollow thump of Papa's fist in the center of her stomach.

We turned right off the highway and passed a huge expanse of land where men were driving stakes into the ground. It was just trodden grass now, but on Monday night, there would be a giant tent with rows of folding chairs, a pulpit, and a cross inside. Papa slowed next to the field before opening the door; stepping outside in his dressy loafers, he approached the tent stakes, walked along the perimeter, and then stopped in the middle. Papa knelt in a bare patch and placed his head in his hands. Though the minivan was a hundred yards away from him, we bowed our heads in reverence. Hannah jerked her chin close to her chest, her body momentarily still. Papa's mouth moved slowly, his lips barely parting to let out sound. Though I couldn't hear his prayer, I imagined his words. *Lord, let me be an instrument of Thy will. Let Your people come to be saved and healed. Amen.* Somewhere behind that prayer, in what he couldn't say to God but held deep in his heart, I knew that he wanted something else like the walking boy in Americus.

After a welcome dinner with the Griffiths, we ambled back to the big house on the church property with full stomachs. Lights illuminated the pillars and bushes, making everything glow. Papa opened the front door, and we began to stumble toward our respective bedrooms.

"Before you go to bed, I have a family announcement," Papa said with the same serious inflection that accompanied his proclamations that Jesus was ready to save your soul. He nodded toward the kitchen, and we trudged through the wide hallway and sat around the cherrywood table, our eyes fixed on Papa, who stood at the head.

"We're having a baby," he said, unable to contain his smile. He looked at Caleb as he made the announcement; Ma, Hannah, and I had somehow disappeared. Even though Ma sat next to me, she preferred to study the table's lacquered grain instead of making eye contact. The last time he'd delivered that news, it had been to tell us that Ma was having Isaiah. Ma had been excited then, had walked around and given each of us a hug. But now she passively accepted the congratulations that spilled from Papa's and Caleb's lips, her palms turned upward in submission, her eyes vacant.

Ma had yet to say a word, even though part of me believed that it was her news to share. But she had lost her voice ever since we entered the room.

"What do you think, Ma?" I found the space to ask in the middle of Papa's praise. I needed to hear her say that she wanted this baby after Isaiah, that she wasn't just riding the wave of Papa's happiness. Papa looked down at us from where he was standing — it might have been the first time he'd seen us since he started talking.

"What a blessing," she finally uttered, with her face turned away from me.

Papa came behind us and placed his hands on her shoulders, his knuckles bulged as he massaged, and she recoiled as though she'd been burned. "It is a blessing, isn't it?"

Two years ago when Isaiah was born, Mrs. Cade and the other midwives had shoved me from the living room before Ma's final push. As I stood on the other side of a wall that separated me from Ma — the first time I'd been away from her since labor began — I waited for a baby's cries but heard silence and shrieking instead. I didn't move, couldn't, not even when Papa brushed by us hours later, carrying a lifeless Isaiah on outstretched palms as though he would break. When my legs finally worked again, I followed Papa into the kitchen, my knees shaky. With a tear-streaked face, Caleb was behind me with Hannah on his hip. In the kitchen, Papa laid the blanket on the table and opened the flap. Isaiah looked like a doll, with a round, bluish face and bulbous eyelids that never got a chance to see the sky. We gathered around the table as Papa filled a small glass with water and brought it over.

"In Isaiah 43:1, the Lord says, 'Do not fear, for I have redeemed you; I have summoned you by name; you are mine.' " Papa's voice cracked at the end of the Bible verse. He lifted Isaiah's limp body into the

65

air. "Isaiah Samuel, I baptize you in the name of the Father, the Son, and the Holy Spirit. Amen." Papa cupped water into his hand at routine intervals and splashed it onto Isaiah's forehead when he said "Father," "Son," and "Holy Spirit." Then Papa did something that he never did with the baptisms he performed in church: he pressed his lips to Isaiah's forehead and clutched him to his chest.

Mrs. Cade led Ma into her bedroom, and she didn't come downstairs for the rest of the day. When I finally got the strength to check on her that evening, she was upstairs at the sewing machine with a tiny piece of terry fabric stretched between her hands. I watched her from the doorway, too scared to take a step inside as she shakily moved the fabric beneath the needle, the glint of sharp silver too close to her hands. Over the coming days, I kept expecting to hear Ma's wails, but they never came. Instead, she sewed baby blankets and scrubbed bathroom floors. I expected Papa to put a stop to it, to tell her that it was okay to express her grief, but they never seemed to be in the same room.

A week after Isaiah's death, we were all gathered at the cemetery in East Mansfield — the same cemetery where Papa had officiated hundreds of funerals. The funeral home had donated a tiny coffin that was no bigger than a shoebox, and Papa had dressed Isaiah in a blue sleeper that Ma had made.

The tiny coffin was lowered into the ground — farther down than I expected — until it was barely visible below. It was the first time Ma had been still since his death, and her legs, seemingly nostalgic for the motion of the past few days, twitched as Papa recited prayers. Then there was a sharp, sudden intake of air that startled me after the week of silent activity. I looked next to me to see her mouth frozen into what looked like a yawn. The sound morphed to sobbing as her folded arms pressed against her distended belly, her toes so close to the edge that the slightest movement would have made her fall in. We lined up to drop handfuls of dirt onto the lid of Isaiah's coffin: first Papa, then Hannah, then me and Caleb. When it was Ma's turn, she keeled forward, her right leg dangling into the hole, her allotment of dirt gripped in a fist that wouldn't open.

Papa turned around to leave, not even looking around to see if Ma was following him on his uphill march to the van. I pulled back hard, dislodging her leg from the hole until the full weight of her body collapsed on mine, her shoe coming off in the struggle and falling to the ground beside us.

"I can't do this again," she said minutes later as sobs interrupted each word. "I can't have another baby."

"You don't have to," I said. "No one says that you have to."

"You don't understand. He's going to want another one." Her sobbing stopped like the break in a storm — or the calm before another one — and her clear voice came through. "I didn't want this one and look what happened." She gestured toward the hole in front of us where Isaiah lay. She was talking loudly, as though Papa wasn't feet away, as though she had forgotten that I was her daughter.

Back at the kitchen table where he'd just made the announcement, Papa's hands hadn't moved from Ma's shoulders, but he wasn't massaging them anymore; it looked like he was holding her in place. A few minutes later, when she still hadn't said anything and the congratulations had faded, Caleb excused himself to bed and took Hannah with him. I hoped Papa would leave us alone and let Ma tell me what she was really feeling about this baby, but he didn't seem eager to let that happen.

"What a blessing." Her tinny repeated words seemed to be aimed at the table rather than at Papa.

"It is a blessing indeed. The Lord has answered our prayers."

"It's getting late, Miriam," he said, turning to me. "You should get to bed."

"I'll tuck you in like old times," Ma offered.

Once we reached the doorway of the bedroom, I pulled her toward me. "Say something, Ma," I whispered inches from her face, my eyes pleading with hers. "Do you want this? After Isaiah, you said —"

She pushed me into the bedroom, closing the door part of the way behind her. "He'll hear you." She was breathless when she got to the other side of the door, and her eyes darted back to the stairs. With her hands light on my shoulders, she guided me into bed. Fully clothed, I nestled beneath the sheets and let her pull them taut around me. Ma stared into the space above my headboard as her hands patted me too hard beneath the sheets.

"I know what I said, Miriam. It's just complicated. Your dad really wanted another baby. And what I wanted — what I want — well, that doesn't really matter. I mean, it matters, but it's hard to explain." Her voice was heavy with sadness.

I opened my mouth to respond when there was a creak on the stairs. Papa. He reached the landing and approached the breach in the door; the visible portion of him glowed in the hallway light. Ma's back was to him, and though she didn't turn around, I could tell from the way she straightened that she must have sensed his presence.

"A baby is always a gift. We are so blessed." Her eyes found their way from the wall back to me; she leaned over and snuck a quick kiss on my forehead. "Now go to sleep, honey. It's getting late." She hopped off the bed and let herself out of the room. When the door was open fully, Papa put his arm around her waist; he pulled her close to him for their walk toward the bedroom.

A torrential downpour pounded Bethel the next day, stopping a few minutes before revival began. Fat raindrops still clung to the tent's roof and slid down intermittently, exploding into the grass like small bombs. Papa stood in front of a revival tent packed to capacity with standing-room-only in the back — his hands were raised above his head to announce the healing portion of the night's service.

"Saints of God, are you ready for a healing?"

Applause churned around us as people crowded into the aisles — they must have been waiting for those words the whole night because they were on their feet before he finished the question. In a couple of minutes, the line in the middle aisle was so long that it almost went outside. A few drunks with their telltale sunglasses covering half their faces were scattered in with the people whose bodies needed to be healed. In East Mansfield, Papa complained about healing the same drunks every week only to see them the following week with the same sour breath, asking to be healed again. His face didn't show his disgust as he stood in front of this line, dispatching the first dozen people and rendering their diseases a thing of the past.

At the end of the healing service, he arrived at the final drunk — a middle-aged man with black stubble and craterlike pockmarks denting his cheeks, whose sunglasses kept slipping down his nose. The man toddled down the line closer to Papa until Papa's hands were on his shoulders, and he swayed on unsteady legs as Papa's lips grazed his ear to ask what ailed him.

Papa brought his forehead close to the

man's and removed his sunglasses. He whispered to him for a few minutes, probably about the evils of drinking and how the Lord could deliver him from his addiction. Then he pressed his right hand over the man's eyes instead of on his forehead, all while tilting his head back. Papa only touched the eyes of people who were blind or losing their sight. A blind man could be just as good for Papa as making a man walk — maybe better. I rubbed my hands in anticipation — this was what we'd been waiting for since Americus.

Papa pressed harder on the man's eyes until the man fell into the deacons' arms, his mouth contorting in a wavy line of agony. As the deacons released his body to the grass, Papa let go in a flourish. The man's cloudy pupils roamed around the ceiling, maybe seeing the fans slicing through the air for the first time, maybe landing on the miniature lights that glowed like phosphorescent teardrops. He was on his back for a few seconds before the deacons helped him to his feet. Once the man was standing, his startled eyes flitted in their sockets as he faced the congregation, never landing on anyone — they just searched as though unable to find what they were looking for. The deacons must have noticed this and abruptly spun the man around to face the pulpit. One deacon clumsily slid the man's sunglasses back on his face, poking him in the eye in the process. While people in the pews were praising the Lord, I could see that the man was growing more agitated. He began wailing as he tried to wriggle out of the deacons' grip, but their arms were grasping him tight.

With a flick of his index finger, Papa directed the deacons to take the man outside. Papa had made his way to the pulpit again, and he raised trembling hands to quiet the crowd. The cheers of only a couple of minutes before had been replaced by confused stares and murmurs. He tried to mumble a benediction, but he was drowned out by the man's bellows coming from outside. Papa, distracted, rushed the service to a close and disappeared through the slit in the tent that led to the darkness outside.

A shout came from the distance. I jumped up before I could realize what I was doing, shook loose from Ma's tight grip that was holding me in the chair, and followed in Papa's tracks. On the flattened grassy path behind the main revival tent, I smacked into an impassable wall of suited bodies that I tried to part with my hands. Another yell off to my left — this one more urgent, more

73

desperate, than the last one. Out of the corner of my eye, a group of deacons had gathered, surrounding the man with the sunglasses. They were trying to lead him into the trees at the perimeter of the property, but he stood in the middle of their circle, swiping the air with punches.

"Get away from me," he shouted. His fists were a flurry in front of his face. Maybe the darkness disoriented him, but his movements were clumsy like he still couldn't see. As he spun around in woozy circles, his sunglasses fell from his head and landed by his feet in the grass.

"He's a fraud!" the man yelled. One deacon grabbed him from behind and tried to bring him to the ground, but the man stayed on his feet. Then there was a parting in the circle, and Papa stepped through. My breathing slowed when I saw him; he would get to the bottom of this misunderstanding.

"Let him go, Robert. He isn't a prisoner," Papa said to the deacon. Then he turned to the man, his voice calm, but the scary kind of calm I always dreaded hearing. "A fraud? Is that what you called me?"

"I know all about you," the man continued. "They may not know about you, but I do."

"You know nothing about me," Papa said,

flexing his hands and then balling them into fists. With each movement, there was a soft crack of his knuckles. As the man continued speaking, it was easier to watch Papa's hands than his face.

"I know about the girl you assaulted last summer. How you got angry when you knew you wouldn't be able to heal her. Just like you're angry now."

The deacons' close bodies held me back from jumping into the center and telling this man just how wrong he was about Papa. Then there was a muffled thump like a rock hitting the ground; when I looked back into the sliver of space, the blind man was on the grass and Papa was standing over him. It looked like he was stomping on the ground near where the man had been. Visions of the pregnant girl flashed in front of my eyes, but I squeezed them shut to rid myself of the memory. My eyes had to be deceiving me now — probably just paranoia from last summer.

The deacons' bodies surrounded Papa, trying to hold him back; I caught a glimpse of him before the circle fully closed. This time, there was no mistake: there was blood streaming down his knuckles as he rained punches toward the ground where the man was writhing. His fists on the man's body made the same sound as the punch he landed on the girl's stomach last summer. He had said that was an accident; this was not.

"You know nothing about me." Papa kept rubbing his blood-covered knuckles. My hands shot to my mouth to block my gasp.

On the ground, dazed, the man nodded.

"There's more of that if you ever come back here." Papa turned to face the circle of deacons. "Now get him out of here."

The deacons moved as one, dragging the man's body with them. I stood in the grass, exposed, my heart thundering in my ears, my legs frozen even as I knew I should return to the tent. Papa turned around in what felt like slow motion; fear and shock flickered in his widened eyes as they landed on me.

"Miriam." My name sounded like a revelation in his mouth. "Why are you back here?" He walked closer to me, and I took a couple of steps back. When there was no more land behind me, I kept my eyes level with the top button of his dress shirt. The stretched fabric was transparent with sweat.

"No one can know about this." His voice cracked like a preteen's would, and my eyes couldn't rise from his shirt to his face. He shook his right hand as though drying errant water droplets from it. With those same hands, Papa had baptized people — he'd baptized all of us too, including Ma — and he'd held Isaiah's delicate body like it was a piece of glass. Standing inches in front of me in the darkness, I stared at the blood that stained the knuckles of his once-familiar hands.

I shook my head. He took a step toward me, and I flinched — a reflex — but he laid his left hand on my shoulder.

"I will never hurt *you.*"

I wondered if the emphasis on *you* meant he would hurt other people. Although Papa had disciplined me many times over the years, his flat hand only struck my bare flesh when I was willful or disobedient, and his spankings were never as angry or violent as what I'd just witnessed.

"Go back inside with your mother. I have more business to see about here."

I turned quickly, running on the path that led back to the main tent. When I blinked in the brightness, I couldn't see Ma at all. I could see only the man motionless on the ground, his eyes searching, the deacons' circle swarming him until he couldn't fight anymore, the red streaks of blood on Papa's hands.

FOUR

In bed that night, I waited for the cones of Papa's headlights to cut through the darkness. All sound had been wrung out of the air; even the crickets seemed to have gone silent. Hours must have passed, but I was still awake when sunrise crept across the horizon's threshold, scattering its rays through the slatted blinds.

Papa had never spent a night away from the house during revival season.

Across the room, Hannah was in the middle of a deep sleep, not even stirring at sunrise, when Ma would have normally been making breakfast. I rose on sore limbs, my neck a knot of nerves, and passed the closed bedroom door where Ma had slept alone. In the kitchen, early-morning sunlight caught the teardrop-shaped glass pieces on the gold chandelier, refracting its brightness into prisms on the walls. My hands, desperate for something to do, opened cupboards that revealed unopened boxes of cereal, packets of hot chocolate, and pancake mix, but my stomach lurched at the thought of eating.

As I sat down at the table empty-handed, Ma walked into the kitchen, a few pink foam curlers askew beneath her multicolored scarf. She walked past me, nodding slightly, and turned to the front door where the lock hadn't budged since we entered last night.

"Morning, Miriam." She was usually chipper in the morning, but this greeting was clipped and emotionless. A minute later, Caleb wiped his eyes and yawned as he came from his bedroom in a ratty second-hand T-shirt and a pair of flannel pajama pants. If Papa had been back, Caleb would have already been dressed in his suit, ready to prepare for another day's service.

"Where is he?" Caleb asked as he began rooting through the cupboard doors that I must have forgotten to close. Ma cleared her throat, preparing an answer for him. What could she say? It was obvious that she had no idea, especially as she kept touching the screen of her cell phone that hadn't pinged since she'd been at the table.

"I'm going to see about Hannah," I said before Ma could open her mouth to give

Caleb some unsatisfactory answer.

As I walked closer to Hannah's bed, she stretched her arms overhead. Scooping her out of the tangle of sheets, I lowered her body to the carpet before opening the duffel bag and scattering a few toys around the room. I held Tiger's floppy body several feet from where she was splayed.

She closed her slack mouth and pursed her lips. One arm was pressed against the gray carpet, and the muscles in her neck tensed as she brought her right arm up to meet her left. Her limp legs spread out behind her as her arms did all the work. Between her grunts, scattered pieces of Ma's conversation with Caleb were audible. Something about *thinking time* and *space.* I realized she knew nothing about why he was still out, what had happened behind the tent.

Hannah made her way to a block and brought it close to her face. Her eyes widened in wonder. Part of me wanted to see the world her way: each ridge in the block the crag in a mountainside, the carpet fibers sea anemones. I wanted to be able to forget last night too — the blood on Papa's hands, the *thunk* from his fist hitting the man's jaw. As Hannah reached me, I tried to smile as I handed Tiger to her.

As Hannah stroked Tiger with her flattened palm, I heard a rumble through the bedroom window. Papa. Crawling to the windowsill, I parted the blinds with my finger. The knot on his formerly perfect tie was loosened; it hung in the middle of his chest like an anchor. His suit jacket dangled from his index finger, and the knees of his new pants were darkened with a thick reddish-brown substance that could have been mud or blood. A thunderstorm percolated behind him on the horizon as he inched closer to the house. He took slow steps toward the front door and rang the bell like a stranger.

At any moment he would be at my bedroom door with an explanation for what had happened. A failed healing could be the result of a faith issue. As for the violence, maybe the man had even attacked him and I hadn't seen it. And even though Papa was a minister, he was a man first, and men needed to defend themselves. There had to be an explanation, and once Papa gave it to us, we could help him string together the right combination of words so that the congregation could understand why he had yielded to the temptation of violence. There was a litany of lines that other preachers had used over the years: *I ask for your forgiveness. I, too, am a sinner saved by grace. Pray for me, all ye gathered here, because the devil is busy.*

I left Hannah in the middle of the floor and rounded the corner just as Ma threw open the front door. Trailing Papa inside the house, Ma caught his suit jacket before it hit the ground and quickly straightened until she was upright. Yesterday, Ma had ironed his clean dress shirt into pristine pleats; now, flecks of blood like polka dots were on his chest and sleeves. His right hand hung limp by his side, his knuckles bandaged with threadbare gauze. Ma must have seen it as soon as I did because she gasped and grabbed his hand.

"Where were you? And what happened to your hand?"

"Nowhere. Nothing." He snatched his hand from her and winced as it snapped back to his chest. "Why do you have to ask so many questions? I have a question for you. Why isn't breakfast ready yet?"

"Samuel, what's gotten into you?"

Papa took another step into the kitchen and slammed his hand on the back of the chair next to where Caleb was sitting. Caleb jumped from the table, knocking over his cereal bowl; pink-tinged milk spilled on the

82

table's wood grain before it dripped to the floor.

"I'm not going to ask again. Where's my breakfast?"

Ma leaped back a couple of floor tiles. Her mouth was agape as she opened the refrigerator; the carton of eggs slipped out of her tenuous grasp and onto the floor.

"Look what you did. Clean that up. Now."

He stayed standing while she bent to scrub the gelatinous mixture of golden yolks and milky whites; with each circular motion of the dishcloth, the stain inched closer to Papa's shoe. I pressed my back against the hallway wall, out of Papa's line of sight, unable to move to help her, even as the ragged hem of my nightgown tickled my kneecaps and urged me forward. I pulled at a loose thread and wound it around my thumb a few times, creating a sudden marble of pain at the tip that was white before turning red and then purple. The strained string broke off in my hand and sailed to the floor, immediately alleviating the pain that I desperately wanted back.

The house held its breath between Papa's solo breakfast and the late-morning hour when he and Caleb should have left for the revival site. I crept past Ma and Papa's ajar bedroom door — a sliver of him sat at the edge of the mattress with his head pressed between his palms, his fingers palpating the quarter-size bald spot at the top of his head. If he would look up, he could explain to me what was going on, why he hadn't told Ma what had happened.

A minute later, the phone blared in the house, but he didn't move to answer it — he hadn't answered it all morning and had ordered the rest of us not to either. Instead, he unwrapped and rerolled the gauze from his knuckles like he was preparing for a fight. In the echoing silence after the phone stopped ringing, the word *fraud* from last night pricked the air like lightning. It wasn't the first time he'd been called a fraud, but Papa had ignored those previous accusations, especially since they'd come from heathens. Something about his response outside the tent made the accusation feel different. Truer somehow.

"Papa?" I said when I'd been standing in his doorway for several minutes. My mind had been a jumble of questions, but when I reached for them now, they hovered out of grasp. Then the words from all of his sermons came back to me. "You said that it's not in God's will to heal everyone. So it wasn't God's will to heal that man. Right?

And you hit him because he lied about you. You were angry. I get that."

I nodded, hoping to coax his response out. "Right, Papa?"

All he had to do was say one word. *Right*. But he kept his head in his hands, not even looking up at me.

"Right, Papa? Answer me!" My voice was rising, frantic.

Papa knew all the verses in the Bible and could recite them on command. He could make small talk about everything, from the weather to car engines. Now he sat in the middle of the sagging mattress, completely silent.

In the empty hallway, the phone started ringing again. As I closed my eyes and knocked the back of my head against the wall, fuzzy images from the night before took shape on the darkness of my eyelids. Bloody knuckles, the screaming man, the semicircle of deacons' hunched, suited backs. The hollow sound of my skull against the wall was like the sound last night when Papa hit the man square in the jaw. I had tried to imagine it any other way, but without an answer from him, the only thing I could believe was that he'd done it on purpose.

He couldn't be a fraud like the man said

— fraud would mean that he'd known all along that he hadn't been able to heal. And he'd healed thousands of people in ways big and small. But the Papa I saw now, the one sitting silently on the edge of the mattress with his head in his hands, didn't look like the same man who'd made a boy walk earlier this summer.

We took one van to revival that night — no separate caravans with men in one car and women and children bringing up the rear hours later. Papa put the air-conditioning on full blast and then rolled down the window. Ma always griped about his habit — *Do you want to cool the outside too?* — but she held her tongue today. A few stop-lights away from the revival tent, Papa's commercial came onto the Christian radio station, proclaiming him "the Faith Healer of East Mansfield." Papa turned the volume dial all the way to the left, and we rode the rest of the way in silence.

A low layer of thick gray clouds pressed against the sky like the heel of God's hand. As we pulled into the space in the lot cordoned off for the revival pastor, I saw that the parking lot was half as full as it was the same time the night before. I watched in the rearview mirror as Papa set his jaw, each muscle in his face straining to make the "faith healer" expression that had been effortless only the previous day. He stepped outside of the van and rested his hand against the top of the open door. As the night air came inside, he leaned over. *Finally, he was going to say something. He had found a way to explain it all.*

"See you inside." He had shrunk since I saw him earlier on the bed — a child in a man's suit.

I took a deep breath and helped Hannah onto the grass outside the van. We moved slowly, passing deacons who looked through us like we were invisible, deacons whose backs I had hidden behind last night. Inside the tent's flaps, the overhead bulbs felt like spotlights as Hannah and I followed Ma down the middle aisle. Faces — though not nearly as many as the night before — turned toward us, staring in the way that people stared at Hannah when they first met her. But there was usually a trace of concern or pity directed at Hannah, whereas these stares were hostile.

"Charlatan," someone hissed from the back of the tent.

"I heard he broke his jaw." Another whisper came to join the chorus.

I could always shake off what faithless

naysayers said about Papa, but this time tears welled behind my eyes. If Ma was surprised by the accusations being lobbed at us, she didn't let on. Her posture was ramrod straight as she bypassed the fourth row where we usually sat and staked out a place in the center of the first row. I slunk into the seat next to Ma, with Hannah on my left. Ma's jaw jutted — it was easy for her to show pride when she didn't know what I knew.

The wait for the sermon to start felt interminable. I kept wanting to turn around, to see if the tent was filling up at all, but I stayed still, not even wiping away a bead of sweat that made its way from my hairline down my face before landing in the collar of my dress.

After an hour that seemed endless, the old keyboardist ascended to the stage and the opening chord of "All to Jesus I Surrender" filled the air around us. A wave of nausea churned in my stomach as Papa made the processional inside. He slipped on a wan smile and stepped behind the pulpit, raising his arms to signal that it was time for the call to worship. The deacons were supposed to join him onstage, but they stayed with the congregation, leaving only Caleb in the semicircle of chairs behind Papa.

" 'Give thanks to the Lord for He is good; His love endures forever.' " These words, usually met with applause, were greeted with cacophonous silence. The microphone screeched, but Papa continued speaking even as his words were inaudible over the crackling feedback.

"What happened last night?" A voice from the back of the tent yelled above the din.

"You put him in the hospital."

Ma stiffened beside me as she wrapped the long strap of her purse around her hand. I shifted my eyes to the right to avoid a conspicuous turn of my head and counted the fast blinks of her confused, glassy eyes, watched the slightest tremble in her top lip. My eyes skipped from her to Caleb, who was seated behind Papa on the stage, gripping both sides of the folding chair as Papa raised his arms to stop the congregation's incessant shouting. But the voices kept coming one after another: "A preacher wouldn't do that to someone!" a woman's voice shouted. "You are no preacher," some man said. With each declaration, Caleb drifted farther away from the stage until his eyes were pointed somewhere over my head at what I imagined was an object outside of the tent's open flaps.

My neck snapped around for the first time

all service. The seats were mostly empty, and the faces that stared back at Papa were full of anger. Papa looked down at his papers as though the answer was written there. He adjusted the wireless microphone behind his ear, but his lips didn't move.

"Saints of God, I want to talk to you about the mysteries of faith." He was yelling now, but their booing drowned out his amplified voice. Ma rooted in the side pocket of her purse until the key ring was in her hand; with each new jeer that rose behind us, she gripped the keys tighter in her fist until only a spike of silver stuck out. She scooted to the front of her chair, planted her block heels squarely on the grass, and stood, pulling me up with her. We had never left a revival early.

The jeers got louder behind us as my hand hooked under Hannah's armpit to bring her to her tottering feet. Soon, we were speed-walking out of the back of the tent. We burst through the line of deacons, and Ma ran at full speed to the car and started it. I was just finishing buckling Hannah in when Papa and Caleb appeared, illuminated by the individual circular ground lights that shone outside the tent.

"What *was* that, Samuel?" Ma asked, after getting out and sliding into the passenger seat so Papa could drive.

"Let's just get out of here."

"No. What were those lies they were saying? You didn't hurt that man. You just tried to heal him. Did something else happen after the revival service?"

"We can talk about this later." He tossed his arm around the passenger seat and looked backward into the rear window. The van zipped away from the tent in reverse.

"We're going to talk about it now." Her words rose at the end with a sharpness that was reserved for times when she was angry with me or Caleb; I'd never heard her use that tone with Papa. Papa ignored her until Ma grabbed the gear shift and jolted the van into park. My head crashed into the back of the driver's seat; I threw out a stiff right arm to keep Hannah in place.

"You need to go back there and tell them that it's all a misunderstanding. We're not going to run away from here like criminals! Tell them!" Ma's words knifed through the minivan's air as she leaned close to Papa's face, her crooked finger pointing in the direction of where she wanted him to go. Papa released his hold on the steering wheel as his shoulders slumped.

They had indicted him back in the tent, so he wouldn't have to admit to anything that hadn't already been said. Besides, we confessed our sins to one another regularly — Ma had told us about her anger at God after Isaiah's death, and Papa had confessed to being prideful. This would just be another confession in a line of confessions. And if he said he was wrong, if he admitted it and repented, we could pray for him and find a way to move forward.

"Tell us, Papa," I finally said with feeble words. I should have said, *Tell them.*

"They don't know anything! They're lying. All of them. There's nothing to tell."

I had leaned forward behind him, straining against the taut seat belt as I awaited his explanation, but I flopped back into the seat after hearing his flat, false words. Ma placed her left hand on the steering wheel, preventing him from driving off, but his two hands on the wheel wrestled it away from her. He jammed his foot on the gas and turned the wheel so hard that Ma's body slammed into the door.

"I saw —" I began.

Ma and Papa snapped around and looked back at me as though I had interrupted their private conversation.

"You saw nothing, Miriam." His eyes narrowed in the red-tinted darkness from the stoplight overhead. As he held my gaze, daring me to defy him, a flash of heat passed through my feet and made the tips of my toes tingle. Then a bubble of rage rose to my stomach and popped. He knew that I wouldn't. Couldn't.

I snuck a glance at the revival tent receding over my left shoulder — I knew it was bad luck, that looking back turned Lot's wife into a pillar of salt, but I couldn't help myself. A ribbon of exhaust streamed from the back of the car, tethering us to the people inside before the tent released us into the dark.

We hurtled onto the unlit two-lane highway that unspooled in front of us as far as the headlights illuminated and no farther. Even the stars' bright pinpricks of light were now hidden behind a veil of clouds. Twenty minutes after leaving the revival tent, we arrived at the Griffith house.

"We need to be out of here in ten minutes, tops." Papa looked at his gold watch that gleamed in the darkness. He didn't say where we were headed — we weren't due to the next revival location until Saturday — four days away. When Ma and Papa went inside the house to pack, Caleb stood by the minivan's open door with creases between his raised, impatient eyebrows.

"What's going on?" he whispered.

"Papa hit that guy, Caleb. He hit him when he didn't heal him."

"What are you talking about?"

"He hit the blind guy and lied about it."

"How would you know? Did you actually see him hit anyone?" Anger — or was it disbelief? — fluttered behind his eyes. Leave it to Caleb to question what I had seen and not what Papa had done. If he had ever questioned Papa, he had never shown it. It must have felt too good to be in Papa's sunshine; he had never experienced what it felt like to be in its adjacent shadow.

"Did you actually see the hit?" Caleb's eyes got wider as he repeated the question, his face hopeful. I wished I had the same faith that he did in Papa.

"Yes. I saw it."

His cheeks slackened as he shifted his gaze to the crack in the driveway. I could practically see his mind racing as he swallowed hard and then massaged his cheeks. He forced air through a pinhole in his pursed lips — the only sound between us for several seconds.

"It was dark. You didn't see what you thought you did. You couldn't have." His voice lacked the conviction it had a few seconds before.

"Five minutes to go." Papa's voice echoed from the bowels of the house.

"You heard him." Caleb turned on his heel and went inside.

We were refugees in the night: there was no map in Ma's lap as we drove through dark streets. Through the van's windows, Bethel was a blur of empty plots of land and vacant shopping centers; only when my knuckles burned did I realize that I'd been holding on to the armrest the whole time. The clock in the car changed from 8:59 to 9:00. Revival would be letting out any minute now, and we were locked in a car moving aimlessly through a city we didn't know. We crossed the border into a neighboring town as Papa put more miles between us and Bethel. Hunger clawed at the edges of my stomach, and I buried my arms deeper into my abdomen to dull its sharp ache. Hannah started to howl and buck against her restraints, but Papa didn't look back in the rearview mirror to signal me to quiet her.

At 10:44, we turned right down an unfamiliar road in a town far away from Bethel, in the direction of an oscillating sign that read TY'S DINER. The inside of the restaurant was bright, with leather booths and a few patrons seated on round stools by the counter. As we sat in the silent, still car, our eyes bounced over T-shirts and jeans before we exhaled sighs of collective relief that none of the people in here had been at the revival that night.

"We're good here," Papa said.

We ordered our food in monotones and fragments: *Eggs sunnyside up, add bacon; short stack of pancakes; French toast; black coffee.* At the other end of the semicircular booth, Papa was jittery in his skin, as though a current was running in his veins. He drummed his fingers next to the coffee mug that the waitress kept refilling, causing black liquid to slosh over the mug's ceramic lip and land in a shallow puddle on the table.

After our food arrived, Papa took one bite of eggs before pushing his plate forward; he reached into his briefcase and spread out the map as though this had all been part of the plan. Papa's shaky hands traced routes from here to places unknown as Caleb nodded without looking over at me. Next to me, Ma speared a triangle of pancake for Hannah and cupped her chin to guide it inside. I nudged her knee while she wiped syrup from Hannah's lips.

"Do you believe what he said?" I mouthed.

Ma looked at me quizzically, and I made sure that Papa and Caleb were still talking before I repeated the words, slower this time, elongating my mouth around the vowels. She peered over my shoulder at them before shrugging.

"I saw what happened," I mouthed again. "I saw him hurt the man."

"What are you two talking about down there?"

I froze as the tendons in her neck became tight cords. The slick palms of my hands slid against the table's surface.

"Just girl talk. Nothing you need to concern yourself with," Ma said.

The tasteless hunk of French toast had jagged edges as it went down my throat, but I focused on swallowing instead of looking at Papa. When Papa didn't believe you, his lips puckered with scorn; I couldn't be on the receiving end of that expression, not after what I had already seen. After what felt like forever, he went back to talking about highway numbers with Caleb. I moved my right foot over inch by inch until it was touching Ma's shoe. She left her foot there and returned to feeding Hannah.

Every few minutes, I caught Ma shooting glances at Papa. Did he at all resemble the man she had married sixteen years ago? The way the story went, she was seventeen when a cocky, twenty-year-old boxer turned preacher came to her town as the Faith Healer of Midland. She gave her life to Jesus on the spot and married Papa six weeks later. We had lived under the canopy of that belief my whole life, eating and drinking faith in God first and Papa second, never questioning Papa's healing abilities, the same way we never questioned the existence of the sun, even when it was hidden behind clouds. Our belief left no directives about what to do if our faith in Papa faltered.

FIVE

The next afternoon, we spread thin bath towels by the concrete edge of the pool at Sleepy Elms Motel. A neon orange sign blinked V CANCY in the lobby window. I laid Hannah on the first towel, and the jarring rip from the loosening Velcro teeth of her leg braces echoed over the shallow water. I stripped her to her cotton under-shirt and panties before lowering her into the pool on top of a floatie. She held the yellow foam noodle for dear life and kicked her thin legs with surprising force. Every so often, she dipped her open mouth below the surface and came back up with full cheeks.

A few kids throwing an inflatable ball by the NO LIFEGUARD ON DUTY sign looked over. They spied Hannah first; then their eyes roved to Ma and me. Our long skirts and loose shirts starkly contrasted their oily torsos that were barely covered by bright strips of Lycra. The moment they made eye contact, I turned away from their brazenness the way Papa had always told us to when we were in the proximity of immodesty. Papa made it clear that God looked more favorably on modest girls like me. He had also told us that nothing happened to the man outside the tent, but I tried to push that thought aside.

A girl who seemed to be the ringleader of the group raised her hands in the air; the tank top portion of her bathing suit rose a few inches, exposing the hollow concavity of her navel. She knew all of the words to an ungodly song I'd never heard, and, as she sang, her arms swayed the way ours did to church hymns. I kicked eddies into the lukewarm water and raised my hands like hers — my shirt slid up a bit, and I raised the hem even more until an inch of my stomach was showing.

"Miriam, what are you doing?" Ma grabbed my shirt and yanked it down before looking over her shoulder. "Don't let your father see you doing that."

But I had seen the cab pick Papa up hours earlier — in the waning moments of gray when night yielded to dawn. Caleb and Hannah were still asleep as I hooked the blackout curtains with my forefinger and saw him open the cab's back door with his stuffed briefcase reliably by his side.

"He's not here, Ma, you know that. Besides, it's hot outside."

"It's immodest." The final word slid out between clenched teeth. "You can enjoy the sun without being naked."

She leaned all the way back — sunbathing, as it were — even though a thick layer of gray cotton shielded her skin from the sun. Stretched on her back with her arms raised overhead, the small swell of her belly protruded beneath the dress's fabric. The faint pink heart tattoo on her right wrist peeked out — one of very few remnants of her life before Papa. While her eyes were closed, I rubbed my thumb on the inky section of skin — the heart's black outline and light-pink interior were indistinguishable from the smoothness of the rest of her wrist. She looked down at my fingers in the center of the tattoo and didn't flick them away.

"Did it hurt?"

"I thought it did when I got it, but then I had children. That was a whole new kind of pain." She ran her hand over her stomach.

"Did your parents know?"

She laughed. "They never knew what the three of us did. And if they did know, they wouldn't have cared. I grew up in a different kind of house, Miriam. My sisters and I practically raised ourselves. If we didn't cook, we didn't eat. We went to bed when we were tired and to school when we wanted to. The only good thing my dad ever did was pay for the occasional dance lesson when there was enough money to go around, but he never came to any of my performances." There were traces of sadness in her voice, but the dark lenses that covered half her face were turned toward a skywriter swooping in the distance, creating indecipherable letters that faded a few seconds later.

"The last time I went to a pool like this, my sisters and I were in high school. During the summer when my mom worked, we stayed at home alone and went to the pool. Claudia's boyfriend was a lifeguard there. We'd pack snacks and stay all day, just to avoid being at home."

"What do you miss the most about them?" Ma was so rarely open with me like this — especially not when Papa was around — so I wanted to take advantage of her candor.

"So many things." She rubbed the indentations that her sunglasses had etched into the bridge of her nose. "Like the way Claudia's eyes crinkled at the corners whenever she told a lie. Or how Yolanda

102

used to feed me her famous chocolate chip cookies fresh from the oven on my birthday, whenever we could afford the ingredients, that is." Her voice caught on the last word. She always spoke about them in the past tense, even though they still lived in Ma's hometown, which was only two hours north of where we lived now. Papa told us that we couldn't have a relationship with them because they weren't saved — effectively, they were dead to us. I'd never questioned Papa's reasons for not letting us around the only aunts we had, even though I knew it was our job to convert nonbelievers.

In public, Ma supported his rules, but on a few occasions, usually when Papa was at the church for a trustee meeting, she slipped into the pantry and shut the door behind her. The muffled sounds of a one-sided conversation echoed through the kitchen — calls that abruptly ended when Papa's car rumbled in the driveway. One day a few weeks before this revival season began, I ran upstairs and got on the other receiver. I didn't remember everything they said, but at one point, Aunt Claudia asked Ma when she would wake up and take her life back. Ma hung up on her instead of answering.

Aunt Claudia's question had haunted me before we left, but I kept the memory submerged. Occasionally, it bobbed to the surface and made many other parts of Ma and Papa's marriage come into focus — how Papa whisked her away from her family at the end of that weeklong revival and asked her to finish the rest of the revival circuit by his side. How he married her six weeks later and told her she couldn't see her family anymore. Or the fact that the only photo I'd seen of their wedding day was of just the two of them in front of a minister, no family or friends standing nearby.

They don't know him like we do. It was what I told myself after the dial tone droned in my ear. But Aunt Claudia's words rose again last night and lingered at the periphery of my mind.

"Tell me the story of how you and Papa met." I had heard the story a few times, but I wanted to hear her tell it again. Maybe I even wanted her loving words about him to rub off on me, to remind me that he had been good once.

Her voice fell away to a whisper as she talked about her pre-Papa life, about how she met Papa the same night that she promised to run away with Claudia and Yolanda if their father came home drunk again, leaving purple handprints on their pajamaed bodies like souvenirs. The evening that she'd met Papa had been a worse night than most, and they packed backpacks and stole their father's truck, vowing never to come back. They drove without a place to go — kind of like what we were doing now — and saw a tent that they thought belonged to a circus.

"I was seventeen when we stumbled on the revival. I didn't even know what a revival was back then, can you imagine that?" She folded her arms over her chest and laughed. "Yolanda, Claudia, and I got there after it started and sat in the back row. I didn't know what I was looking for when I came inside. An escape, maybe. But when I first heard the music, I felt like I'd been transported to another place. I had never experienced anything like that before."

I knew what she meant; I had grown up in the church, yet there were still moments when my soul rode the highest chords to unimagined places. I imagined hearing that mixture of keyboard and tambourine and drums alongside a choir for the first time — it probably felt like her soul had been snatched out.

"And then he started speaking. I couldn't take my eyes off him. He was barely older than me, but his presence filled the room like he was twice my age. I didn't know the God that he was talking about, but I wanted to know everything. By the end of his sermon, I jumped out of my chair and ran to the front of the tent before it was time, before the benediction. The deacons held me back, but I fell onto the altar and gave my life to Jesus in that moment. And I met my husband."

I turned and looked over at her. Her eyes were still hidden behind her glasses, but there was no smile carved in her cheeks.

"What happened next?"

"He asked me to stay after the service, and when the entire tent emptied, he invited me to revival the next night. I couldn't tell if I was doing it for Jesus or to get your father's attention, but I went back to revival every night that week — making up excuses when my sisters asked where I was going. He was supposed to go to another revival in some new city that Sunday, but he showed up at the diner where I worked on his way out of town. I still had three hours left in my shift."

"Did he wait for you?"

"Some things about your father have changed." She laughed. "But some things haven't. He never liked to wait. Even back then. So, I told my boss I was taking my break and left. Your father took my hand and led me to the parking lot. I remembered the way he opened the car door like a gentleman — he seemed like a real adult, not like the boys I was used to."

"Where did he take you?" I tried to picture my parents as people close to my age — as people at all. As she spoke, silhouettes of their pasts sharpened into clear pictures. I imagined Ma in a powder-blue waitress uniform with her name on the lapel, the slow way that she reached behind her back and untied her apron — folding it in thirds the way she now folded our laundry — before leaving it next to the cash register. I imagined her taking Papa's hand, callused from all those years of boxing, and sinking into his car.

Ma kneaded her hands against her thighs while she spoke. Then she sprang upward like a latch snapped closed inside her. She tucked her skirt between her parted legs and tented her knees before patting the small piece of cement in front of her. I climbed into the cove left by her skirt, sliding my shoulders between the peaks of her raised knees. The protrusion from her growing stomach pressed into my back as her fingers parted my hair in the center and whizzed across my scalp. My head lolled in her deft hands as she tugged and braided. She hummed as she leaned close to my scalp, her lips buzzing by my ear. I was too old for her French braids and would unravel them tonight, but right now, I loved the feeling of her hands in my hair.

"We went to a nearby lake. He didn't even know if I would go with him, but he had packed a picnic basket in the back seat with a blanket next to it. When we got to the lake, he asked if he could do something. He led me to the water and stepped inside. I stayed on the bank and told him that I didn't want to swim. He said that he wanted to spend the rest of his life with me, but in order to do that, he would have to baptize me first."

"He baptized you on your date?" She'd never told me that detail before.

"It sounds ridiculous now, but it was romantic then. I knew I was in love as soon as he dropped my head back into the water. He proposed to me on that blanket." She spun her gold band on her ring finger as her voice faded. "We got married six weeks later, on my eighteenth birthday."

Hannah inched closer to the edge of the pool, ready to come out. I yanked her from the water and placed her on the towel.

"What did he do?" Ma asked, her voice suddenly deeper. Nearby lawnmowers buzzed a soft soundtrack to Ma's barely audible voice. I leaned closer while rubbing Hannah dry. Caleb was a few feet away, his feet crossed on the chair where he was reclined, his hand above his eyes providing shade from the sun.

I paused. Part of me wanted to protect her from what I knew. But lying — especially to Ma — was a sin. "He beat the guy up, Ma. Then he stomped him into the ground and told the deacons to take him away." The shock in my face was reflected in her sunglasses.

"I've never seen him like that. It was terrifying. It was almost like it wasn't him," I continued.

"Mmm." It was a knowing moan — one that conveyed no surprise.

"Have you seen him do that before?"

Ma exhaled — a stream of pressure being released from a balloon. I reached forward and pulled her sunglasses from her face. Her eyes were red, like she'd been crying before we even got to the pool.

"Your father is a man like other men. It's important to remember that. God has chosen your father for a special calling, but he is also human." She reached for her sunglasses and clumsily placed them back on her face. Suddenly, she stood up behind my unfinished braids; her dress unrolled like a curtain closing.

"I'm getting hungry. Let's get lunch."

Gas stations and supermarkets dotted both sides of the wide street that led away from the motel. Even though Ma said she was hungry, we passed the diner where we'd eaten the night before and kept driving without slowing down. Ma seemed like she knew where she was going, so I rolled down the back window and leaned outside. A truck barreled by us in the right lane; I shielded my eyes against the flecks of debris that it stirred into the air.

Ma slowed the car to a crawl at a stop sign. She looked both ways and squinted, seemingly deciding the best way to turn to get lunch. In that moment, a familiar voice came through the open window.

"Ma. Do you hear that?"

"Hear what?" She angled her ear toward my open window behind her. A siren blared nearby, obscuring the voice.

"Wait a second."

A car honked and then sped around us with a screech. Ma and Caleb rolled down their windows. The voice came back — still faint.

"I don't hear anything."

Ma passed through the stop sign below the speed limit, and the words got louder as we crept closer to their source.

"I hear it," Caleb said. "It sounds like Papa."

Ma gripped the wheel tighter as the voice was soon unmistakable. My eyes bounced from trees to brick facades to concrete slabs of sidewalk before they found a suited figure half a block away on the left side of the street. There was no way that could be Papa, even though he wore one of Papa's suits and sounded like him. Ma pulled over and turned on the hazards. I could hear him clearly now; he was reciting verses from Revelation 6 about the end days and the four horsemen of the apocalypse. It was the sermon that he would have been giving if we were still in Bethel. But we weren't in Bethel, and he was on the side of the road with a sheaf of papers in one hand and a microphone in the other, looking to all the world like a crazy person.

"What's he doing?" Caleb's words stumbled over one another.

"Shh!" Ma's finger shot to her lips before she furiously rolled up the windows to cut off any sound he was making. My heart stuttered as I jerked forward to see more, but the seat belt pressed me back: a reprimand. Through the front window, the sharp edges of his silhouette got blurry. Papa always called street preachers madmen: according to him, what differentiated him from the lunatics on the street was a denomination behind him, the word of God on his side, and a pulpit.

The man — Papa — looked in our direction for a split second, and I reclined my seat until I was almost horizontal. My heart froze as his eyes fixed on the minivan and then looked away.

"Drive," I yelled. "Drive!" The words propelled themselves out of my lungs.

Ma let out a gasp that she immediately squelched with her hand — the resulting sound was like someone being suffocated.

"What's he doing? What's he doing?" Caleb had been repeating the same question into the window since we got there, emphasizing different syllables and blurring the words together so it sounded like one rapid-fire phrase.

A lump rose in the back of my mouth that I tried to swallow, but it lodged in my throat instead. Ma jolted the car back into motion and jerked away. Papa disappeared from view; I focused my eyes on the double yellow line in front of us until it became wavy in my vision.

■ ■ ■ ■

Back in the motel room, lunch was a hot dog wrapped in foil that Ma had plucked from the greasy metal rollers at the gas station. She had even turned on the television — breaking one of the cardinal rules of our house. Usually, the smallest transgressions were thrilling, especially when we got away with them. But this was not the same as stealing an extra slice of pie at dessert or returning home from Micah's house a couple of minutes after curfew.

No one had spoken Papa's name or offered an explanation for what we had seen. The television's vivid pictures couldn't dilute the memory of him shouting on the side of the street like a madman. How had he turned from a man whose congregation had been in the thousands into this? Maybe it had all started with his hitting the pregnant girl — I had told myself it was a mistake, that he was sorry for it. But everything changed that night in Bethel. And if I hadn't seen it for myself, I would have sworn that the man at the corner wasn't him either. There had to be other things about him that I didn't know — other things that I hadn't let myself see.

113

My untouched hot dog was still mummi-fied in its foil wrapper on the end table. Ma chided me to eat over high-pitched laughter on the television, but a few bites of the cold, slick link didn't quell the burn in my stomach. Who was this man we were fol-lowing everywhere, trusting the words that came out of his mouth like gospel? And what else was he capable of?

The desk clock said 11:03 p.m. when I heard a car pull up. Ma was back in her room next door as footsteps against the pavement made a cadence that was distinc-tively Papa's. The room was awash with the television's blue glow as I scrambled out of bed and jammed the power button until the screen went dark. I crept to the door; my breathing quickened as I placed my hand on the lever and pushed it down a mil-limeter or two. Then all the way.

I stepped into a wave of heat, smack into the impenetrable wall of three vertical gold buttons drooping from his suit jacket. He jolted forward as though he'd seen a ghost; his briefcase dropped from his extended palm, clattering to the ground between us in slow motion. As I dragged my eyes from the scuffed brown leather of his briefcase to his wrinkled suit jacket to the smudged glasses that were halfway down the bridge of his nose, the hot dog tossed in the pool of grease in my stomach.

"Miriam. Why are you still awake? What is it?" His words were blunt at the edges. He moved to get past me, but I widened my stance as he maneuvered to the left to get by. He sighed his annoyance as he looked over my shoulder. The words I wanted to say vanished the way they always did when he was close. I searched his face — reconciling this version of the man I barely knew with the one we'd seen on the street and the one from the night in Bethel.

"Why did you hit him?"

"What are you talking about, Miriam? Get back to your room." His words were flinty as he flung out his right arm and pushed the air aside to dispatch me.

"Was it because he said you couldn't heal?" I took one step closer to his hands that dwarfed the key card. *I will never hurt you; I will never hurt you.* I needed to believe it now, but those words rang as hollow as his other ones. I knew that talking back, especially to Papa, came with consequences. But this man wasn't Papa anymore.

"You don't know what you're talking about." With each word, the muscle in his jaw twitched as his eyes darted in their sockets.

"I know what I saw. You lied about this. What else have you lied about?" His anger made me bolder than I really felt; it braced my spine as I sandwiched myself between him and the hotel room door.

"Who are you to question me about any of this?" he growled. "I've been doing this work longer than you've been alive. You know nothing about what it takes to make a successful revival. There are months of planning — years — behind every minute that you get to witness." He raised his arms to emphasize his point; his hands inched closer to my face, and I slid away from where I stood between him and the door, backing toward the railing.

"So don't you dare question me. I have nothing to explain to you. Nothing." On his final word, he swung a fist in my direction. I leaped back, out of range, landing with my back against the railing's vertical bars. I cowered with hands in front of my face as he came closer, unable to get to my unsteady feet. *I will never hurt you; I will never hurt* you played on repeat in my head. His eyes were closed as his hands swung in the emptiness. He couldn't have been fighting with me because his punches whizzed in

116

the air, faster and with more force, with none of them landing anywhere close to me.

When he finally opened his eyes, he looked around in the darkness as though expecting to see something, but his head flinched at a lone mosquito that sailed in front of his face. He finally looked back at the ground, and his face collapsed as he saw me in a pile, my knees to my chest, my arms around my knees. But a moment later, he straightened to his fullest height and slid his glasses up to the bridge of his nose. Only when they were back on his face did he seem to realize where he was.

A door clicked — I tried to scramble to my feet, but they wouldn't grip. Caleb stepped outside, rubbing his eyes with his fists. He furrowed his eyebrows as he looked at me on the ground and back up at Papa.

"What's going on?" Caleb reached out an arm to yank me to my feet.

"Nothing. We were just talking." Papa spoke up even though Caleb was still only looking at me.

"It sounded like you were arguing."

"Miriam had a misunderstanding."

"There was no misunderstanding." My steady right hand against the railing belied the wobble in my knees. My voice came out strong, clear of the cottony fuzziness that

117

had been in my head. Papa stared at me, but he wouldn't do anything in front of Caleb.

"It's late. We should get some sleep. We can talk about it in the morning."

Papa slid his key card into the reader and slipped inside. Caleb and I stood in the hallway watching the bronze numbers — 211 — long after the door closed.

"Are you okay?" He finally asked when we both realized that Papa wasn't coming back out to explain anything.

"Not really."

"Where are you hurt?" He scanned the common places for physical injuries — elbows, knees.

"I'm not hurt like that." How could I tell him that the hurt was in a place he couldn't see? That only a couple of days before I still believed that Jesus Christ was Lord, Papa had the healing gift from the Holy Spirit, and we had to follow his lead. But those final two truths had been splitting themselves in my brain, like cells during mitosis. One truth became two possible truths, and then four, and then eight. By the time we arrived back in Texas next month, it would be impossible to know what was true anymore.

Six

In the six remaining revivals after Bethel, I expected Papa to seem chastened, but rather than admit fault for anything that had happened, he told us that God was using this test to strengthen our faith. All the while, he raved about the end days in front of mostly empty tents in Tennessee and Oklahoma, becoming the corner preacher all over again. By the time we pulled into the garage back home with 3,253 new miles on the odometer, Papa stepped onto the driveway as a shell of his former self. We spilled out of the car, our feet desperate to be on familiar ground again. I slipped off my shoes and stood on the warm concrete. It was my ritual for returning home, even though the house didn't look like the one we had left.

"Gather around," Papa said to all of us, cupping the air with his arms to emphasize his statement. We circled him and knelt next to oil stains on the driveway. Papa bowed his head and we all followed suit.

"Lord, thank You for another successful revival season," he began with a voice louder than normal. "Thank You for all the souls that You brought into the tents for deliverance, and thank You for the power You have given me to continue doing Your will."

I opened my eyes to see Ma and Caleb nodding at Papa's words as though their desire to believe him made what he was saying true. It was easier to accept things without questioning them, but wasn't that just blind faith — the very thing Papa had preached against for so many years?

"Amen," Papa said.

"Amen," Ma and Caleb repeated in unison. I struggled to make the words pass through my clenched lips, but Papa didn't seem to notice as he brushed the dirt from his pants and stood.

As they headed into the house, I dawdled outside for a few minutes before lying down on a patch of grass. A pillow of blades prickled my back as clouds churned above, evidence of the earth shifting even though I couldn't feel its subtle movements. Then there was a darkening in my field of vision. Ma's face entered my view, lines of concern etched on her forehead. A few seconds later,

Hannah appeared next to her.

"What's wrong?"

How could I tell her that I wasn't okay when everyone else was? That I needed a bit of what she and Caleb had taken to forget what I had seen. Or maybe I just needed an extra dose of belief because that was always the answer when doubt crept in. But belief didn't work that way, not for us. It wasn't the answer to an on-demand question — *Lord, please give me more belief* — and then bam. Belief required trial and prayer and faith and conviction. But all the Bible verses that I knew by heart were retreating the more I tried to remember them.

I sat up slowly, my head still swimming. Ma must have seen the questions that flashed behind my eyes because she crouched on the parched grass next to me.

"What's going on?"

"It's hard to be back here with everything. I thought it would be easier to be home, but it's harder."

Hannah held a dandelion inches from my lips as though a wish could make my uncertainty and anger disappear. When its thin stem bent in the slight breeze, I blinked for a stutter longer than normal and then pursed my lips. With one blow, tiny, cottony puffs scattered in all directions; some went overhead, where I traced their trajectory until they got lost in the sun's blinding rays. A few remaining puffs hovered close to Hannah's face before landing on her skirt and my nose. She burst into laughter and something rumbled deep inside me too before pouring out — the first laugh in weeks.

On Sunday, the morning of Papa's triumphant return to the pulpit of Living Waters Baptist Church, we dressed for what always felt like an unofficial holiday. We knew that there would be crowds that rivaled those of Christmas and Easter, with overflow in the multipurpose room. I wondered if Papa would give the deacon board specific numbers about how many he had healed this summer, ignoring the ones he hadn't.

Papa slowed down at the stop sign at the end of the street and waved to Mr. Finley, who was walking his dog. "See you at church today." Papa's voice didn't rise at the end of the question because it wasn't a question at all.

Mr. Finley nodded. Mr. Finley was a heathen, and we had two options when encountering heathens: we delivered them the word of God or we kept our distance —

there was no in-between. Papa had been inviting Mr. Finley to church for years, and even though he never came, Papa never gave up.

Papa pulled into the parking lot of his new church that had been built last fall. I waited for the familiar feeling of pride to churn in my chest, but a weight tethered me to the ground. I wanted to roll down the window and tell everyone what had happened, to tell them to go to one of the other churches in town because the person they'd put all their faith in wasn't who they thought he was, but then Papa put the car in park and we all got out.

With an hour to go before the start of services, the church was still almost empty. But Mrs. Cade, the senior usher and resident church midwife, was there setting up. She smiled as she saw me, and I relished seeing her familiar face that was the color of Papa's perfect cup of coffee with a swirl of cream. With a hurried pace, she shuffled over to the door where I was standing and ran her gnarled hands across my face, as though my moles were braille. Her knobby fingertips stroked the bridge of my nose and ran across the Cupid's bow of my top lip. Her movements were steady, methodical, as though she were trying to keep track of how much I had changed in the three months since she'd seen me.

"Miriam," she finally said. "Welcome home." She pulled me close to her chest, and I inhaled her strong scent of lavender. When she released me, she reached into the pocket of her suit jacket and unearthed a few peppermints. She passed them to me like contraband, and I shoveled them into my pockets.

"Hi, Mrs. Cade."

She leaned in close and pressed both hands against the sides of my face. She had been one of the earliest members of Papa's first church when he was a twenty-year-old preaching prodigy, following him across Texas until he arrived in East Mansfield. As kids, Caleb and I made a game of guessing how old Mrs. Cade was, but we knew better than to ask. From our estimation, she was about sixty, because not only had she delivered me, Caleb, and Isaiah, she loved to brag that she had also delivered Papa.

"How was revival this year?"

I wanted to tell someone, anyone, about what I had seen in Bethel, someone who wouldn't pretend that it was an anomaly. Mrs. Cade kept my secrets — she was the only person I had told about the dark days in the house after Isaiah's death. She had known Papa before he was a holy man; surely, she could know the depths to which he had sunk in Bethel.

"Great," I began. Words stirred below the surface, but I swallowed them.

She tilted her head to the right as though to spur me on. I gave her a wan smile instead and turned down the long hallway toward the multipurpose room before she could ask another question. The hallway's bright walls were lined with pictures of Papa and awards he had won: "Texas Baptist Preacher of the Year" from 2010 until now. There were polished plaques from ceremonies he'd attended and pictures of the old church back in Midland — the one that he preached in when Caleb and I were born. I stopped in front of the final picture, of Papa with a big pair of scissors in his hands the day before this building held its first Sunday service. We stood next to him with our faces permanently frozen in expressions of delight. He had come so far in a short amount of time; there was so much to lose. Scandals had rocked other churches around this area, leaving large shuttered buildings where vibrant, bustling congregations used to be. In no time, we could lose this church and be back in the storefront in Midland.

"Miriam!" Micah, my best friend for as

long as I had memories, shouted as she barreled toward me. Her father was the longest-serving deacon in the church — he followed Papa out to East Mansfield from Midland, and the story went that Micah and I had been friends since we slept in adjacent cribs in the nursery. She ran over to me like she was unaware of how the pieces of her body worked together — her stride halting and interrupted, her back permanently slouched, her knobby knees protruding from opaque tights as she almost knocked me over with the force of her hug. It looked like she'd grown about an inch since we'd been gone, and now she was almost my height.

"Welcome home!" she squealed as I was enveloped in the tangle of her arms. Before more words could make their way out, her hand shot to her mouth — we couldn't be too loud in earshot of Papa's office. I led her by the arm away from the multipurpose room into the sunlight outside. When the door eased shut behind us, she fired off a series of questions: *How was it? How are you? When did you get back? What did you bring me?* Her questions sailed above me as more cars turned into the parking lot — it was still early, which meant that we were on track to have another massive post-revival crowd.

126

As we leaned against the wall with the backs of our dresses snagging rough bricks, I started at the revival in Americus. Micah's face brightened as I gave the elaborate retelling of Papa making the boy walk; the auspicious revival beginning seemed like a lifetime ago. But, as I recounted the details, I wondered if it hadn't actually been quite the miracle we'd all thought.

"What about the rest of revival season?" she asked at the end of my story. I fed her a rehearsed, sanitized version of the cities we had seen and the souls that had been saved, omitting the fact that the numbers had plummeted after Bethel. Before she could ask a question about healing, I reached deep into my pocket and fingered the soft edges of the postcards that I had purchased at various gas stations. I fanned the bright skylines and sunset landscapes — it was the closest that she would get to seeing the rest of the world, which was what we called everything that wasn't here.

Ten minutes before service started, Micah and I took our seats at the back of the sanctuary. Hannah sat between us, coloring, and Micah reached down every so often and brushed Hannah's bangs out of her eyes. With no siblings of her own to care for, Micah relished the role of surrogate mother. She never used baby talk with Hannah, and she never saw the intricate braces on her legs as impediments. I watched them from a few inches away, my hands resting on my lap in a rare moment of having nothing to do.

As service started, I wanted to be anywhere else, especially as the congregation jumped to its feet before Papa entered the sanctuary. People closest to the aisle grabbed on to his suit like it was the hem of Jesus's garment. With each grasping hand, I slunk deeper into the divot in the seat. Micah was on her feet before Papa entered, her face aglow with admiration as he walked down the aisle next to us. While everyone clapped, I wrapped my hand around Hannah's and pressed the brown crayon into the paper until it tore, the waxy nub crumbling in my hand.

Hannah and I made trees and clouds and rainbows and birds during the white noise of the sermon; I looked up for a few minutes each time Micah mouthed for me to pay attention, but before long, my gaze slipped back to Hannah's picture.

"What are you doing?" Micah was loud as the percussion provided a backdrop for the climax of Papa's sermon. Her eyebrows were raised in confusion — she and I were the ones to take notes during every sermon, but my notebook and Bible were closed next to me. "What's gotten into you?"

I shrugged and forced myself to watch Papa jump around on the stage — the movements not unlike what he'd done on that street corner. When Hannah's picture was complete, a line of junior deacons came to the front of the congregation to serve communion — there were a few boys among them who I recognized, boys who used to run around the church and terrorize me and Micah. These boys, who I was supposed to call young men now, fanned off from the front and positioned themselves behind the table piled high with gold serving dishes. Senior deacons like Micah's dad presided over the solemn ceremony.

A boy I didn't recognize stood at the end of my row; although he was wearing a white dress shirt and black pants — the usher uniform on first Sundays — it looked different on him than on the others. The blue crayon fell from my hand when I looked at the whisper of stubble that dotted his top lip and the broadness in his shoulders that strained his shirt. A bronze nameplate pierced the right side of his dress shirt: Jason Campbell. *Campbell, Campbell, Campbell.* I had no memories of his family, so they were either new or his parents weren't members. The blunt edge of his stubby nail and the coarseness of his flesh grazed my hand as he passed the communion plates. I gave the plate a little tug and he tugged back for a second before letting go, ending our mini-game before it really started. On the surface of the plate, the warmth that his hand left behind still lingered; my skin flushed as I pinched the plastic cup of grape juice in one hand before grabbing the cracker. I pressed my legs together to extinguish the tingling in my crotch, but it made the feeling sprout outward to my hands and feet instead. His right knee nudged mine in the slightest, knocking my knees together. The glass of grape juice sloshed, and I held it aloft to keep it safe. When I finally looked at him, he was staring down at me with his cheeks stretched into an almost-smile. My neck snapped back into place.

As Jason shuffled to the pew behind me with now empty hands, I remembered when Micah and I had gone to the playground last year and seen a pair of unsaved kids with their limbs intertwined beneath the trees. I'd wondered what it would feel like when my husband touched me like that one day, but I'd never thought about it during church. If Papa knew what I was feeling, he would call me a harlot before making me recite Bible verses about the evils of lust.

"The body and blood of Christ," Papa said over the microphone. In the pulpit, Papa's laser vision was directed at me, his eyes singeing my skin. I'd always wanted him to notice me from the stage, but not like this. His eyes bounced back to Jason and then to me. "Confess your sins to the Lord and you shall be forgiven. Do not eat and drink damnation unto yourself." He was supposed to scan the congregation, but his neck stayed fixed in one direction, his eyes igniting my flesh. Had he really seen the lust in my eyes from that far away?

Forgive me of my lust, I confessed in my heart after an eternal low buzz on the microphone. The feeling that had just blanketed my body was snatched away, leaving behind a chill as Jason exited the sanctuary. Papa had drilled into us that lust was a gateway for other sin, that sin in the mind corroded everything it touched. But as we waited for Papa to announce the healing part of service, I desperately wanted the feeling back.

"I know that many of you are waiting for healing, but this summer the Lord has told me to change the way I do things here. I will not heal on Sundays anymore. We will have separate healing services starting in a few weeks. All rise for the benediction."

A stunned silence settled over the congregation, many of whom had probably been waiting for months to be healed. Even Micah couldn't hide her wide-eyed disbelief as she stood in slow motion. It would've surprised me before Bethel, but nothing where Papa was concerned shocked me anymore. As I recited the benediction, Micah looked over at me, her eyes begging for an explanation. But all I could do was feign surprise as the congregation dispersed.

Quietly, we started the routine of first Sundays, of collecting the communion dishes and washing them, of folding the tablecloth and storing it for next month. I followed Micah outside and into the annex, where the deacons had left behind a messy pile of communion trays and half-filled glasses of grape juice. Hannah clacked behind us with her crumpled picture in tow. When we got inside, I settled her in a chair with a new, clean piece of paper.

The whir of the ceiling fan made background noise for our work — Micah sealed the remaining crackers in plastic bags while I dunked each communion tray in soapy water.

"Why didn't he heal today?" Micah asked the question rhetorically, and I wished I could tell her the truth. "Did something happen?"

I froze and watched the sponge in my hands making sudsy circles on the gilded plates. "What do you mean?"

The ceiling fan's swift oscillations answered me. I turned my head to look at Micah at the very moment when she pitched forward on the sink. Before I could catch her, she fell in a heap on the ground, her arms raised above her head in some odd position of submission. The faint red glow of the exit sign illuminated a damp line of sweat that had collected on her top lip like a mustache.

"Micah!" The plastic bag in her hands had fallen to the floor, scattering cracker crumbs on the ground. I crouched by her side, noticing the pale sheen on her normally deep-brown skin as I slipped two fingers below her chin — the same spot where I checked Hannah's pulse after seizures racked her body and left her lifeless on the ground. A steady heartbeat thrummed under the pads of my fingers as her chest rose and fell beneath her dress. On her left wrist, the thick links of a silver bracelet were attached to a rectangular panel with stencils:

TYPE I DIABETES. During homeschool, we made short trips from my basement to the bathroom; I watched as she pricked her fingers, swiping blooms of blood that swelled from her fingertips onto test strips and inserting them in the machine that she kept with her at all times, but I had never seen her faint.

"Help!" My voice reverberated back to me from the closed door and the stained-glass windows. Behind me, Hannah's folding chair had tipped over, and she was crawling toward us. Over Hannah's earsplitting wails, I placed my cheek next to Micah's open mouth and felt the puff of her shallow respirations. Her face was clammy as I slapped it to get her to wake up, but it only made her head flop one way and then the other. I jumped up and ran to the door, forcing it open.

"Help! In the annex." The second scream drained my lungs. Then the doors to the multipurpose room pushed open and Mrs. Nesbitt, the Sunday school director, looked around.

"What happened?" she called.

"It's Micah. She passed out. Call an ambulance."

Mrs. Nesbitt nodded before disappearing through the closing door. I rushed back to

Micah's side. Hannah had made her way over too and was tugging on Micah's ankle.

"You're going to be okay." Singing the sentences to Micah the way Hannah liked, I lifted Micah's limp body onto my lap to rock her. The room was still and mostly silent as Hannah's wailing had now become barely audible moaning. My hands needed something to do to displace the anxiety — I placed my right hand in the middle of Micah's forehead, spreading my index finger by her hairline and my pinky by the bridge of her nose.

"Lord, touch and heal Micah. Restore her to her full power in You." Or was it *Return her to her full power in You?* Prayers that I hadn't said in weeks — hadn't thought about saying to a God who had forsaken us — clattered in my mouth like stones. I pressed harder on her forehead. If I kept talking, she would hear me and wake up. I snatched the Lord's Prayer and the twenty-third Psalm out of the ether to speak over her, relieved that I hadn't lost those trusted prayers.

"In the name of the Lord Jesus Christ you are healed." My hand flew from Micah's forehead and shot to my lips as the forbidden healing words reserved for Papa and men like him — only men — slipped from my tongue. My chin immediately shot to my chest in penance; just then, the door pushed open, and my prayer ended mid-sentence. Micah's eyes were open in my lap, and her pupils were fixed on me.

"What happened?" Mrs. Nesbitt rushed to my side. She peeled Micah's torso from my lap and rested her on the carpet. Someone must have called Ma; she was standing under the glowing red letters of the exit sign, making the room suddenly claustrophobic. Somehow Hannah had gotten to her, and she was wrapped in the folds of Ma's skirt, staring at me with a focus I had never seen before in her eyes. A chill shot through me, then a wave of heat.

"She passed out a few minutes ago, but she just woke up."

"I'm okay," Micah said. Her voice was strained as though each word had to push through a sandpapery throat to get to her lips. She tried to sit up, but Mrs. Nesbitt pinned her shoulders to the ground.

"Don't get up. The ambulance is coming. Your mom is coming from the sanctuary too."

"You didn't have to do that, Mrs. Nesbitt. I'm feeling better. I think Miriam —" Micah tilted her head to look over at me.

"What happened with Miriam?"

"Nothing," I chirped. Micah was the worst at keeping secrets. "I just sang to her. That's all. Hannah likes it, so I thought she would too."

The blare of sirens in the distance grew louder until it sounded like they were right on top of us. Micah's mother entered the room in a cloud of perfume and crouched next to her. Seconds later, the paramedics burst in and strapped Micah onto a stretcher. She mumbled something that I couldn't hear as they placed a clear dome over her nose and mouth and took her away, her mother clinging to the edge of the stretcher like a barnacle.

A blue uniform walked closer to me. His lips were moving but words didn't seem to be coming out. The face came closer, inches from mine, and the lips moved again. "You were with her when she passed out. We need to ask you some questions."

Some questions. He pulled out a clipboard even as my legs wavered beneath me. My eyes bounced around the room's familiar walls before landing in the corner where Ma and Papa stood. When had Papa gotten here? I tried to wave him away, to tell him that we had sorted it all out, but my arms — too heavy for my body — hung by my sides. I couldn't answer the paramedic's questions in front of them, but it would be more suspicious if I asked to speak somewhere else.

"What did you see?"

"I didn't see anything. But I heard her fall."

"Did she hit her head?"

"I don't know."

"And about how long was she unconscious?"

They were asking the questions so quickly that I had a hard time keeping up. "Don't you need to take her to the hospital? Do you need to keep asking me questions?"

"Answer him, Miriam." Ma's voice was stern.

"I don't know. A couple of minutes."

"We'll follow up if we need more information." The paramedic wrote down my name and phone number before tucking the clipboard under his arm and walking through the open doors to the waiting ambulance. Papa jogged away from us and leaped into the back of the ambulance — we all watched as he laid his hand over Micah's head and spoke words of healing. Words that I had just uttered a few minutes earlier. He stayed inside until the paramedic gently motioned for him to go. There was no siren as the ambulance pulled away —

the engine gunned and the tires screeched over the parking lot. Then silence.

There had been so much activity and noise, and now my ears rang in the echoing cavern that the ambulance had left behind. Everyone stayed in the position they had been in when the paramedics left: Ma was by the door with her hands pressed against her cheeks while Mrs. Nesbitt was crouched on the ground, kneading the carpet as though Micah's body was still in front of her.

Soon Mrs. Nesbitt rose and opened the annex door — I followed her, Hannah, and Ma into the late-summer breeze that stirred the trees, feeling each tendril of wind curl under my skin as though it had been ripped off in one sheet, leaving the fleshy pink parts underneath exposed. As we walked across the lot to the entrance of the multipurpose room, I peeked at my arm in the sunlight. The skin still looked intact — there was no rash or other outward sign of the fire raging beneath.

"What happened back there?" Ma asked when we reached the hallway outside the multipurpose room.

"I think —" My mouth formed around the confusion that had resided in my body for the past half hour. Papa's voice came

139

through his closed office door down the hall.

"What were you saying, honey?" She leaned closer. Her nods coaxed words out of me, but Papa's voice echoed as though he was speaking into a megaphone.

"Nothing. I wasn't saying anything." I shook my head to dislodge the thoughts of Micah's body in front of me, the words that had come out of my mouth.

"Maybe we can just go home."

Later, the house was claustrophobic with the laughter and suited bodies of a dozen deacons and elders. They always came over for dinner after the first post-revival Sunday service. It was my duty to help Ma in the kitchen. I stood, waiting for her marching orders, until she handed me the foil pan of lasagna and directed me to bring it to the table.

As I carried the steaming tray in, I overheard Deacon Farrow saying they'd had the biggest crowd in years. A few elders estimated that a thousand people had attended service — a new Sunday record. Their cackles swelled as I placed the foil pan in the middle of the table and let my fingers linger on its crimped edges. This world of revivals and faith healing was a small one, so I waited for the conversation to shift to

Bethel and what they'd heard from the deacons who'd been in attendance there, but no one said anything. The briefest glance at some of their laughing faces was proof that they hadn't heard the news. Or that Papa had spun a narrative to explain whatever they might have heard. I knew not to listen in for too long: *Children should be seen and not heard.* And as Papa paused in the middle of accepting his accolades to look at me, it was clear that he didn't want me around.

I started cutting and serving the lasagna when Papa was still staring in my direction. Ma worked next to me with a pitcher at her side, filling each glass to the rim with lemonade. On my way to the perimeter of the dining room, I threaded through elbows as Papa's voice, light and unburdened, cut through the laughter like a bell.

"Gentlemen, let's begin dinner with a prayer for the healing of Micah Johnson."

At the mention of Micah's name, the heat from the annex surged through me once again. *Heel toe, heel toe.* I inched closer to the wall where Ma and Hannah were already standing for the prayer with dipped chins, but they seemed to get farther away as I got closer. When I finally arrived, I pressed my back against the wall, leaning into it to keep me upright as Papa's prayer voice covered us like a blanket.

"Amen." The men sat as one with their ties loosened, hands straddling their plates. Caleb sat toward the end of the table, next to Papa, too shy to speak among the men's baritone voices. We said amen and ducked into the kitchen to eat the crispy corners of lasagna that we deemed not good enough for the men.

"Are you okay, Miriam?" Ma whispered, careful that her voice didn't cross the wall that separated us from them. My eyes wandered to the dot of cheese on her top lip, knowing that if I looked directly in her eyes, I would have to tell her what had happened in the annex. *I said healing words, and Micah's eyes opened.*

"Joanne. More lemonade, please!" Papa barked. Ma jumped up with the pitcher. I watched as she cupped a protective arm around her stomach before bending to fill the glasses of men who acted as though she didn't exist. And the secret that had been so close to the surface receded.

SEVEN

The thin latex skins of red, blue, and yellow balloons shielded me from the hospital hallways and provided a millimeter of remove from the medicinal smell. I stayed a few feet behind Ma and Papa as we approached the glass doors to Micah's unit — 4B — that wheezed open and swallowed us inside.

Micah sat upright in bed with a faux wooden table positioned over her legs. She scooped runny eggs from a deep crater in her plastic tray.

"Good morning, Mrs. Horton and Reverend Horton. Hey, Miriam." Her voice was quiet, formal, over the constant pinging of heart monitors in nearby rooms. Next to her bedside, a skeletal IV pole was empty when it should have been laden with swollen, opaque bags. I'd expected to see tubes everywhere and the erratic green lines of a heart monitor, but she was just sitting up in bed like nothing had ever been wrong. The only difference was that she looked smaller amid the pillows. I kept a wide berth as I walked around her bed and placed the balloon bouquet on the windowsill next to a vase of tulips whose heads were already drooping.

"Thank you. That was nice."

My whole body tensed as I turned around with empty hands and no barrier between us. Our parents had ventured into the hallway, and Micah patted a spot on the bed next to her swaddled legs. I stood motionless in front of the same Micah who saved the maraschino cherries on her banana splits for last. The same Micah who had the embarrassing habit of laughing when she heard sad news, causing her to be the recipient of countless pinches during church services. As I climbed in beside her, I felt knees that were too angular as Micah's unfamiliar body pressed me against the railing.

"What have you been up to?" It was the only thing I could think to say when she was inches away from my face. But as soon as the words came out, I realized how stupid the question was.

"Just hanging out here." She gave a polite laugh but then started coughing, her body jerking forward in bed. I grabbed a plastic cup from her tray and pointed the bendy straw toward her parched lips. She took a long sip of water before rolling over to face me again. My body recoiled but I forced myself to stay still.

"What happened in the annex?" she asked. Her voice was thick and phlegmy, her breath sour. This was the question I had known — and feared — she'd ask.

My skin was a shirt that was becoming too tight, forcing air out of me with each breath. I slid away from her, but the bed's low metal railing pinned me close. Hoisting myself over the side of the bed, the tray that held the remnants of Micah's breakfast clanged to the ground. A shallow pool of milk leaked from an open cardboard spout and clumps of eggs dotted the checkerboard linoleum squares.

Ma's head peered around the corner after the crash, followed by Papa's and Deacon Johnson's. "Are you girls okay?" Ma asked.

I looked from their faces to Micah's. Micah's was creased with confusion, while theirs were full of concern.

"I'm okay. It was an accident."

I squatted to scoop the eggs back into Micah's tray and swiped at the milk with my hand. The floor was as clean as it was

145

going to get, but I waited until their feet retreated into the hallway to stand up.

"Miriam," she whispered as I backed away from her bed. She beckoned me over with her index finger, and I inched closer until her mattress was pressing against my abdomen. My ear angled close to the line of dried blood that bisected her cracked bottom lip.

"What did you do in the annex?" Her voice was faint.

"I don't — I didn't do anything."

"I woke up and your hands were on me —" she began.

"It didn't mean anything."

"What did you do?"

I looked over my shoulder at our families; they were on the opposite side of an open door just a few feet away. "I don't know. It was all a mistake."

"I heard you say something. What was it?" Micah's voice was getting louder. I took a step back, but she grabbed my wrist and pulled me closer. Papa's voice got quiet in the hallway, and we both paused.

"You can't tell anyone," I said when Papa resumed his conversation.

"But if you didn't do anything, what would I tell?"

"Drop it, Micah."

"Drop what? That I heard you say something and then I felt something happen in my body and now you're acting weird?"

I let my wrist go slack in her hand. She had felt something. I had felt something too. The tingly heat from the day before was still close.

"Just tell me what happened!" Her frustrated voice rose an octave as her grip tightened on my wrist. Suddenly the window air conditioner blasted on, making the balloons dance. A line of sweat formed on my top lip even as the rest of my body shuddered.

"I don't know! I didn't do anything."

Just then, Deacon Johnson entered the room, followed by a doctor in pale blue scrubs.

"Can you excuse us?" The doctor encroached on our space with a chart in his hand; on his heels, Micah's parents wore the worried faces of people who didn't believe in an all-powerful God. Papa was right behind them like he was a member of the family. In the commotion, Micah let me go and I took several steps back toward the door, near where Ma was standing. Two more steps and I would be out of there. Free.

"They can hear whatever you have to say,"

Deacon Johnson said.

My shoulders must have dropped, but I yanked them back up before Ma could see. Soon, we were standing at the edge of the bed next to Papa.

"Micah's A1c levels are better than they've been in two years. I can't say for sure right now, and we need to observe her further, but it looks like she's in what we call partial remission."

"What does that mean?" Mrs. Johnson chimed in.

"We usually see this right after a patient is diagnosed, when they require less insulin and their A1c level remains low. But we don't usually see it with patients like Micah who were diagnosed two years ago. But it is good news."

"Praise the Lord for His healing," Deacon Johnson exclaimed.

"I didn't say that she's been healed, Mr. Johnson. Type 1 diabetes is incurable. But for some reason, it looks like the disease is in remission for now. I'll want to keep her here one more night for observation in case something changes, but if it stays like this, we'll be able to release her tomorrow."

"Hallelujah!" Deacon Johnson shouted before the doctor was even finished. My mouth shot open, and my eyes kept slipping back in Micah's direction even as I wanted to pull them away. Deacon and Mrs. Johnson swarmed the sides of Micah's bed, smothering her with hugs until her face disappeared behind her father's suit jacket. Each shriek and praise seemed to pull a little more oxygen out of the room. I tugged Ma's arm, dragging her away from the edge of Micah's bed.

"Let's get out of here. They should be alone."

"Did you hear that? Micah's been healed." Her feet were rooted by the edge of the bed as she raised her hands toward the ceiling in a mini-praise.

"The doctor didn't say that." It was supposed to come out in a whisper, but it must have been louder than that because the room went silent. Micah breached her parents' embrace and sat up in bed, her face aghast like she had just been struck.

"Well, it's a good thing we don't serve doctors, isn't it?" Deacon Johnson said after the room had been silent too long. "Our doctor is the Lord Jesus Christ, hallelujah! And He has declared Micah healed in His eyes, not necessarily in man's."

"Samuel, I can't thank you enough," Mrs. Johnson chimed in. "You came into the ambulance and healed her. Praise God for you."

The doctor, still trying to emphasize a point by gesturing to Micah's chart, finally gave up as the praises rose in volume. He stepped out of the room in the middle of their whoops and cheers.

When Micah's parents faced her again, Papa shot a glance at Ma. His eyelids fluttered with validation, or even confirmation, and Ma nodded as though to verify his understanding. With their wordless conversation, they seemed to agree that he was indeed back, that Bethel had been a fluke. Ma shuffled over to him and threaded her hand in his, and by the time he squeezed back, they were on one accord. All the while, my skin prickled under Micah's gaze, even as she was being smothered by her parents.

"You healed me," she mouthed at me in slow motion. With each word, her eyes widened with wonder, as though she hadn't believed them until she had just said them and made everything real.

After Ma and I left Papa at the hospital to make his weekly rounds, I sat next to Ma in the passenger seat, trying to silence Micah's words that played on a loop. When Ma turned up the radio on her favorite hymn, Micah's words morphed into the throaty alto's lyrics, her refrain of *you healed me* playing over the plaintive chorus of this woman's love song to God.

"You seem restless," Ma said. She eased the car to a stop in front of the house. I followed her eyes to my fidgety right leg, and as I pressed it down with my palm, something else was rising in me. A memory from years ago came back like it was yesterday, like someone had opened the door of a long-closed vault and let the air and light in. It was an image of Papa laying hands on Hannah as an infant. It had been early in the morning, hours before I was supposed to be awake, when the door to the bedroom I shared with Hannah opened. I pretended to be asleep as Ma and Papa tiptoed over to Hannah's crib and whispered inaudible prayers through the wooden slats.

Papa lifted a floppy Hannah in the air and cradled her — her legs swung like a rag doll's over his forearm and her neck lolled to the side. Ma passed him a bottle of holy oil as he readjusted Hannah to support her head. He emptied the entire bottle on her forehead and lifted her, glistening, toward the moonlight. She stirred and started to cry, but her limbs never stiffened, and she didn't lift her head. Ma and Papa stayed there, motionless, for what seemed like hours, even as Hannah fell asleep in Papa's arms. They placed her into the crib and left the room; Ma's head was downcast as Papa put his arm around her shoulders.

In the days after the healing attempt, Ma and Papa seemed to watch Hannah carefully, waiting for Papa's words to take hold, even though the mere practice of waiting meant that it hadn't worked. Nonetheless, she continued to miss milestone after milestone. And though they smiled and said that Hannah was "taking her time" learning to roll over or crawl as other babies her age were babbling and toddling around the sanctuary, their visits at night became more frequent. Even as their prayers grew more fervent, they never took her to the front of the church or to the doctor. It was only when the seizures started that they took her to a specialist. They should have been relieved that they would finally get a diagnosis; instead, each time Papa strapped her in the car seat and drove her four cities over, he looked defeated. In public, Papa started preaching about the nature of suffering and the mystery of God's ways, while in private, he announced that no one in the family could come to the altar for a healing.

As Hannah grew, Papa inched away from her — at first emotionally and then physically. Now that she was eight, all of her tasks had been delegated to me and Ma. Papa was only around when she celebrated big achievements, clapping in the corner of the room when she took her first steps with orthotics and crutches, but then receding into the house when the celebration ended. For Papa, looking at Hannah must have been like staring failure in the face, realizing that the dark shape that he always feared had eyes and teeth, was more human than spirit.

As the unearthed memory of Hannah merged with the pregnant girl last summer and the blind man in Bethel, I looked over at Ma, who was still watching my jumpy leg. She placed her hand over mine, and I let her steady pressure subdue me.

"This should be a good day, Miriam. Your father just healed your best friend. But you look like you're carrying the weight of the world."

The love song to God on the radio ended, and Ma turned up the volume on an updated version of "Amazing Grace." She sang with lightness that I envied all while tapping a slow beat on my knee.

"I'm okay," I said as the song ended. "And it is a good day."

■ ■ ■ ■

The next night, Papa arrived home from the hospital with buoyancy in his steps. Ma rushed to greet him and took his briefcase before he could close the door.

"Hortons! Come downstairs for some good news."

There was thunder on the steps as Caleb came down. Hannah trundled in from the living room, and I stayed inches away from the front door.

"Micah has been released from the hospital with no sign of diabetes on any of her tests. The doctors couldn't believe it, but the Lord has used me to fully heal her! It's a miracle." His words were definitive: a proclamation.

I stared at him as he spoke, waiting to see a twitch in his right eyelid or a quiver in his lip — any tell that would betray his words. But his face was stony. He had been the last one to place his hands on her, long after she had opened her eyes in my lap. He must have known that the feeling that passed through his hands as he touched her was different from the other times he'd actually healed someone. He wouldn't have felt the same electric sensation that I did when I'd touched her only minutes before.

"I knew there was going to be a miracle on Sunday," he was saying to Ma. "I just had no idea that it would be Micah."

"Oh, honey," Ma said as she tossed her arms around his neck and buried her face in his collar. "I'm so proud of you."

By the time he stepped out of her embrace, his shoulders were square, not slumped, and he walked down the hallway with a newfound confidence.

"We're going to the Johnsons' for dinner tomorrow night. A thank-you of sorts. They've been praying for Micah's healing for years, and they want to celebrate with me. With us." He caught himself, but Ma didn't seem like she heard the mistake. I stood at the edge of the kitchen as he rummaged in the refrigerator and drank directly from the carton of orange juice.

"That sounds wonderful, honey." Ma planted another kiss on his cheek before she playfully elbowed him in the shoulder for brazenly engaging in a habit that she hated.

We stood on the Johnsons' porch the next evening — I jammed the illuminated doorbell in rapid succession while Ma held a glass container of cornbread aloft next to me.

"Coming," Mrs. Johnson called over the familiar chime. I heard her slow, lumbering footsteps and tapped my fingers against the doorjamb to get her to move a little faster. The questions I needed to ask Micah had been buzzing around my head since I saw her on Monday.

"What's the hurry, Miriam?" Papa asked behind me. I couldn't turn around to look at him; I'd barely been able to look at him since he came home the day before and declared Micah healed.

"Come in, come in!" Mrs. Johnson appeared in the doorway. "I'm so glad you could make it." She took the dish from Ma, and we followed her inside. Before I could even greet her, I bounded up the thirteen stairs that led to Micah's closed door.

"Micah," I whispered into the raised letters of the mini license plate that bore her name — a souvenir that I brought her from a revival in Oklahoma two summers ago. Hearing nothing, I balled my hand to knock, but that gesture was foreign. Instead, I opened the door slowly into the pink of Micah's room — the pillows and comforters on her bed, her desk in the corner with the sparkly lamp on it. She knelt beside her comforter, head in hands, a prayer leaking from her lips.

It felt like I was eavesdropping on something I shouldn't have been part of, but I knew better than to interrupt when someone was talking to God.

"Thank You for my healing. Thank You for the hands that healed me. Let me be obedient enough to be worthy of Your favor. Amen."

She stood up from the edge of the bed and looked startled, stepping back as though she hadn't heard me call her name or come inside. "Miriam."

Suddenly I didn't know where to start.

Micah clearly wasn't feeling tongue-tied though. "Now can you tell me what you said in the annex?" She whispered *annex,* as though that word made her aware that only a thin floor separated us from our parents. She stood in front of me, shifting in her pantyhose the way she always did when she was uncomfortable.

I closed my eyes and felt the heat of the annex again, heard the noise from the fans. "They just slipped out."

"What slipped out?" Her voice wavered as she looked down at the sheer fabric that bound her toes.

I was only confirming what she'd already heard, but my heart raced as though I was confessing something new. I took a deep breath. "The words Papa uses when he heals people. That's what I said."

"That's what I thought. Do you know what'll happen if your dad finds out?"

With one step, I closed the gap between us. "He can't find out because it's a sin, and you know it as well as I do."

"But I'm healed. And you did it." Her voice, light and victorious, didn't match the frantic pace of my words.

"But you know as well as I do that women don't have that gift."

"Then how do you explain that I didn't feel anything when your dad healed me, but I felt it when you did?"

Until now, I'd been pretending that she was mistaken. I hadn't let myself imagine what it could mean if what she'd said in the hospital was, in fact, true.

"Micah, Miriam, dinner!" Mrs. Johnson's voice from downstairs shook the silence in Micah's room.

"I don't know. Just promise that you won't say anything to anyone."

Micah and I stood across the room from each other, still as statues. She stared at me for what felt like an eternity.

"Please, Micah," I begged.

Micah moved away from me and stepped toward the door, and I was frozen as I

158

watched her leave. When I could finally make my legs move, I followed her downstairs and sat in the empty seat between her and Caleb.

After Papa prayed for the meal, Micah's body was rigid next to mine as she took small nibbles of her mom's chicken and dumplings. On the other side of me, Caleb took loud, indelicate bites, even slurping the broth, before complimenting Mrs. Johnson on the meal. I looked at my spoon in my bowl, unable to say a word to anyone.

"So I know I'm not supposed to ask this," Papa began, his mouth full of Ma's cornbread, "but I figure I can break protocol because I've known you since you were a baby. What did it feel like?" Papa's voice was loud and brash over the dinner table. His question was improper, self-serving. *Aggrandizing* was the word Papa used when he called out other men for it.

Micah quickly shot a glance in my direction before turning back to Papa. She seemed to think for a second, and I looked down as she spoke, wincing before the first word came out. "You placed your hand on me in the back of the ambulance, and a tingle passed through my feet," she began. "Then the rest of my body got warm. When you prayed, said healing words, it was weird.

159

Like I felt the disease leaving me all of a sudden." She shoved a spoon in her mouth at the end of the sentence. I didn't realize that I'd been gripping mine so hard until I let it go. I took one bite and then another as I relaxed into the chair, listening as Papa feigned interest in Micah's story. As he nodded and gave the occasional *mmm-hmm,* I knew what he was thinking: *It feels good to be back.*

"Praise the Lord," Ma said. She'd been saying it nonstop for three days — ever since we were clustered at the foot of Micah's hospital bed — and it was losing power with each iteration. Especially since she was saying it about Papa.

"What a testimony," Papa finally said. "The Lord is good." I wondered if the rest of the table noticed the way he said *Lord* like it was a stand-in for his own name. My attention flickered during parts of the conversation — *I felt the healing in my hands the second I left the ambulance. I knew that God would give me the ability to heal Micah, so I'm grateful that my prayers have been answered.* My chest started to swell, pressing against my shirt when I wanted to take a small amount of credit for what had happened. But I knew that I couldn't, and each word from Papa's mouth made my neck

160

bow over the plate of cheesecake that Mrs. Johnson had brought out for dessert. There was no gratitude to God in my stooped posture — just defeat as Papa spun a story that he and I both knew couldn't have been true.

In the days right after Micah's healing, Papa's voice boomed in ways that it hadn't since we left Bethel. The more he proclaimed it over the mic on Sunday mornings and paraded Micah onstage next to him, the more he seemed to believe in his renewed power. And even though home-school was Ma's domain as our teacher — the one place in our house that Papa steered clear of — he ventured into the basement where we were gathered, interrupting Ma in the middle of a lesson. He ordered all six of us — me, Hannah, Micah, Caleb, and two other elementary kids in the congregation — to gather around him and praise God for Micah's healing, completely ignoring Micah, who stood beside him.

Weeks later, buoyed by the healing that he had so desperately needed — a healing whose extra emphasis seemed strange given the fact that he had healed so many people before — the congregation anxiously waited for the announcement about when the

161

stand-alone healing services would start. For someone who felt so much power after healing Micah, it was odd that he didn't seem to be in a hurry to start them again anytime soon.

And then finally, on the first Sunday in October, a month after Micah's healing, Papa announced that the first post–revival season healing service would happen on the following Friday. He seemed nervous in the days after the announcement, never sitting at the dinner table long and changing the subject whenever we brought up the healing service.

One night, I caught him standing in the backyard after dinner, arms raised in a V above his head, the doubtful slouch from Bethel still in his shoulders as he prayed. I flicked the latch of the patio door and slid it open before crossing the wooden deck planks and descending the steps into the backyard. I stepped closer to the guttural remnants of a prayer.

"I know that You have not forsaken me, Lord. The power is still there. Continue restoring me in time for the healing service. Use me to do Your will. Amen."

Papa must have heard my sharp inhale because he immediately stopped speaking and turned around; his teeth and half his face glowed in the blue moonlight.

"What are you doing out here?" he asked.

"I just wanted to see what you were praying about."

"Prayers are private. You know that."

"Are you nervous about the healing service?"

"Why would I be nervous?"

"I don't know. I'd be nervous after this past summer."

Papa lowered his arms. I waited for him to take a step toward me the way he did outside the hotel room in Bethel, but he just glared at me.

"What do you mean you'd be nervous?" I was close to the edge of his patience — the clipped end to the question assured it — and I couldn't make myself look in his eyes anymore. I wanted to push, to get him to admit that he knew he hadn't healed Micah. But in the prolonged silence that formed, it became clear that he'd never confess.

"I just think that healing would be hard. I wouldn't be able to do it." The last words got caught in my throat — even putting *healing* in the same phrase with my name seemed like too much of an admission. But Papa, none the wiser, seemed relieved by what I'd just said.

"Yes, it is," he exhaled. "But all I can do

is shepherd the power that God has given me. And if Micah is any indication, many will be miraculously healed this year." He looked up to the sky as he spoke, his hand rubbing the mini–mountain range of razor bumps on the underside of his chin.

"Pray with me for these upcoming healing services." He extended his arm across the chasm of grass. I had prayed with him hundreds of times, had listened to him pray even more than that, but now as his hand beckoned me over — his thick fingers curling, his wedding band glinting in the darkness — I was reminded that I'd have to swallow what I'd done so he could believe in himself.

I walked over and stood next to him, my chest heaving with each breath. His hulking body was inches away from mine, and I could feel his presence even with my eyes closed and head bowed.

"Kneel," he commanded. As I knelt, each blade of grass knifed into the tender skin of my knees, and my body listed forward as he spoke.

"Heavenly Father, thank You for the gift of healing. I pray that You will bring many souls to the church for healing services so that I may reveal the power that You have given me. Use me to make bodies whole. In

164

Your holy name, I pray. Amen." He looked down at me when he finished, his expectant eyes blinking hard as they waited for an *amen.*

"I'm going to bed, Papa. I'm tired."

"Miriam." I knew he wanted me to say *amen,* but I couldn't utter those words for a prayer that I didn't believe in. Anger that I couldn't hold back much longer swelled inside me. I stood up to walk away, letting his words pelt my back until I stepped safely inside and closed the screen door on his entreaties. Away from his gaze, I wiped at a tear that had fallen down my cheek.

On Thursday afternoon, the day before the first healing service, the facade that I had attempted to keep up for the past couple of weeks was falling away. I tried to focus on the Bible verse inches away from my face, but the words kept shifting on the page. Even Ma seemed off: during homeschool, she got distracted in the middle of her primary lesson about Noah's ark, forgetting part of the story that she knew by heart.

Micah looked over at me as Ma messed up the Noah's ark story for the third time, and a chuckle forced its way out of my mouth. Micah laughed too, before biting her lips like she was embarrassed of her reaction, like she was as uncomfortable around me as I'd been around her lately. Even though the basement walls around us had evidence of our former friendship — yellowed crayon drawings with our stick-figure bodies tossing too-long limbs around each other's necks — things hadn't felt normal since the dinner at Micah's house. Our timing was off — we interrupted each other now, often cutting off the end of each other's sentences and apologizing in unison. But she hadn't shared my secret, and I was grateful for that.

Ma talked about the elephants coming onto the ark two by two. Next to me, Micah swayed a bit in her seat.

"Mrs. Horton, can I be excused?" she asked. By the time Ma looked over, Micah was already standing, her face the pale grayish-brown of a fish belly as she slung her backpack over her shoulder and walked upstairs. There was a steady, slow cadence to her steps before she stopped — it sounded like she'd paused halfway up the flight. A minute or so later, she started walking again. We used to have a signal when her blood sugar was low — a nod of her head and I'd be by her side, getting snacks or a glass of juice — but she hadn't looked at me as she asked to be excused.

Micah's footsteps overhead took her to the bathroom. And then minutes stretched where there was no sound at all. Normally she would check her blood sugar in the basement. I bolted from my chair and ran upstairs to grab a candy bar from the pantry before pushing the bathroom door open without knocking. Micah was crouched on the closed toilet lid, her knees spread apart, the glucose meter balanced on one thigh. She looked over her shoulder at me as the meter spit out the number fifty. We both knew this was a dangerously low level, and I slipped the wrapper from the candy bar, broke off a tiny brown square, and presented it to her. Her shaky hands gripped her knees as I took another step closer.

"Take it," I implored. Her hands stayed in her lap as the shaking intensified.

Tears welled behind her eyes. It was hard to tell if she was incapacitated by low blood sugar or the fact that the healing hadn't worked. A shock of disappointment passed through me at this realization too, but I quickly pushed it away. Micah needed me now. Her whole body quaked as I knelt in front of her and squeezed the hinge of her jaw, forcing her mouth open. She shook her head vigorously as I pressed the chocolate through the tiny gap between her rows of teeth.

She blinked slowly. Once and then twice. Her eyes took in the room, the towels on the rack, and me standing next to her. Removing my hand from her mouth, I stepped away from her and pressed my back against the wall, sliding to the floor. My raised knees were the only thing separating us as she inhabited her skin again. She looked at the open pouch of testing paraphernalia on her legs like she'd forgotten what had just happened.

"I was healed for a bit, wasn't I?" Her thin voice brimmed with desperation.

Part of it had been real, hadn't it? There could be no denying that I had felt something that day in the annex and so had she. And for the past five weeks, she had been healed. But now, the thing that she feared so much, that I didn't realize I was afraid of until now, had happened. Had Micah even been healed at all? Would it have been a healing if Jesus put mud on the blind man's eyes only for his blindness to return? Or if the leper's newly smooth skin erupted back into scabs and scarred flesh? Did Papa also harbor these fears — that behind every healing was the possibility of a tumor metastasizing, abnormal cells splitting during a pregnancy, a relapse?

My impotent hands hugged my knees as I waited for a feeling of relief to settle in. I had never meant to heal Micah, was never supposed to have the ability to heal her, so this should have been good news. It meant that everything could go back to normal. But even as I'd told myself that it hadn't worked, that women like me weren't allowed to heal, I'd wanted to be wrong.

"Wasn't I healed?" she asked again. My eyes traced her pigeon toes before moving up over her bent knees and to her chin that was resting against her folded arms.

"I think so."

"It felt so good to not have to prick my finger." Her voice floated away as she spoke. "I guess I always knew it would come back. I was afraid of it."

"I'm so sorry you're sick again, Micah. I really wanted you to be healed."

"Me too." The words had barely left her mouth before heavy, racking sobs filled the room. I stood up and bent over to put my arms around her. She curled her body into mine as I stroked the oiled spaces of scalp between her orderly cornrows.

"Can I be alone for a bit?" she said when my knees cramped from crouching beside her. Every joint ached as I stood up and walked toward the door.

"I'll see you back downstairs."

"Miriam," she eked out at the crest of another sob. "Don't say anything to your dad."

EIGHT

The night before the first healing service, Ma, Hannah, and I sat at the table with orderly rows of small white bottles between us. Forty was the magic number of bottles to fill — the same number of days and nights that Moses was on the mountain with God. Ma looked at me from the other side of a thin, gold ribbon of oil that flowed from the industrial-size bottle of Crisco into the smaller bottles.

There was no special ceremony as we filled each bottle, stopping when they were about three-quarters of the way full. I wondered if the people who lined up for healing knew that the cross Papa traced on their heads was really Crisco. Papa said that the power came from the prayer, not the oil.

Wordlessly, Ma and I finished and placed the bottles into the cardboard box that Papa would take to church with him tomorrow.

Before Bethel, Ma and I used to play a game where we guessed who would be healed by this oil. *A woman with cancer,* I sometimes offered. *An older man with arthritis,* she would say. But I was too busy thinking about Bethel to bring up the game.

"That's forty," Ma said as she folded the box's cardboard flaps closed. She drummed her fingers on the lid like there was more to say. At the table, Hannah lifted the bottle of vegetable oil in front of her face. She shook her head, perhaps in disbelief that the table and chairs could look so distorted behind the viscous yellow substance, or perhaps she thought that there was magic in the liquid somehow.

Later that night, I heard three soft raps on my door. Before I could answer, Ma slipped into the crack that let the light in. She approached my bed with her arms behind her back — a sly smile spreading across her face as she presented the newest library book on outstretched palms. She hadn't come for our secret reading sessions since Bethel, and the fact that she was back meant that things had returned to a semblance of normalcy. I put my prayer journal on my nightstand and straightened in bed, holding her elbow as she climbed over me. She'd been slowing down more now than during her pregnancy with Isaiah, but I tossed the thought aside.

"Look what I have," she whispered, her eyes darting to where Hannah was sleeping a few feet away. "It's the one that you requested a couple months ago. It just came in." I held the cellophane wrapper and fingered the embossed letters on the cover. *Song of Solomon.* It crinkled open and I pressed my nose against the new pages. Even though we were surrounded by books at home — Bibles in multiple translations and biblical commentaries — those books weren't mine. And though I loved the stories of Miriam, Moses, Deborah, and Esther, the books that I got with Ma from the library were different. It felt good to try on lives that weren't mine, lives that didn't involve traveling every summer. I fell in love on those pages and felt the ache of heartbreak that I'd never experienced.

"When did you get it?" A pang of jealousy rose in my throat, and my words came out more accusatory than I intended. The library was a place we went together when Papa was at the church for trustee meetings. Under the guise of getting more Christian books to replenish the homeschool baskets in our basement, we always chose one secular book that we hid in the middle of the larger stack to read late at night. The title of this one made things easier, though — if Papa saw it, he would never suspect that it wasn't about the Bible.

"Let's read a couple of pages," she said. "We have some time." She glanced at her watch as I slid closer to the nightstand to give her more room.

In the puddle of light from the desk lamp, I read aloud, letting my tongue taste words that Papa could never know I was reading. I felt the slip of Mr. Smith's blue silk wings on my bare arms, imagining his leap to his death and the way his stomach must have plunged to his feet on the way down. Ma leaned her head into my shoulder and nodded with pride when I read words like *bereft* and *transfixed* — and in an instant, I was five again, only this time her finger wasn't dragging beneath letters on the page, bouncing each *b* or releasing a tiny spit stream with each *p.* And since she wouldn't read these books aloud herself, she got some joy at hearing me tell her about a life that she had once lived. A life I never had.

My face grew warm as I read about Macon undressing his wife, Ruth, and my words halted.

"Did you fall in love before him?" I asked the wall. I crossed my legs to quell the tingle in my crotch that rose when I thought about

Jason Campbell, but the feeling dissipated soon thereafter when I remembered Papa's withering gaze.

Ma paused for a minute, seeming to weigh whether to answer me. "My first love was when I was twelve. He was my next-door neighbor. Curtis." His name was closer to a giggle than a word when it came out of her mouth.

"Anyone else?"

"There were other crushes before your father," she laughed. "Kevin and Christopher. But they weren't real. I knew it the second I met your father because they all vanished — their names and faces. And for an instant, nothing else had any meaning in my life."

"What was it like? Falling in love."

She stretched out her legs in my twin bed, her toned dancer's calves twining around each other like cords in a rope, her pointed toes emphasizing her high arches. It was clear what he saw in her — a beautiful dancer who clung to his every word as though it were gospel. And she saw someone who could save her from her life. She told me that her heart burst when Papa pulled her, soaking, from the murky lake water, but lately I'd wondered if she had been desperate for anything to take her away from the house where she grew up. The boy who came to town wearing a suit that was two sizes too big happened to be in the right place at the right time and distorted her sudden love for God into a love for him. For a moment, all the power that she let him wield in the house made sense — she had never known Papa without God and never known God without Papa.

"Keep going. It's getting really good," she said, nodding to the book.

I turned back to the open book and continued reading even though my brain wasn't keeping up with the words. Ma put her hand on my knee; I must have paused too long.

"I know this hasn't all been easy, Miriam. And I'm sorry." Ma was inches away from me — her scent of laundry detergent and floral soap faint in my nose — but I couldn't look at her as she spoke.

"Sorry for what, Ma?"

"Oh, I don't know. Nothing. Everything." She tossed her hands in the air; as they fell back to the comforter, her voice dropped. "He's different. I can't think of another way to describe it. The man that I married never would have hit the man in Bethel."

I willed my chin to look in her direction. She was looking straight ahead, at the closed door, at Hannah in the bed across from us. "And I brought all of you along on this ride. It hasn't been easy for any of us, but particularly you. If I had known then what I know now —" She cut herself off before the inevitable end of the sentence.

"What would you have done differently?"

There was no reply, but I felt her shoulders rise and fall in a shrug. "I was really young. I was in love."

"Are you still?" I snatched the words from the bottom of my throat. I expected her to chastise me for asking such a thing, but in the long pause that passed between us, the Ma who was always so certain about God and Papa didn't seem certain at all.

"It's not as simple as that, honey. It's not a yes or no. You'll see." She pulled her knees up to her chest and hugged them.

We heard a door open downstairs, and Ma quickly kissed me on the forehead before wishing me good night. I slid the book under my mattress after she left.

The air felt heavier when she was gone, like someone had left a window open during a passing storm. Now that I'd seen Papa for who he really was, it was hard for me to understand how I'd once been one of his staunchest defenders. Perhaps Ma just had more faith in him — or faith in general —

than I did. Or perhaps it was that she'd known him for a whole lifetime before I'd even been born, so for her to suddenly see him through different eyes might have felt impossible.

The next evening, a few dozen cars were in the parking lot for the inaugural healing service. We stepped inside the sanctuary to see a hundred or so people already there; they wore jeans, T-shirts, waitress uniforms, and dingy sweatshirts that they would never dare to wear on Sundays. Whatever illness had made them come out tonight had stripped away all desires for vanity.

Caleb, Hannah, Ma, and I walked to the front of the church and slid in the pew next to Micah right before service was supposed to begin. I didn't know what to expect as Papa walked to the pulpit. Several deacons were scattered on the carpet below in the same assigned positions they had on Sunday mornings. Papa bowed his head, and his lips moved in some form of prayer that we couldn't hear; a few people around me looked up in concern. As Papa continued mouthing inaudible words, the doors at the back of the church opened and slammed shut, jolting me in my seat as the sound echoed off the empty pews in the back few rows. I couldn't turn around until he ended the opening prayer, even as the pews creaked under the weight of the new people who had entered.

"In Jesus's name, I pray. Amen."

On the *amen* I spun around to see several more stragglers coming into the sanctuary. A few older women moved slowly down the aisle in thick-soled shoes. Among them were Mrs. Deveare and Mrs. Lewis: names that had been on and off the sick and shut-in list for years. Names that we claimed to pray for even when they were displaced by newer names — the accident victims, the young mothers who'd had complicated deliveries — the ones who had been in the bloom of health a few weeks earlier, whose deterioration had been so sudden that it made the rest of us draw in breaths at the mention of their names.

Behind them, Dawn Herron stepped inside, her arm gripping her father's crooked elbow for support. The Herrons weren't really members. Even though Papa had made house calls to convince them to change their minds, they resisted his overtures, only coming on occasional Sundays right before healing and leaving before the offering. Dawn was the only nonmember on the church prayer list for her many surgeries to repair a congenital heart defect, and an air of mystery surrounded Dawn and her dad. From the few facts I could piece together, I knew that her mom had died from a heart condition a few years ago, that her dad worked two jobs and still couldn't quite keep up with Dawn's mounting medical bills, and that Dawn was a senior at East Mansfield High.

Soon, Papa raised his wobbly arms and the hundred people here flooded into the aisles as he took his time walking down to the ground. I waited for Dawn and her father to creep into my peripheral vision, but I didn't see them. When Papa emptied holy oil into his hand and placed it on Mr. Tucker's forehead, I peeked around. I wondered why they weren't coming up to the front like they always did. Next to me, Micah's leg twitched like she wanted to go up too but knew that she couldn't. I placed my hand on her knee, and she covered it with her hand, tucking the medical alert bracelet back in when it slipped from beneath her sleeve.

If Papa noticed Dawn's absence in the line, he didn't let on. He seemed more confident in his movements while he made his way through the sixty or so people who were left in the aisle. Soon, all the people he had healed were lying on the ground, some of them just starting to get to their feet when he returned to the pulpit to announce the offering.

"Give as the Lord has given unto you." It was Papa's standard offering line, but asking people to give after they had just been healed seemed like they were paying God — or Papa — for something that God would do for free. When the buckets had all been collected, and the benediction was delivered, Papa dispatched me, Micah, and our mothers to the multipurpose room with a sleight of hand. He'd told us that we'd be responsible for preparing dinner after the first healing service, and on Papa's command, we rose in an orderly line and followed Ma outside.

"Miriam, can you grab the cups from the car?" Ma dangled her key ring from her curled index finger. I swiped it and walked out of the double doors leading to the parking lot. The car alarm to the minivan chirped as I popped the trunk and rifled through cardboard boxes in search of plastic tumblers.

"Can I talk to you?" a breathy voice asked as I stood under the trunk's open canopy. I turned around slowly, catching a glimpse of

Dawn's face, which was cloaked by darkness.

"To me?" I was the only one out there, but she'd never spoken to me before.

"Yeah."

"Sure." She was half a head taller than me as she folded her long, willowy limbs in front of her chest. A few tightly coiled strands came loose from the bun at the top of her head and flopped in her face. She raised her eyes to look at the hair but left it there as though it took too much energy to push it away.

"Can you do me a favor?" Her words were labored and slow as she took deep breaths every other word or so.

"Sure." I leaned closer.

"I need you to fix me."

I grabbed her arm and pulled her toward me, instinctively looking around to make sure no one was nearby to overhear. Goose bumps sprouted on my exposed flesh even though the October air was warm.

"What did you say?"

"I heard about Micah. I need you to fix me too." Her voice was partially eaten by a passing wind.

"Where did you hear that?"

"I just heard it around."

In those early days, Micah was swarmed

by people who were waiting to hear about how she had been healed. She soaked in the attention from people who'd never talked to her before — it had been agony to walk by and hear sections of her embellished story that took a new shape each Sunday as the crowds got larger. Maybe one of Dawn's friends who went to the church had been nearby one of those days, and maybe that was the day that Micah had accidentally said my name instead of Papa's.

"I never healed Micah." What I couldn't say was what I wanted to say. *Micah isn't healed anymore.*

Dawn looked up to the sky, where a band of dark clouds trailed across the moon like a bride dragging her veil. She didn't speak for a while, as if the answer were somewhere up there.

"Please." Her voice was faint.

"I can't do what I did with Micah," I whispered. "I don't even know what happened."

"You can try." In the moonlight, the whites of her eyes glowed. "What harm could it do?"

"I don't think I can. I gotta go. They're waiting for me." I grabbed the sleeve of cups and slammed the trunk, turning to walk toward the rectangles of light that the multipurpose room windows spilled on the pavement. Dawn grabbed for my wrist, but I wrenched out of her grip and ran toward the building — one parking space became three, then five, as my breath raced out of my lungs. I didn't turn around to see if she was walking in after me.

"Look," she said.

My hand was on the door and her voice was barely audible — one turn of the knob would mean safety in the multipurpose room. But the same curiosity that made me sneak behind the tent in Bethel swept over me like a storm surge. Caleb always said that it would get the best of me. *Go inside,* I told myself.

I shifted my head to the left, where she was now standing under the low-hanging branches of a weeping willow. She took slow steps toward me and removed her jacket before unbuttoning her shirt; she pulled the fabric apart with her hands until the top of her sternum was exposed.

"Look," she said again.

The gape in her shirt collar revealed a red, raised vertical scar that burrowed into her sternum like a worm. The furrows radiating from the main scar made the entire wound look like outstretched tree branches thrown into relief against the flatness of her chest.

There were at least a dozen surgeries behind those scars — we had prayed for each of them. In all of that time, Papa hadn't been able to make her heart whole again. Who was she to think that I could?

"Help me," she pleaded after my eyes hadn't moved from her chest.

I turned the knob all the way to the right and stepped into the glow of the church hallway.

Later that night, the veiled moonlight was replaced by an inky darkness that was thick and heavy as it poured inside the open bedroom window. My bedspread was a lead blanket as occasional lights from passing cars danced across the wall. I closed my eyes, and Dawn's features — the hollow in her cheekbones, the unexpected dip of her Cupid's bow — materialized. The burning emptiness of my stomach ached in the place where dinner would have been, but I hadn't been able to eat after Dawn's questions.

What harm could it do? The question carelessly dropped from Dawn's lips as though it was just about harm. But I knew it was bigger than that — it was about sin. According to First Corinthians, spiritual gifts were doled out to men and women equally, but according to Papa, women weren't allowed to exercise those gifts over men. So even if a woman could speak in tongues or heal, it would be sinful to act on this ability. When Papa preached those sermons, I had written down his words as gospel, nodding as he spoke. Sitting awake in my bedroom, the words to his sermon ricocheted in my skull, louder than they had been when he preached them. But there were other questions that followed: *Why would God give us gifts that we couldn't use? Why had my words over Micah worked — even if just for a little while?*

Dawn had asked me what harm there was in trying. She didn't understand that it would cause a scandal along the lines of something the church had never seen. My father, the head of the church, had tried to heal Dawn on multiple occasions. Anything I did to discredit him would disrupt the delicate ecosystem of our church, throwing everything that the Lord had established, and Papa had built, into chaos.

In the days that followed, I tried to forget Dawn's request, but my attempts to push her to the back of my mind only meant that I thought about her with every Bible recitation and before-meal prayer. By the time we stepped out of the car at the next Friday's healing service, I spun around when I heard a crackle, only exhaling when I discovered that the sound had been branches in the wind.

I bowed my head and said a prayer before stepping inside the sanctuary — the selfish prayer that Dawn wouldn't be in service today. On the other side of the heavy sanctuary door, Dawn was nowhere in sight to hear my mumbled prayer of thanks. Papa took his box of holy oil bottles from Ma — brand-new for today's service — and marched into the pulpit with more confidence than he had last week. As each minute ticked closer to the beginning of service, Papa's movements were looser and more languid as mine contracted until my muscles became ropes pulled too tight.

" 'Give thanks to the Lord for He is good,' " Papa commanded.

" 'His mercy endures forever,' " the congregation responded.

"All who have come to be healed, come to the altar for a touch from the Lord."

The usual suspects got out of their seats — next to me, Micah shifted and leaned forward. I looked over at her — this would be the worst time for her to have another episode.

"Are you okay?" I tapped her leg, reaching into my pocket reflexively for a piece of candy. Papa was making his way to the ground — too busy to see Micah having a relapse. But she was still, not shaky, and her skin wasn't clammy to the touch.

"Micah," I repeated. I held the wrapped candy in my lap for her to grab. But she didn't see it as she craned her neck forward and made eye contact with her dad. Deacon Johnson looked back at her and winked. Micah stood up and stretched her legs, then she took careful steps into the aisle.

"Micah," I thought I whispered, but it must have been loud enough for Ma to hear two rows in front of us. Her finger shot in front of her lips, but her eyes widened when she saw Micah standing. She shook her head, but it was too late — Micah was already in the aisle. Papa had placed his hands on an older woman's head, completely oblivious to Micah, who was now at the end of the line.

I kept my eyes on where Micah had shifted two steps closer to the front of the line. My heart sped up as Deacon Johnson came from the altar to stand by her side. As he put his arm around her shoulders, I waited to see him lean over and tell her that she was making a mistake. But instead, they inched closer to the front where Papa still hadn't looked up.

Unlike her traditional slouched posture, Micah stood with her shoulders pulled back. I had just seen her that morning, and in all the time we'd spent together, she'd given me no inkling of what she was about to do. I had kept my end of the bargain — I hadn't told anyone that she had gotten sick again. And she had kept my secret about healing her. So what was she doing?

Papa saw them when they were in the middle of the line — a flash of confusion passed over his squinting eyes and creased brow. He managed to compose himself for the next few healings, ironing his rutted forehead as people fell to the ground in heaps and stepping over them to move down the line. Finally, Micah and her father reached the front.

"Deacon and Micah Johnson," the words sputtered out. "I must admit that I'm surprised to see you here." His eyes darted in their sockets, and his bottom lip quivered with rage. His jittery hands made oily stains on his suit pants. The congregation that had seen him march Micah to the pulpit during his triumphant return tour grew silent.

"What ails you, Micah?" He was breaking with precedent because healings were always quiet and never meant to be broadcast over a microphone.

"She got sick again, Reverend Horton."

Papa took a big step back as though Deacon Johnson's words had force. "What do you mean, *got sick again?*" He was supposed to be talking to Micah, but the angry words that he spat through clenched teeth were directed toward Deacon Johnson.

"You healed her, and we're grateful, but there's been a setback."

As I stared at the graying patch at the back of Deacon Johnson's head, I imagined the hope in his eyes at the renewed request for his only daughter's healing. But only new Christians believed in do-over healings, and Deacon Johnson had been a Christian longer than most people in this church had been alive.

"A setback? You have to be mistaken."

"No mistake. It came back. The diabetes. About a week ago." Deacon Johnson flung words out at a frantic pace.

"We just wanted you to try it again. Please."

"You know that healings are as much about faith as anything else."

"I do know that. But I figured it wouldn't hurt to ask you again."

"How weak is your faith, Ray?" Papa roared. The microphone's feedback obscured his words and droned louder, even as he seemingly tried to yell over it. A hollow tap on the mouthpiece was a thunderclap. Papa must have just realized that he was speaking into the microphone because he pulled the black wire from behind his ear, and it clanged to the carpet with a wave of static.

He was backed into a corner: he could either walk away or heal her. And with all those people watching, he wasn't going to walk away. So he flipped the lid off the bottle of holy oil without removing his gaze from Micah and her father. Then Papa took quick steps toward her, and his healing words soon reached a crescendo.

His hand all but smacked Micah's head, making her reel backward into her father, who caught her. My fingertips tingled as he pressed his hands on her forehead, and I slid them under my thighs. The healing words were faint, but even though I couldn't hear anything, I could tell the cadence was off. He wasn't even trying. And Papa didn't close his eyes to summon the power of God: he stared at Deacon Johnson even as he declared Micah healed.

Papa knelt to pick up the microphone. He closed his eyes for a moment, then threaded the wire behind his ear before walking toward the edge of the sanctuary and exiting through the door that led to his office. A few seconds later, Deacon Johnson rushed from Micah's side and followed Papa through the door. A handful of deacons and Caleb stood in front of the congregation and helped people to their feet.

Micah was in a daze as she walked back up the middle aisle — her forehead gleamed in the overhead light. Her stiff movements were slow and rehearsed as she returned to the seat next to me. She refused to meet my gaze.

"What did you do back there?" It was Papa's voice from the other side of the wall. He must have forgotten that his microphone was still on. "Are you trying to make a fool of me, Ray?"

"It's a healing service. I wanted you to heal her." Deacon Johnson's reply was muffled at first, but it got clearer and louder as I imagined him stepping closer to Papa.

"You could have come to me privately. How dare you show me up?"

"How could I be showing you up? You're a healer, right? Unless you're not. Correct me if I'm wrong." On the last word, I imagined Papa lunging at him like a rabid dog before getting jerked back by a chain.

"It's my daughter, Sam," Deacon Johnson

continued with uncharacteristic boldness. "My only daughter. Did you expect me to do nothing? What would you do if it had been Miriam?" At the mention of my name, my skin prickled like all the eyes in the room were on me.

"Or better yet, Hannah?" Deacon Johnson knew that Hannah was always off-limits. Papa's Achilles' heel.

Hannah looked around for the origin of the voice saying her name, and I pulled her hand into my lap. Caleb rushed toward the door while the rest of us were pressed into the pews in some form of collective paralysis.

"Get the fuck away from me, Ray. Get the fuck out of my office and out of this church. Now. And I never want to see you back here again."

Papa's curses slapped the air, followed by shrieks and gasps from the crowd. Ma sank into the pew.

The door leading into the sanctuary was thrust open, and Deacon Johnson walked toward the congregation with an ashen face. Micah had been sitting next to me, wooden, but as Deacon Johnson slid back up the middle aisle, she came to life, grabbing her Bible and standing up to meet him. I reached for her; my fingers wrapped around the protruding bone of her wrist before sliding to her hand. She looked down, puzzled, like my hand was a foreign appendage.

"Micah." It was hard to know what to say to her in that moment. I squeezed her wrist tighter. We had a million silent languages — she'd be able to understand if she would just look at me, but she was still surveying my hand.

"Micah," Deacon Johnson's voice snapped from the aisle. She looked over at him.

"I'm sorry," I mouthed, tugging her back toward me. I wasn't sure what I was apologizing for: for her sickness, or my dad's pride, or the fact that she wasn't healed after all. Or that she was walking away and all I wanted to do was follow her.

"I'm sorry too," she mouthed before pulling away. I let her go, my hand falling to the still-warm empty space on the pew next to me.

Long after Micah and her father left, I abandoned Ma and Hannah in the sanctuary's cavernous emptiness and followed the departing parishioners into the parking lot that shimmered in the fresh rain. It was tempting to pretend, even if only for a few seconds, that I could jump into one of their cars and drive far away from here. When the parking lot was empty, save for our van,

I stared at the crescent moon that dangled overhead like a fingernail in the starless night, reveling in the stillness and silence that would shatter as soon as we got home.

Back home, I pressed the cylindrical lock on the bedroom door when Hannah, Caleb, and I were inside. When we were younger, Caleb would come into our room on nights like this, saying that he wanted to comfort us when he was the one who really needed comfort. Through the thin floor of safety, I heard Ma pleading with Papa to sit down and have a cup of tea. Then their voices shifted to a lower register. I slipped Hannah into pajamas even as she complained about being hungry, her hand pointing to her stomach. *There will be no dinner tonight,* I wanted to tell her, my mind bouncing back to the way the women left with their foil-covered pans long before the deacons exited.

A crash of dishes. Ma's pleas rose through the vents, curdling by the bedroom carpet. Another crash — a harder one this time — followed by a plaintive scream from Ma. Hannah rustled against the tight bindings of her comforter and sheets, howling even as Ma kept screaming and more plates and cups shattered downstairs. Papa yelled in between the crashes. I shuddered with each roaring swell; then there was a deafening crash that sent my head into the detergent smell of Hannah's pajamas. I waited for it all to stop while Caleb buried his head into my pillow.

Papa's rage subsided sometime later; in its wake, I twisted the knob until the lock popped and cracked the door open. One step into the upstairs hallway, past the study on the right, and then another few steps toward the stairs. Downstairs, I rounded the corner by the open front door, and then I was at Ma's side, placing my hands on top of hers on the broom handle as she continued her work of sweeping ceramic shards into a pile. She swiped at long rivers of mucus that glistened on her face.

"Where is he?"

She shrugged as she released the broom. "Gone, I guess. He didn't say where."

"Did he — ?" I couldn't get the final words out. She wrapped her arms around her expanding stomach and shivered. I scanned the visible parts of her — her wrists, her neck — for bruises. She pulled her sleeves down as though feeling the heat from my gaze.

"No."

Images of him in the middle of the mob in Bethel came back. Then I remembered her knowing moan by the pool when I'd told her about his violence.

"Can I see?" I tugged her wrist, but she tugged back harder.

"There's nothing to see, honey." She choked on the last word. "I'm okay. I'm going to bed."

Her kiss on my forehead was a reflex without feeling before she turned away and walked upstairs. A few seconds later, her bedroom door clicked, and I surveyed the damage in the kitchen. Jagged shards of all our dishes were on the floor, and kitchen cabinet doors had been flung open. I knelt in a square of linoleum next to a beige dish that I'd made for Mother's Day a few years back. *We are all clay in the Master's hands,* Ma had said as I dug the heel of my hand into the wet clay and left behind an imprint that my hand currently dwarfed. Now a ragged fault line ran through the center of the hand. I dropped the piece back on the floor where I'd found it and swept it into a pile.

The sharp hunks fell into the trash bag, making the thin plastic bulge and tear. The patio blinds were open, and the rain outside had become more violent over the course of the evening. I slid the patio door open and stepped into the driving rain as a streak of lightning split the sky in two. A clap of thunder resounded overhead; I balled my fists and screamed once, and then again and again until my throat burned. My weight pitched forward until I fell on my knees on the wooden planks of the patio, the splinters digging into my skin. I used to think that storms were evidence of God's wrath at His people, and though I knew now that the God of famines and floods didn't punish people that way anymore, there had to be some message in the way the clouds roiled and the sky illuminated in patchwork flashes. God was punishing all of us for Papa's sins now. Or maybe he was punishing me for the sin of healing Micah.

Another jagged ray of lightning made the house white and then indigo before returning it to black. Somewhere out there, Papa stood under the same rain, raging against a God who he thought was taking away his ability to heal. Meanwhile, Ma was probably upstairs cleaning cuts on her hands and icing other wounds that she hadn't let me see. Ma's words came back again — *We are all clay in the Master's hands* — we only had one Master and that was God. Ma had always used that saying to remind us of who was in control of our destiny, but on nights like this, it felt like we were clay in Papa's hands rather than God's.

The news would pass quickly in the church — the families who'd been gathered at the healing service had probably already told their friends, who were calling their friends now. *He had gotten too big too quickly,* they would say. *A fighter can never really be a preacher.* It was the salacious news that they salivated over, not thinking about what that fall meant for Papa's family. And now that other people knew what I knew — that he hadn't been able to heal for a while — what would that mean for the sick people who still needed to be healed? For the Dawns of the world?

I stepped back inside the house in my rain-soaked pajamas; a puddle collected on the kitchen floor below my feet. I didn't have Dawn's number, but Papa had it in the log where he kept the contact information for anyone who had ever been to a service. I crept upstairs to the study, where I flipped through the log and found the number. It was too late for calls, but I wouldn't have the nerve in the morning, especially when Papa would be back.

The phone rang several times — it was silly to think she would answer this late. I pulled the phone away from my ear to hang up when a man's voice, scratchy with sleep, answered.

"Hi, Mr. Herron. It's Miriam Horton. I know it's late, but it's urgent. Can I please speak to Dawn?"

He called her name into the echo chamber of a house that sounded empty. Then the rustle of a phone being passed.

"Hello?" Dawn's breathy voice finally said.

"I'll do it. Next Wednesday."

NINE

I woke up the next morning with the residue of my words to Dawn still on my lips — *I'll do it.* A sleeping Caleb was in a heap in the middle of the floor, and I stepped over him on the way to the hallway. The study door was closed — not how I left it last night. Papa must have come home when I was sleeping.

Muffled words came through the door as I passed. I leaned closer to hear them. "I don't care what you need to do, but remove him from all positions at the church immediately."

I'd hoped that he was all bluster last night, that he would have a cooler head when he returned, but he was doubling down.

"Figure it out," he chimed in again. I assumed he was speaking to Deacon Farrow — the head of the deacon board. Papa would need his support to remove Deacon Johnson from church leadership.

"I don't want to see him at the church again. End of conversation."

The phone slammed down on the cradle, and I heard Papa stand up. Before he could reach the study door, I slipped back into the bedroom.

"What's going on?" Caleb rubbed his eyes and rolled over, blinking me into focus.

"He just fired Deacon Johnson." As I said it out loud to Caleb, it hit me that firing Deacon Johnson meant that Micah would be gone too. I collapsed onto the edge of my bed and placed my chin in my hands.

"He can't do that."

"He can do whatever he wants. I just heard him."

"Did she tell you?" Caleb rolled over on his back and slid his hands beneath his head.

"Did she tell me what?"

"That she was sick again."

"What does that have to do with anything?"

"He felt blindsided by it. Deacon Johnson is his best friend. Was."

"Whose side are you on?"

"There are no sides, Miriam." Caleb rolled over onto his forearms and released an exasperated sigh. "You always see a problem when there isn't one."

"There's no problem? Did you hear what

happened downstairs last night? How he hit Ma?"

"Wait, what?" He shot up to a seated position. Hannah stretched in bed. We both froze, silent for a few moments until she rolled over and resettled into sleep.

"He hit her, just like he hit that man in Bethel," I lowered my voice.

"How do you know? Did you see it?"

My stomach fell at his accusation. I hadn't seen what happened with Ma, but how could I tell him that there were other ways of knowing beyond seeing? "Why are you so blind?"

"You don't know what you're talking about."

"Why do you think that you know him so much better than I do?"

Caleb massaged his temples. "He's going through a lot right now. You need to be more understanding."

"But what about what he's doing to us? To me?" My voice broke at the end, at the thought of never seeing Micah again.

Caleb reclined on the floor. "Give him time, Miriam. You know that these things blow over. In the meantime, we have to give it to God."

I looked at Caleb, at his eyes, which were farther apart than mine, at the spray of moles over his nose whose pattern I knew by heart, and at the faintest shadow of stubble that clung to his chin and cheeks. As he spoke, his face didn't indicate even the smallest bit of shock about what I'd just said. He'd already chosen not to believe me about the man in Bethel, but I figured things would be different when he knew that Ma was the recipient of Papa's violence.

Papa had been drawing lines between us ever since Bethel — but also long before that, as soon as he'd decided that Caleb was old enough to become his apprentice. Recent dinners involved whispered secretive conversations between Papa and Caleb that were too important for me, Ma, or Hannah to hear. I remembered a time when Caleb and I were the keepers of our own secret language; these days I couldn't even rely on him to stand up to Papa. I stood back up and walked to the door.

"Miriam, don't do anything stupid. You're overreacting," he said.

I opened the bedroom door and stepped into the empty hallway.

"Or you're not reacting enough," I said, closing the door behind me.

Ma tried to pretend that everything was normal, despite the fact that we ate our meals that day off paper plates while Papa worked nonstop in the study upstairs. As we bowed our heads to pray, Ma's words about gratitude didn't mesh with my anger toward a God who was letting this happen to us, but I said *amen* anyway. No one brought up the previous night.

For the rest of the day, we found ways to busy ourselves on the first level of the house — I made paper dolls and did puzzles with Hannah while Ma folded endless stacks of laundry. As each minute passed, it got harder not to pick up the phone and call Micah, but it was too risky. Plus, Papa was on the phone all day with deacons and members. We went to bed late, and I must not have been the only one who lay awake under the covers dreading Sunday's arrival.

At church, I waited for Micah in our usual place in the foyer even after service officially started. But soon I couldn't wait any longer, couldn't watch Mrs. Cade and the rest of the ushers holding piles of bulletins that they normally distributed to parishioners who hadn't come. I pushed the foyer doors open into a half-full sanctuary. Ma was by herself in the front row — I started to walk toward her, but instead opted for my normal position with Micah in the back of the sanctuary. It would be an easy place for her to find me when she arrived. But Micah never came, and maybe it was good that she and her family didn't get to see Papa, broken, as he tried to string together an incoherent ten-minute sermon from notes that had spilled on the floor. Then he claimed that he wasn't feeling like himself and left in the middle of his sermon.

From Sunday until Wednesday, I went over the motions for Dawn's healing until they became muscle memory. I had studied Papa during so many healing services that I knew how high he lifted his hands when he prayed — about six inches from the forehead — or how he traced signs of the cross from top to bottom, left to right. There were so many slight gestures to remember, and missing one of them could invalidate the entire healing. I imagined how I'd catch Dawn before she hit the ground, how the holy oil would feel warm and viscous on my fingers before I applied it to her forehead.

Thoughts of healing Dawn helped distract from Micah's absence in the basement, from her stack of books that still sat on the table, her work that was posted around the room. Someone had left a cardboard box on the chair where Micah was supposed to be, and in between teaching kids on the primary side how to blend syllables, Ma ripped papers from the walls and placed them inside the box. She didn't even make eye contact as she made the memories of Micah disappear the same way Papa had done with the photos of Ma's sisters.

"I'll do it," I said on Ma's third trip over. I couldn't continue to watch her drop Micah's things into the box with such indifference. I grabbed Micah's binder from Ma and placed it on my lap instead.

"Your father wants me to drop it off at the Johnsons' tonight."

"You don't have to. I'll take it to her on Wednesday." I hadn't thought about it before, but it would be the perfect excuse to leave the house and get to Dawn when Papa was out for his weekly hospital visits.

"Fine," Ma relented. "Take a break from the lesson and do it now. Please."

I sifted through the pages of Micah's notebooks, letting my finger trace the loops of her *j*'s and *y*'s before dropping them into the box. When the box was finally full, I pushed it deep into the shadows under the desk. For the rest of the afternoon, I nudged it with my feet to make it seem like she was still there as I plodded through my lessons alone.

■ ■ ■ ■

On Wednesday morning, Hannah stirred on the other side of the bedroom — it had been a good few nights for her, with no seizures or nightmares. A positive sign. And even though Christians weren't supposed to look for signs, something had to get me through the day. I willed my knees to bend for morning prayer — it had been harder to pray ever since the healing service, but I went through the motions each morning in the hopes that my belief would catch up to my words.

"Dear Lord," I started. I waited for the words to come as they always did, even though today's task was different than any other day's. I didn't know what to ask. For the strength to heal Dawn? For God's will to be done? For forgiveness in advance of the sin I was about to commit?

"Lord," I began again. "I pray that You anoint my hands today and use them to do Your will. And forgive me for my sins." I waited for the feeling that God had noticed me — to be underneath the warmth of His gaze — but my room still had a morning chill coming from the open window.

"Amen."

The clock started when I left the house at

noon — the box was clumsy on the handle-bars of my bike, making it hard to steer to church. Soon, the steeple inched closer above the trees and I arrived in the parking lot, threading my bike between the few cars there. The door to a red hatchback opened and a foot stepped onto the pavement. I shot around to see Dawn's legs, then her torso and face.

"Hey." She sounded scared, a far cry from the bolder version of Dawn who had asked me to heal her.

"Hey." I didn't know what else to say, but her wide, terrified eyes matched how I felt. For a moment, I was grateful that a box separated us. "You ready?"

She nodded.

I was still out of breath when we got to the side of the church where the lock on the outside door leading to Papa's office was broken. He had been telling Ma that he was going to get it fixed, but he hadn't yet. Inside, our footsteps echoed on the spar-kling linoleum that looked as though it had just been waxed. In its emptiness, the church's familiar interior felt disorienting. Dawn and I walked past the empty pastoral offices and toward the double doors of the sanctuary. I took a deep breath and pushed the doors open. Rows of orderly pews cast long shadows into the aisle while the lonely organ sat on the edge of the stage. Jesus looked down from behind the altar with mournful eyes that followed us as we found a spot on the carpet in front of the pulpit. I placed Micah's box down and reached around in my backpack for the bottle of holy oil that I had plucked from Papa's stash.

"Stand here." I touched Dawn's shoulders and adjusted her position. Not directly in the path of the cross but a little to the left of it, exactly where Papa conducted his healings. When she was in place, I took a step back and felt breath enter my lungs as the weight of what I was about to do fell on me.

"Dawn Herron, do you believe that I have the power to heal you?" A noise rattled the windows: the whoosh of tires, followed by the rumble of a shaking load. A semi, not Papa's car pulling into the parking lot. *He's not here; he's not here.* I repeated it as my hands bobbled the bottle of holy oil.

"Dawn," I began again. I was standing upright, but it felt like I was collapsing, like I would fall if the slightest thing touched me — a feather, a hand, a gust of wind. I dug my toes in the carpet, hoping to root myself to the ground. Dawn looked up at me with eyes that were simultaneously desperate and pleading, and my gaze danced from the cleft in her chin to the smooth dome of her forehead. I kept my focus on her face even when I wanted to stare at the scar on her chest.

"What ails you, Dawn?" I had to ask the question even though I already knew the answer. It was part of the healing, and I couldn't deviate from the plan now.

"I have a bad heart."

I gripped her shoulders; either she was trembling, or I was. She crossed her arms over her chest before I even told her to. She had done this for Papa so many times that she knew the drill by heart.

"Do you believe that I have the power to heal you?"

Papa's voice had a shape that filled up the space around it as it rose to the rafters and pressed on the eaves; my voice was a whisper in comparison. My watch glinted to the right of my face — ten minutes had passed. Dawn's eyes were now wide open as they fixated on the ornate chandeliers. And even though some air that came from the nearby vent made the chandelier's glass orbs dance, Dawn's pupils weren't moving.

I closed my eyes and willed the movements to come back to me, but now that

Dawn was in front of me, the practiced ritual felt elusive. Was this the moment when I was supposed to trace the cross on her forehead or bow my head and say a prayer? I flipped the cap on the bottle of holy oil and doused my fingers with the warm liquid, watching a few drops escape to the carpet. In the thousands of healings Papa had performed, an errant drop had never slipped out of his holy oil bottle.

"In the name of the Lord Jesus Christ, you are healed." I traced a slick sign of the cross on Dawn's forehead — top to bottom, left to right — and pressed my palm against the cross to seal the healing. A wave of heat came into my arm as my hand lingered on Dawn's head for longer than Papa's generally did; my hand burned as though a fever was seeping out of her body and igniting mine. I yanked it away from her head, but the heat was still there — radiating from my palm to my fingers and from my fingers through my arm and to the rest of my body. I shook my arm, but that only made the fire rage hotter inside. Dawn loomed in front of me; beads of sweat mingled with the glistening remnants of holy oil that dripped into her eyebrows.

Dawn swayed on her heels. I swallowed the pain and hurried behind her, sticking my knee out and straightening my left arm to brace myself for her fall. White heat flared behind my eyes, darkening the room little by little. I took deep breaths in and out, training my eyes on Dawn, even as she started to fade. The room grew darker in stages as Dawn's swivel slowed and then her body flexed. She was supposed to fall — all of Papa's people fell into his arms — but Dawn got steadier the longer she stood in front of me. I walked around to face her. Still standing, Dawn's eyes snapped open, and she looked at the room around her. She didn't have the glazed-over look of the newly healed.

She took a few slow steps toward the front pew and sat. Fifteen minutes had passed. I eased myself down next to her on the pew, but some kind of electricity flowed through my body along with the heat.

"Dawn?"

"Hmm?" She turned her neck ever so slightly from where her gaze was fixed on the altar — like a breeze had tickled her cheek — but her eyes landed over my head. Her lips were pressed together, as though opening them would require too much effort.

"Are you okay?"

She nodded. I wanted to ask her what she

was feeling, but we had to leave — there would be time to talk later. It took more effort than it should have to pick up Micah's box with my left arm and help Dawn to her feet with my right. She leaned into my quaking body, and we walked toward the sanctuary doors and out into the hallway, where the faint tapping of computer keys resounded in the otherwise empty corridor. Had someone been in there all along? Had they heard us?

I turned to Dawn and placed my finger in front of my lips. With our backs pressed to the wall, we inched down the hallway. Papa's door was still closed, so it wasn't him, but if anyone saw us, word would reach him before I got back home. Mrs. Nabors's door was open at the end of the hall; I could have sworn it had been closed when we arrived. I pointed down the left side of the hallway, and Dawn nodded. This was not the way it was supposed to happen — I'd planned an escape via the sheltered privacy of the back door, not the exposed front door where anyone passing on the street could see us. We didn't have a choice as we tiptoed past the closed doors of the nursery and Sunday school classrooms. The tapping stopped, and I held my breath, drawing my belly button close to my spine. I wanted to run; instead, I took slow, measured steps toward the main doors and heard Dawn's ragged breathing behind me. I shoved my shoulder into the door and winced; the rubber squeak of footsteps replaced the faint sounds of typing. Dawn and I ran out the front door and hid behind the bushes by the edge of the building.

A few moments later, Mrs. Nabors came outside and scanned the parking lot, a concerned look on her face. A rogue branch stabbed my cheek before droplets of coppery blood fell into my open mouth. I tried to quiet my breathing, to make everything still so Mrs. Nabors wouldn't hear me. Dawn trembled next to me, rustling the bush. Mrs. Nabors craned her neck in our direction but must have heard nothing because she receded — a turtle's head returning to its shell.

Each brick scraped my spine as we melted down the side of the building. Dawn didn't move — she still looked dazed. Then she got up and slowly walked away from me, her arms stiff by her sides.

"Bye, Dawn," I whispered.

She tossed up a hand without turning around. I watched her get back into the red car and drive away before I peeled myself from the concrete.

Each downstroke of the pedal to Micah's house sent a fresh wave of pain through my body. By the time I got to her front door, it was almost 1:00 p.m.; Ma was expecting me back any minute now. I stashed my bike by Micah's garage and forced myself to knock when I usually let myself inside. The lilt of Micah's voice said that she was coming, and then the door cracked open until all of her was standing in front of me.

"Miriam. Hi." It wasn't her normal cheerful greeting, and she didn't swing the door open to invite me inside. She scanned me from head to toe. "What's up with your arm?"

I realized that I was holding it against my body at a funny angle. "Nothing. It's fine." I tried to lower it, but a shooting pain passed from my elbow to my hand. "How've you been?"

"Okay, I guess." She looked down at the box.

"I wanted to bring you some of your things from school. Your favorite pencil is in here somewhere." I scrounged around the bottom of the box for the metallic pencil that she used for everything, anything to keep from looking at her.

"You don't have to do that. I'll find it. Thanks for bringing my stuff." She took the

216

box from me and rested it on the floor inside her house.

"I miss you." I crossed my left arm over my abdomen.

"Yeah, I miss you too. It's been hard not to talk to you."

"That's been the hardest part." I didn't tell her all the times since last Friday when I'd lifted the receiver to dial her number and been deterred when Papa picked up the other end.

"What's going to happen to you guys?" I asked. When I spooled time back to the day in the annex, I wondered if we'd be where we were if I hadn't spoken those forbidden words over her.

Micah shrugged. "I think my dad is looking to work for another church, but that's been hard. And I have to find another homeschool. My mom's been calling people."

Deacon Johnson's voice calling Micah's name came from the belly of the house. Micah tilted her head toward the low sound. "Coming," she yelled back.

"So what does this mean?" I asked.

Micah shrugged, her eyes brimming with tears.

"We'll see each other again, right?"

Micah gave a halfhearted nod.

"Promise me we'll see each other again." I stuck out my pinky to link with hers — she lifted her hand but placed it on the door and pushed it closed.

"I gotta go, Miriam."

As the bronze doorknocker swung closer to my face, I wondered if Ma had felt something similar when she had to leave her sisters. If she'd had a similar conversation with them while Papa was waiting in the driveway with the engine running. If she had the same sensation I was having now, where I felt the parts of myself that had always been solid leaking through my shoes.

TEN

The congregation dwindled as November marched on — first the Smiths left, and then the Markhams and then the Loomises. It must have felt like betrayal for Papa — he had welcomed the twin Loomis boys into the kingdom last year, dunking their identical bodies deep below the surface of the lake. He took comfort where he could, in the fact that most of the regulars who'd been members since the church was founded — save the Johnsons — were still in attendance. In the midst of it all, Deacon Farrow stood by Papa's side Sunday after Sunday, while Mrs. Cade and Mrs. Nesbitt vocally supported him.

In the first couple of weeks after the Johnsons left, offerings reached a new low. At the end of the third Sunday service in November, the baskets made their way down the rows and returned to the front still almost empty. Afterward, as we were loading up the car to leave, the head of the usher board brought a Post-it with the written tally out to Papa. Papa took it and didn't seem to register what it said, but when we got home, doors slammed all around the house, knocking pictures from the wall. We tiptoed around the house for the rest of the day, grabbing fallen pictures and returning them to jutting wall nails.

For each Sunday that more pews were empty, living in the house was like standing on a tightrope — small things, like too much syrup on the pancakes, sent Papa's whole plate flying off the table. By the end of the month, when the multipurpose room showcased amateur hand turkeys with what we were thankful for, church attendance was a third of what it had been when the congregation had welcomed us back from revival season.

I tried to see Dawn's absence from the past month's healing services as a good sign, that maybe she was no longer in need of healing, but as each week passed without information, my uncertainty grew. And then Papa officially canceled Friday healing services — it was more out of formality than anything else. They had been all but dead since the Friday with Micah, and none of

220

Papa's attempts to resuscitate them had worked.

Somehow, through the tangled grapevine of church news — a congregant to an usher to a deacon, or something like that — Papa found out that Deacon Johnson had started serving on the deacon board of his rival church across town. It was a week before Thanksgiving when the phone call came. Ma made dinner while Papa was sequestered in the study — every few minutes, his angry voice surged downstairs.

"Bring your father up his dinner," she said to me, fear barely hidden on her face. She held a heavy plate — from the replacement set she had bought — in front of my face, a fillet of grilled fish set on its center. Curlicues of steam tickled my nose as I walked up the stairs and heard Papa's loud whispering from around the corner.

"Have I done nothing for him for all these years? How dare he? He acts like he doesn't owe me a bit of loyalty."

Whoever he was speaking to didn't have much of a chance to say anything as the rise at the end of one question bled into the first syllable of the next.

"He owes me everything. This place wouldn't exist without me, and he knows that." He pounded his fist on the desk at the final word. I bobbled the plate, sending a few asparagus spears into the air before they landed on the carpet. I crouched and picked them up, blowing them off before replacing them on the plate's edge, not touching the other food — just the way he liked it.

The study door flew open, almost sucking me inside the room on a gust of air. Next to my hands, Papa's socked size-thirteen feet stretched the thin navy-blue fabric, revealing the mountain range of corns on his scrunched toes.

"Miriam. How long were you out here?"

"I — I just got —"

"Don't lie to me."

"I'm not lying." I swallowed the last syllable and dug my hands into the carpet to stand, but my legs threatened to let me fall. A tight grip like a blood pressure cuff constricted my upper arm and yanked me to my feet.

"What did you hear?"

"Nothing, Papa. I promise."

"What does the Bible say about lying?"

"I'm not lying."

"Then you need to repent."

Repentance meant that I was supposed to pray or recite Scripture, loud enough for him to hear. I dropped to my knees near where his dinner plate was sitting; the butter had slid from the top of the mashed potatoes and was congealing under the asparagus. Papa took a step closer — I hadn't started praying yet.

"Repent." His breath was hot and stale on my face as he bent over me. Downstairs, Ma and Caleb had stopped talking.

His favorite Scripture for disobedience was Ephesians 6:1–3, which was about honoring your mother and father and your days being long on earth. He took another step closer and then another until he was so close to me that I couldn't see all of him. *I will never hurt* you; *I will never hurt* you. I clung to his words from a lifetime ago, needing to believe them.

I closed my eyes and brought my hands to my face, pressing the pads of my fingers together in front of my nose. Saying the Bible verse out loud would appease him, and I would have to repeat it until my voice was gone or he was satisfied; it was never certain which one would come first. But my tongue felt thick in my dry mouth.

"I'm waiting, Miriam."

I kept my lips pressed firmly together, even as I heard his knuckles crack behind me. A loud *whap* on the back of my head thrust me into the hallway wall. My hands flew in front of my face and made contact with the wall first. The plaster and drywall gave a little as my head reverberated from the force of his slap.

"I'm waiting, Miriam."

His words echoed between my ears as though my head had been hollowed out. He struck me again — right on the space where my ponytail holder gathered my cottony curls at the back of my head. The pain came sharp and fast and radiated to other parts of my head. I squeezed my eyes shut behind prayer hands.

Above me, his breathing became more erratic. We stayed there like two statues as the silence dragged on. I imagined him closing his eyes and taking a long breath to compose himself the same way he did before starting a long sermon, his shoulders rising and falling beneath his T-shirt. The pain began to ebb as I waited for the next hit.

The hallway throbbed with our breathing — mine burning as it filled my lungs, refusing to steady even as I focused on long inhales and exhales. Finally, I twisted my neck and looked up at him. His eyes were red, and the vein in his forehead was pulsating. But then I saw the anger in his eyes transform into something softer — regret, perhaps. As he turned around and walked into his bedroom, I slowly stood up. All of the pain that had gone away earlier swam to my head. The dizzy floral wallpaper supported my unsteady palms as I waited to hear Ma or Caleb come up to see if I was okay. But no one moved downstairs. Alone, I stumbled to my bedroom and locked the door. If Ma wanted to come and check on me later, she would have to knock.

I reached for the Bible on the nightstand, fingering my name embossed in gold on the worn leather cover. That night's reading was from Deuteronomy, but I couldn't make myself open it. I put the Bible back on my nightstand and reached for my prayer journal instead. The early questions of my youth mocked me with their simplicity. *Does Jesus prefer Baptists because he was baptized by John the Baptist? Is there a different heaven for Baptists?* With the journal perched on my legs, I didn't even know what I wanted to ask — what were the words to explain the feeling that pulled at the core of my stomach and sent a bitter wave of vomit to my throat? My pen hovered above the page, unable to make contact. I pressed it closer to the sheaf of paper and a blob of ink pooled onto the faint blue lines. Suddenly, a hatch opened as my pen skimmed over one page, then another and another. When I finally finished, I was breathless, gasping over the page as though I had just finished a race.

The kids in our neighborhood who had grown up with myths of Santa Claus and the tooth fairy must have already experienced this emptiness after feeling a hand linger too long under the pillow or upon witnessing their parents placing carefully wrapped presents under the tree. We had been shielded from that — Ma kept our teeth in a little wooden box and we each picked a name to buy a Christmas present for. Papa had told us never to believe in transient things for happiness because our hope was in eternal life. But Papa had carefully cultivated our belief in him. He never said it outright — *Believe in me as you believe in God* — that would have been obvious blasphemy and idolatry. But he was the all-consuming presence that had filled my entire life, taking up all the space in the house and in revival tents. In its absence was a black hole that seemed bigger than the presence that had inhabited it. Like the gap left behind after losing a tooth — the ragged, sore space in your mouth always felt larger than the tiny bit of enamel that fell out.

The annual Thanksgiving service was always held on the Sunday before the holiday, and this year's was to be no different. We separated at the front doors: Caleb and Papa walked to the sanctuary while Ma, Hannah, and I went to the multipurpose room to prepare the Thanksgiving meal. Most years, we cooked with Micah and her mom; together, wearing turkey hats and oven mitts, we served members of the church and the neighborhood. This time, when we stepped inside the multipurpose room, I felt the absence of Mrs. Johnson's ebullient hello and hug that usually squeezed the air out of me. Instead, we were greeted by silence and a crooked banner that read HAPPY THANKSGIVING stuck to the wall behind a crystal bowl full of punch.

Ma and I got to work on the string beans. Her arms jostled mine in the small space as snatches of the sermon came over the loudspeaker.

"We're popping all these beans, but I don't know how many people will come this year. I guess it's always better to have too much than too little." She laughed.

I shrugged. There was nothing funny

about the small congregations and the way they precipitated Papa's anger. And she had felt it too, which made her laugh even harder to understand.

"What's with the silent treatment lately, Miriam?"

If she had still been the person I remembered, she would have noticed that I hadn't been able to laugh with her since the day she sacrificed me to Papa's rage and left me alone while he hit me in the hallway. We hadn't had our late-night reading sessions either; the few times she'd knocked, I'd pretended to be asleep. I glanced away from Ma's desperate face and looked behind me, where Hannah was punching soft balls of dough. Hannah glanced toward us, her mouth opening for a soundless laugh. I joined her as she slapped the dough onto a cutting board, placing my hands on top of hers and adding gentle pressure as we moved the rolling pin over the airy mound, creating a jagged shape. Her hand curled around the glass as we cut perfect circles into the dough, and I dropped each disc onto the greased cookie sheet. When I closed the oven door, Hannah stood next to the rectangular window and watched the heated coils glow red as the dough rose.

Caleb's hesitant voice through the loudspeaker announced that Papa would give the benediction; I imagined him in the pulpit next to Papa, his clip-on tie askew. I'd asked him to say something to Papa one night when they were in the study together, to tell him how bad his anger was getting at home, that I wasn't sure how much more we could handle. *What do you want me to say?* he'd responded to my pleas. *Tell him the truth,* I'd said. But for all I knew, he hadn't said anything.

" 'The Lord bless you and keep you; the Lord make His face shine upon you and be gracious to you; the Lord turn His face toward you and give you peace. Amen.' "

I poured green beans from the pot into the colander and watched through the wall of steam as people started to trickle through the double doors. Normally, the line would be in the hallway before Papa said the closing prayer, but people came in one or two at a time. Per Ma's request, I had already made Papa's plate with a turkey leg, a heap of green beans, and two biscuits.

Papa entered the multipurpose room, and I grabbed his plate so he didn't have to wait in line. Some motion near the side window rustled the bushes — the profile of a man and a girl who was a head shorter. Dawn and her father. With Papa's plate in my hands, I elbowed my way past Ma.

"Be careful, Miriam," Ma squeezed out of clenched teeth as I pressed past her awkward third-trimester body, jolting it into the open cabinet door. I let myself out of the kitchen and wove through the short line of people who were picking up plates and grabbing cups. On the way outside, I bumped into Papa and handed him his plate.

"Where are you going?" Papa called as I jogged out of the multipurpose room, his voice echoing in the hallway.

The wind outside had picked up since we had arrived that morning, and my heart was beating faster than my shoes slapping the concrete. The driver's-side door was open as Dawn's father lowered himself inside.

"Dawn," I yelled.

We had been standing close to this exact spot on the night when she'd asked me to heal her. Breathless, I approached Dawn's closed passenger door and banged on the window. She opened it and stepped outside; I followed her around the side of the car to the rusted trunk. Her face had more color in it, her cheeks chubbier, her breathing at normal intervals as she spoke to me.

"Hi, Miriam," she said. "I tried to find you earlier but didn't see you during the service."

"I was cooking in the back."

She looked at the front of my flour-covered apron and nodded. I hadn't thought about what I would say to her when I saw her; I grasped the apron's fabric and ran it between my fingers as I tried to formulate the right question. "How are you feeling?"

"That's why I wanted to find you." She leaned closer to me, and her voice dropped. "I felt weird right after the — you know — so it seemed like all the other times." Another gust of wind ripped through the parking lot — she paused and looked around. A few other parishioners mingled outside, making small talk that wafted over to where we stood.

"I went back to my cardiologist for a checkup. Do you know what they told me?"

I shook my head. Dawn's father rolled down the window and poked his head out. "Hurry up, honey. We're running late," he said.

"Coming."

"What did they say?"

"My heart function is normal. I can't remember the last time I had a normal checkup. The doctors couldn't believe it, especially since I haven't had the latest surgery yet."

"Honey!" her father called.

"Gotta go. Thanks, Miriam. See you around."

She wrapped me in a hurried embrace and jogged back to the car door as though she'd been jogging all her life. That had to be proof of something. I held on to that picture as she looked around once again with a wan smile before sinking into the car's upholstery.

I played her words over and over again. Maybe, like with Micah, a normal checkup could just mean that an abnormal one was on the horizon. But maybe it had worked. Euphoria should have felt like all my neurons and synapses firing at the same time — something that should have made my body feel lighter — but I sank onto the ground. My hands grasped small piles of gravel next to the tiny rainbows that appeared in the shiny black oil puddle. I closed my lips around a prayer that I couldn't utter aloud, the prayer that ran counter to everything I'd ever learned or been taught: *Thank You, Lord, for healing Dawn through me. Give me the strength to seek You and do Your will.*

In bed in the middle of the night, I couldn't stop thinking about how my hands had

232

touched something and made it whole again. But then my thoughts were interrupted by music that wasn't gospel riding the heat currents through the vent beneath my bed. At first I thought I was dreaming, but the music continued even after I got up and crept downstairs, passing the front window where I saw an empty driveway. Papa had been leaving early a lot more these days, staying gone for hours at a time and offering no explanation about where he'd been when he returned. I imagined long, closed-door meetings with the deacon board as he tried to replace Deacon Johnson, meetings that were too volatile for him to let us overhear.

When I got closer to the kitchen, the music slid into my veins — the hi-hat's tinny tapping was persistent as guitars and drums faded, leaving nothing but a woman's mournful voice singing about a man who left her, her high notes breaking away from the music and modulating until they landed on a sound more animal than human. A pair of feet padded a syncopated rhythm in the kitchen's dimness — quick steps that were out of pace with the slow words and music. When I craned my neck around the corner, all of the weight of Ma's growing body was raised on the balls of her feet. Her eyes were closed, and her right arm was bent several inches in front of her as though she were holding someone who wasn't there. She looked younger than I'd ever seen her, unencumbered by the heaviness of pregnancy and revival season that had stooped her shoulders. I watched her reflection as she passed the black mirrored pools of the kitchen windows; my eyes slid to her undulating hips that drove her from the cabinets to the stove, buffeting her against the refrigerator and back toward the sink, her face tilted upward. Her limbs threaded together in front of her, swimming their way to the light. *Carnal,* Papa probably would have muttered if he had been here, but this wasn't the evil of the flesh that he said was sin. For a moment, I saw the dancer that she'd been before she met Papa.

I leaned against the doorjamb, my shoulder touching the wall. I couldn't shift my eyes from her, from the smile that tickled the sides of her mouth as her lips formed words to lyrics that I'd never heard her say: "I'll be your lover. Better than any other. I'll make you moan and scream with ecstasy." Her lips should have stumbled over these words, but there was only unfettered joy behind her closed, fluttering eyelids as her languid limbs moved like they were floating underwater. I wondered how many nights she went downstairs while we slept, a thin floor the only thing separating us.

The song ended and her eyes opened and focused on me as the opening chords to a new song filled the room. Her mouth widened in shock, and she wrapped her hands around her nightgown as though she were naked.

"Did I wake you up?" She transformed in front of me, jamming the screen of her phone until the room was quiet. Her scared eyes darted as her neck craned around me.

"He's not here."

Her shoulders relaxed, and she collapsed in the kitchen chair — all the vibrancy in her face and body slowly left the room. I took the chair across from her.

"I've never seen you dance like that, Ma."

She shrugged.

"Can you teach me?"

A sparkle in the corner of her normally dimmed eyes provided a glimmer of the Ma I'd just seen. She pressed both hands against the table and turned toward the door once more. When she got to her feet, she stretched out her hand toward me. I grabbed it, and she pulled me to a standing position — soon we were in the middle of the kitchen floor. Her phone began another song with a quicker beat like the *rat tat tat tat* of sudden rain against a windowsill. She crooked her arm around the small of my back and pressed me against the hard, protruding mound of her stomach, flattening her breasts against mine as she collapsed the gap between us with one swift jerk of her arm. Our bodies moved as one, her hips rocking a couple seconds before mine caught up. My clumsy body was off-kilter as it rammed into hers, bouncing us off each other and sending me away from her in a twirl — when I stopped spinning and found her again, she was extending her arm across the kitchen toward me.

She spun me again, all while singing along to the lyrics. We danced until that song ended and then through another few songs until I lost count.

By the time the sun burned the sky orange, we fell to the floor breathless, spread-eagle beside one another. My laugh intertwined with hers until they were inextricable from each other, and her chest heaved and fell in rapid succession. I'd heard her laugh before — at Caleb's dumb jokes over dinner or Papa's impressions of church members. But this laugh was different — it was bright and bold. The first real laugh since what had happened with Papa the night after Micah's healing service. I looked over next to me at where she lay with eyes closed and hair splayed against the floor like a sunburst.

"You're pretty good," she said to the ceiling when her breathing returned to normal.

"You're not so bad yourself."

"It's all the contemporary classes I took in high school. Before things got bad." She rolled over on her side and perched her chin in her palm. Her laughing eyes became mournful as they searched mine. She reached out and placed a palm on the side of my face, her fingertips grazing my cheekbone that was prominent like hers. Our twin faces in different bodies, she liked to say.

"I kept saying that I couldn't marry a man like my father. And your dad was different in the early years. But I feel like I don't know him anymore. And I've been meaning to say that I'm sorry."

"Sorry for what?" I asked.

The front door clicked. We sprang from where we were sprawled on the floor — Ma opened cupboards, clanging pots and pans together in an elaborate charade of making breakfast as I pressed the pause button on her phone and shoved it in the pocket of my robe. Papa's loud footsteps came down the hallway, and Ma's trembling hands made the heavy cast-iron skillet handle rattle against the burner. As he stopped at the edge of the kitchen, I folded and re-folded a dish towel into sections, watching the thread loops line up like a row of tiny nooses.

I sidestepped to the edge of the kitchen until my spine flattened against the refrigerator door. Ma greeted him with a tentative embrace, her face seemingly trying to gauge how long he had been waiting on the porch, what he had heard. His arms were relaxed by his sides even as Ma hugged him hello.

"You're back early. Do you want some breakfast?"

"I'm starving."

With Papa's focus on Ma, I slowly crept upstairs. Back in my room, I sank into my bed — feeling some comfort that I wasn't the only one with twin selves. Ma didn't heal, but she kept a whole other side shielded from Papa. I would have to follow her example and separate my selves as well. When alone, I would drape my power around my shoulders like a cape, but before leaving the sanctum of my room, I would have to revert to the Miriam I had learned how to be — the Miriam who held her tongue and stayed quiet the way Papa expected.

■ ■ ■ ■

The following week after services, I felt a delicate hand on my shoulder. It was a girl from the congregation whose round face I recognized even though I didn't know her name. "Nadia," she whispered before asking me to heal her. There was another girl after that — Suzette — who made her request as I snuck to the bathroom, away from Papa's presence but still within earshot of the loudspeaker booming his words about obedience and submission. Papa would have wanted me to turn them away, would have struck me in the face if he knew what I was doing. So I kept my secret from him, from all of them, as I moved away from the danger of the main sanctuary for the later healings. I healed Nadia of her psoriasis by the sink in a locked bathroom while erratic knocks interrupted us from outside. Suzette's migraines were harder — we were crowded in the closet of the claustrophobic annex where Micah had passed out. At the end of each healing, when I saw double and they reeled in front of me, I told them to say that Papa had done it if anyone asked.

Later the night of Suzette's healing, I lay awake in bed, the words that had declared her migraines a thing of the past wet on my lips. A hollow in my stomach felt like hunger, but it couldn't have been, since I'd just devoured Ma's fried chicken — the ravenousness a new side effect of healing that Ma, as she scooped me another helping of corn, chalked up to growing pains.

Outside the open window, a baby's plaintive cry caught the night wind and entered my room — its boldness a reminder that Isaiah had never had the chance to cry. I conjured him back. No one knew I had touched him as he passed from Papa to the paramedics, had felt the curve of his swollen belly that never ate, had traced the edges of his mute, open mouth. My hand had fallen to my side at that moment, not expecting the rubbery coldness of his scentless skin, but I could have kept it there and whispered a prayer over him then, tracing a dry sign of the cross over his eyes that probably would have been deep brown and pensive — like Caleb's — if only they had opened.

ELEVEN

Ma pulled the Advent calendar — the same one we'd had since I was a baby — out of a tattered box marked "Christmas." The calendar's twenty-four tiny cardboard doors didn't shut anymore, prematurely exposing that day's Scripture and gift of mangers, Jesus figurines, and nativity scenes. Caleb, Hannah, and I stood in a semicircle around her as she placed it on the mantel; this once-breezy gesture, now laborious for Ma, officially marked the beginning of Christmas season. Only this year, it was almost two weeks late.

Ma made up for the missing nightly Advent celebrations by pouring four mugs of hot chocolate that we sat around the table to drink. Hannah wore a foamy mustache when she pulled her lips out of the mug, and we laughed until there was a thud upstairs. Our laughter came to an abrupt end as Ma padded up the steps. A minute later, the silence was shattered by a shriek.

Caleb placed his palms on the table and jumped up. Then another scream came, more chilling than the first. He looked over at me, his pupils contracting into periods.

"What's he doing up there?" His voice broke and spilled over as he asked the obvious question. Another scream shot to the first floor. Before I could answer him, he jerked away from the table, knocking the chair to the ground. He must have taken the stairs two at a time because seconds after he left, muffled footfalls pounded above me. I fingered the whorls in the table's fake wood grain as the bedroom door flung open, glad he was going up to help Ma, but wondering where all of this concern had been when Papa had hurt me in the hallway a few weeks ago.

After some minutes passed, Caleb's heavy footsteps were on the stairs with Ma's trailing behind a few seconds later. Needing something to do, I jumped from the table and dumped half-full mugs of tepid hot chocolate into the sink, steeling myself to face her when she rounded the corner. Then she was behind me, as close as she had been when we were dancing. She reached around — startling me with her touch — and pulled the mugs from my sopping hands before laying them at the bottom of the sink. I dropped my head and watched the water wash the brown away until Ma shut off the tap.

I blinked back tears as I turned around; she angled the left side of her face away from me, even though the visible right side was caked with layers of foundation. Caleb was in front of her now too, pinning her in place with a wide stance. With the gentlest grip, he turned her chin so he could see the side that she was trying to hide.

"It looks worse than it is." Tears clogged her throat as she spoke. She pulled her face away from him and winced. I didn't know why she was explaining something to him that he had just seen. Before he could respond, she pushed her way between us and walked toward the cupboard, jangling pots and pans for a dinner that was hours away. We followed her as she pulled out a cutting board and started chopping an onion — the repetitive motion of the blade against the hard plastic surface blunted the edge of Caleb's repeated questions. "What's going on? How long has he been doing this?"

She looked over at me. *Tell him,* I told her with my eyes, nodding to punctuate the point. I put my arm around her waist; she was as close to confessing as she had ever been.

"Things have been hard on your father," she began. Hannah had been playing at the table; she stopped moving when Ma spoke. "He doesn't mean it. He just can't control himself."

Caleb's mouth got wider as he tried to make sense of how the man who he had placed next to God was capable of such brutality. I thought back to the day behind the tent in Bethel when I had to see him with different eyes. How hard it had been to reconcile what I had seen with what I had always known.

"How can you say that? There's no excuse."

"It won't always be like this."

Caleb's hand snaked inside of mine as he hugged Ma from the other side. She stopped chopping onions as her neck bent.

Later that night, Ma whistled a tuneless song from far back in memory as she made four plates of burned meat loaf for dinner and brought them to the table. The leftovers stayed in pots on the cooktop. We ate dinner without him at the head of the table, and I stuffed myself with the charred meat even though I wasn't hungry. Afterward,

Hannah, Caleb, and I curled under Ma's outstretched arms on the couch as night fell. Her hardened belly protruded into my ribs, and I leaned close enough to it to feel the occasional kick. We pretended to be excited about the impromptu slumber party, shivering in unison whenever there was a loud noise upstairs.

I woke up in the middle of the night with Hannah's arm below my back. I sat up on the couch and tried to readjust myself under Ma's armpit, but the space where Ma had been sleeping was empty. Caleb and Hannah's necks were at odd angles as their snores competed with each other for airtime. Pushing myself off the couch with a stiff arm, I walked through the empty hallway. There was no sign of her.

Upstairs was the faint noise of a zipper — a sound that always reminded me of revival season — followed by a rustle. I stayed by the landing as Ma crept downstairs in the dark with a suitcase by her side. When she was halfway down the staircase, I came into full view. Ma froze in midstep like a caught child; she shifted the suitcase by her side, as though she could somehow hide it. Even in the darkness, her face was wet, her eyes glassy.

"What are you doing?" I asked, as soon as

I could find my voice.

She set her suitcase down on the step before her body crumpled next to it, her shoulders raising into a shrug. A car approached the house and slowed down before killing the lights. Ma lurched to her feet with the suitcase swaying by her side and slid past me on the staircase, tossing the front door open like she was expecting company.

"Who is that?"

She turned her head from me to the glinting car on the other side of the screen door, then back to me. Her hand gripped the door's handle.

"I have to do this. I'm sorry." Pain creased her voice, folding it into hundreds of tiny pieces like the origami birds I used to make with Micah, the ones that crashed into the carpet whenever Micah and I tried to make them fly. The door opened, and Ma straddled the threshold — one foot outside with the suitcase while the other foot was planted inside a square of ceramic tile.

She peeked over the back of the couch at Caleb's drooped head — for a moment, we both listened to his snore, which sounded like a car whose engine wouldn't start. I glanced over Ma's shoulder into the driveway where a woman I'd never seen before sat behind the wheel. Her face looked just like Ma's.

She took another step outside, toward where her sister — one of the aunts we'd never been allowed to meet — waited for her. I wanted to move toward them, but my feet had grown roots. Time unspooled itself — first moving quickly and then shifting to slow motion — as she opened the back door and threw her bag inside. As she moved to the passenger door and opened it, her hand glided over the door's steel curve, then down the straight edge. She looked back at the house — at me inside the front door — weighing the life that she had with us with whatever was on the other side with her sister.

She lifted her hand and wiggled her fingers slowly — a wave that I was unable to return. But instead of stooping into the car and disappearing into the passenger seat, she stayed upright, her dress floating away from her body on the breeze, her gaze still fixed on the house.

Prickles traveled up my stationary legs as I stared at her, willing her to move one inch closer to the house. A low voice from the car chided her as Ma took a longing glance at the woman in the driver's seat and then back at the house. With a jerking motion,

Ma closed the door. Behind the sloped windshield, her sister pressed her head against the steering wheel as Ma opened the back door and retrieved her bag. Ma's sister shook her head and then started the car. As silently as she came, she pulled onto the street and left Ma and her suitcase in the middle of the driveway. I released the breath I hadn't realized I'd been holding and propped the door open for her as she came back inside. She paused on the threshold as though considering her decision, her left hand on the doorjamb, her right arm crooked against the small of her back as she fell forward into the screen.

"Are you okay?" I didn't know which version of the question she would answer.

"I don't know what's going on anymore." She hadn't closed the door yet and looked back out to the street, where the car was retreating. "I don't know what to do. I can't go with her, but I can't stay here like this either."

The foundation that she had so carefully applied before dinner had melted away from her face while we slept, revealing blue puffiness and a left eye that was almost swollen shut in a wink. She had borne the brunt of all he had to offer, her soft body a convenient receptacle for his rage.

The car was still on the street, its hazards lighting the night in flickering yellow. Ma hadn't yet brought her bag inside, hadn't yet stepped over the threshold. I couldn't move to bring her in or shut her out, so I kept the door open as an invitation.

"What will happen to us if you leave?" It was the most selfish question, but it was the only thing I could think about, especially as Caleb and Hannah slept only feet away.

"You don't think I've thought about that? You three are the first things on my mind each morning and my last thoughts at night. How to love and protect you. How to keep you safe. And I've failed at all of it. I'm so sorry for that . . ."

Her voice trailed off as she spoke, each word bringing her farther inside the house. By the time she stopped talking, both feet were on the tile. When the screen door closed on her, the car turned the corner with its hazards still on. Ma sagged in the doorway with her hands pressed against her stomach, breathing harsh exhales through pursed lips. It seemed like a contraction, but her due date was a month away. I helped her onto the couch and carried her suitcase upstairs, stowing it in the back of my closet behind a cardboard box of old Bibles and Sunday school drawings.

■ ■ ■ ■

Later that afternoon, the house suddenly swelled with wailing. The low hum from Ma's early stage of labor lifted through the vents and curled its way beneath doors. It was too soon, and when I rushed to the couch to check on Ma, she was grabbing her stomach and rocking, as though that action would slow things down.

"You're okay, Ma," I said as I scampered into the kitchen to call Mrs. Cade. I tried to keep my voice neutral, but Mrs. Cade must have heard something in it that scared her because ten minutes later, her car tires screeched into the driveway. I opened the door to her familiar, welcome face, and stepped aside while she rushed to Ma.

She entered the living room and gasped when she saw Ma's swollen face; a moment later, she reset her expression into a look of practiced calm and hurried to Ma's side.

"You're okay, Joanne," she said over and over. I stayed far behind her, looking over her shoulder as she placed her stethoscope to Ma's stomach.

"The baby's okay, too," she said. "Everything's going to be fine."

Caleb took Hannah upstairs while I

turned on the teakettle in the break between contractions. Its whistle mingled with the noises that Ma was now making in the living room. I checked the kitchen clock: 3:04. The house paused to catch its breath as Ma caught hers; in the brief silence, I gathered an armful of towels.

My body sprang into action, the movements deep in muscle memory. I'd done this with Isaiah, wiping Ma's brow at regular intervals and feeding her ice chips, counting the minutes between the contractions and, finally, when the time came, telling her to push with my hand propped on her sweaty knee. But Mrs. Cade must have seen something that wasn't right, because just when I was about to tell Ma to push one final time, she sent me away.

I'd watched from the hallway when Ma was having Hannah, too young and scared to enter the room. Ma's cries were different back then, more like a cat's breathy mews than wails. At first I thought those noises were normal, until a look of concern crept across Mrs. Cade's brow and she stepped in the kitchen to make a call. Before we knew it, the house flooded with intermittent flashes of red light. While Papa stood there, the paramedics placed a plastic dome over Ma's mouth that silenced her cries. They belted her to a gurney and whisked her off, the stretcher's back wheels skittering like a wayward shopping cart's. Papa went away in the ambulance with her. When I finally got to see Hannah, a wall of glass and a tangle of tubes separated us.

In the kitchen, I soaked and wrung out the towels that Mrs. Cade had directed me to get. For a moment, it was quiet. My internal timer counted the seconds between contractions. *One, two, three.* Ma screamed out at almost ninety-four. *Go time,* as Mrs. Cade called it. Normally, she would tell me to go upstairs and bring Papa down, but she must have gotten a good enough look at Ma's face and decided not to extend the invitation.

"So we're going to do this, huh?" Adrenaline pulsed through me when I realized that it would be the three of us for the first time. Ma switched from her laboring position on all fours to the birthing position, which meant that her raised, bent knees were on either side of Mrs. Cade's head.

"Hey, Miriam." Her thready whisper was barely audible with the noise of Mrs. Cade removing things from her bag.

"Hey, Ma." I crouched by her head, wiping her brow with a cool cloth. Her dry lips cracked into a smile before I rubbed a piece of ice over them.

"When the next contraction comes, you need to start pushing," Mrs. Cade directed from between Ma's knees.

Ma lifted her head from the pillow in acknowledgment of what Mrs. Cade had said. Like a wave, the next contraction rolled in. Ma curled around herself. I grabbed one of her knees and guided it back, focusing on the way the bruise seeped across her left eye as she winced, listening to Mrs. Cade's steady movements rather than the irregular patter of my racing heart.

"Push," I coaxed. *One, two, three, four, five, six, seven, eight, nine, ten.* I paused a beat between each number, just like Mrs. Cade had taught me. Ma's screams threatened to shatter the windows. I grabbed her hand tight, hoping to take away some of the pain. She squeezed so hard I thought my fingers might come off, but I kept counting.

"Good, Joanne. A few more like that and we'll have a baby."

"Good job, Ma," I whispered. I took the few moments of quiet to wipe some of the accumulated beads of sweat from her forehead, avoiding the tender space near her eye, and moved my hand down to the thick white glue that had gathered in the corners of her mouth. Everything around her — the pillow, the couch — was soaked with her sweat.

"I see a head, Joanne! One more good push."

Ma looked like she didn't have an additional push to give, but she nodded, or shook her head: the movement so slight that it was hard to classify. The baby crowned, and Mrs. Cade invited me to peek between Ma's legs to witness the miracle of life. In the dark cove between Ma's thighs, a damp thatch of hair surrounded the wide opening that was giving way for a baby to come into the world; then I looked back up into Ma's tired eyes and squeezed her hand tighter.

"Don't push," Mrs. Cade counseled. She bent down and I heard a tiny snip of scissors, then a sharp drawn breath from Ma as her eyes pleaded with the ceiling for release.

"Okay, Joanne. Push now."

"One more push." I tried to be encouraging, but it was obvious that Ma didn't have much left. Her eyes fluttered under pale lids as I counted to ten slowly, trying to place a bit more distance between when all of our lives would change once again. Before I got to ten, a rush of thick liquid and blood poured onto the towel followed by a long pause, but no cry.

"Mrs. Cade?" Ma and I both said in

unison. This couldn't be another Isaiah. *Please God, let this baby live.*

Before Mrs. Cade could respond, a cry filled the room, more like the bleating of a lamb than a baby's screech, but it was the sweetest sound.

"It's a boy!" Mrs. Cade announced the words that Ma had been waiting to hear. Papa's footsteps upstairs stopped as Ma's head collapsed against the sodden, canary-yellow pillowcase. Mrs. Cade placed the baby on Ma's chest; Ma stared at his tiny, wide nose that was a replica of Papa's and touched the cleft in his chin that was identical to hers. I waited for singing and cooing as she met her newest son, but each time she opened her mouth, nothing really came out.

"Do you want to cut the cord?" The glint of Mrs. Cade's silver scissors pulled my gaze away from the mournful look in Ma's hooded eyes. This should have been a joyful time — God had seen fit to bring a new baby to this house after so much suffering. But looking at Ma, who was holding the baby to her chest with mechanical arms, made it feel like less of a blessing.

A coiled spring like a slick, stretched phone cord connected Ma to the baby. Mrs. Cade directed me to cut between the two places where she had clamped the cord. She handed me her scissors, and I pressed down hard before the sharp blades finally cut through the thickness.

"What do you think his name should be?" Ma finally asked. Even though her voice sounded stronger than it had a few minutes ago, it was tinged with sadness.

"I get to name him?"

"Well, you helped me, didn't you?"

Papa was normally the one to name babies, not me. But Mrs. Cade and Ma were both looking at me expectantly. The baby pursed his perfect set of pink lips as I grazed the silky layer of black fuzz that covered his pale brown scalp.

"So what is it?"

"Isaac." The only son of Abraham and Sarah. Their miracle and the reward for their belief.

"Isaac," Ma repeated. "Isaac it is."

It felt strange to name him without Papa — but Ma's mind was made up; even Mrs. Cade nodded from between Ma's legs as she delivered the placenta. She lifted an armful of dirty towels and marched toward the laundry room. Ma eased her legs back to the couch — just like that, all the evidence of the birth was swept away into trash bags and the washing machine. Then there were erratic footsteps on the stairs — Papa's presence took some of the air out of the room as he entered.

"Do you need me to cut the cord?" he asked. But then he must have seen the baby, already swaddled and wrapped on Ma's chest. He stopped suddenly, his torso jutting forward with inertia before he pulled himself back. Caleb came down with Hannah; they rushed past Papa and went to Ma's side.

"I see you have it covered." Papa seethed from the periphery where he stood, his foot not crossing the dividing line between tile and carpet, his eyes raging at Ma beneath half-open lids. Mrs. Cade stood by Ma's side like a guard.

"This is your new son. Isaac." Mrs. Cade's voice — daring with its defiance — emphasized the last word, the pact that the three of us had agreed on without consulting him. No one talked to Papa like that in here.

"Isaac, huh?" Papa rolled the name around in his mouth. He pursed his lips and lowered his eyes — the same face that he used when he consulted his sermon notes — at that moment, however, crinkles of defeat settled beneath his eyebrows. Then he looked back up at me and Mrs. Cade flanking Ma. Mrs. Cade's gaze was steely on him, even as my legs wobbled. I took a step closer to Mrs. Cade, hoping that proximity would give me some of her boldness.

"Isaac it is," he relented.

As Papa took a few steps forward to get a better look at Isaac, Isaac started to wail. Ma, ashen, nestled him under her shirt, letting a swollen breast flop out of her nightgown rather than covering herself the way she normally did when Papa and Caleb were nearby. My cheeks burned at them seeing her like that, and I concealed her with the corner of a blanket as she negotiated a large brown nipple into his mouth.

"Thank you, Gladys." Papa walked over to Mrs. Cade and stood by her side. He bent down and started to put away some of the supplies that she had taken out of her bag. She wrested her bag away from him, shoving a blood pressure cuff and amber vials of medication inside before sliding the zipper closed.

"Can you help me bring some things to my car, Miriam?" Without waiting for my reply, she handed me the bag, and I followed her to the driveway, where she popped her trunk.

"How long?" Mrs. Cade asked when we shared the trunk's shadow. I rearranged

258

some of the cardboard boxes to make her birth bag fit.

"I think it was three hours this time. The shortest."

"Not the labor, Miriam. The bruises." Her voice shot down an octave. She reached up and placed a hand on the trunk lid but didn't move to close it.

I recoiled — even though I'd been waiting for someone to give voice to what had been happening with Papa, her words landed in the center of my chest like a punch. We weren't supposed to talk about family matters outside the house. That was especially true now that Papa's reputation was on the line.

"It's me, Miriam." Her hand moved from the top of the trunk to where mine was resting by my side; she interlaced her fingers with mine and squeezed. With her other hand, she cupped my chin and guided my face level with hers, snatching my eyes from where they were searching the cracks in the ground. I finally looked up at her, and she tilted her head to the side as her eyes brimmed. My lips trembled.

"I can't, Mrs. Cade."

"I know what I saw. You can either confirm what I already know or lie to me. And I know you're not the kind of person who lies."

Mrs. Cade knew me as the person who recited memory verses in her kitchen over plates of homemade cookies; the person who always stood by her dad and believed him to be infallible. Mrs. Cade had no idea the kind of person I had become. The kind of person who healed but lied about it, who had seen and heard unspeakable things. I wasn't ready to tell Mrs. Cade what was going on at home — saying it out loud would make it real.

Mrs. Cade's phone buzzed. She pulled it out of the duffel bag and touched the screen. "I have to run. A high-risk mother is in labor. I'll be back to check on your mother and Isaac. And to finish this conversation."

As she got in the car and put it into reverse, I looked back through the screen door. I could make out the shape of Caleb rocking Isaac in his arms. Since Bethel, it had always been me to come to Ma's defense, even when she and Caleb hadn't come to mine. Caleb had ignored my warnings about Papa until the night before, when pretending everything was okay was no longer possible. So maybe it was only fair that he would have to be the one to stay

260

and protect her rather than me.

"Wait!" I yelled when Mrs. Cade had backed halfway down the driveway. Her car jerked to a stop, and I ran to open the passenger door before sliding inside. Mrs. Cade turned off the radio, presumably to give me space to say what I couldn't before. The car's doors and windows pressed in tighter as we veered under a canopy of trees. It would be easier to tell her everything when I got farther away from the houses I recognized, when the car outran the looming shadow of Papa's congregation.

"For about five months. He hit a man on the revival circuit, back in Bethel. He hadn't been able to heal him, and . . ." My voice drifted off. It should have been harder than this to betray Papa, but, after I took a deep breath, the truth spilled over the dashboard. "He's been hurting us — me and Ma — since we've been back. Ma's gotten the worst of it."

Mrs. Cade nodded as she swerved right down a narrow dead end. Then she reached over the gulf of empty travel mugs between our seats and rested her hand on my knee.

"It's worse than I thought."

"You knew?" I looked over at her, but she was squinting at the road, nodding.

"He hasn't been healing for a while. I

know that he used to heal — at least I think that he did. He started forgetting who had the power — him or God. And that's where he started to go wrong. And I've seen some other troublesome things around the church, even before what happened with Micah and Deacon Johnson. He's had the deacons covering up for him, pretty much eating out of his hand, until they couldn't hide what was going on any longer. When he got rid of Deacon Johnson, that was the last straw for most people, and that was his last real defender except for Deacon Farrow. People are losing faith in him for the first time in his life. A prideful man like your father can't hear that truth about himself. And he can't take that sitting down."

Mrs. Cade must have been talking about another preacher in another church in another town who had gotten too much power and forgotten who gave it to him. As I tried to process the first phrase, there was another one beneath it — *deacons covering up for him* — and beneath that another one — *losing faith in him.* Each phrase echoed in my skull. I wanted to ask Mrs. Cade so many questions, but before I could, she pulled into a driveway.

"This is it." She popped the trunk and jumped out before I could ask her anything.

By the time I stepped out of the car, Mrs. Cade was already up the driveway, the duffel bag thumping against her right leg. A few steps behind Mrs. Cade, my heels sank into the rotted-out wooden boards on the porch before following her inside. Thoughts of Papa disappeared in the claustrophobic, labyrinthine hallways whose walls were cluttered with pictures of unfamiliar faces. At the end of the hallway was a closed door, which Mrs. Cade opened without knocking.

The howl in the room swirled around us. Mrs. Cade rushed to a lump on the ground. She leaned her ear close to the mummified frame that barely moved. For a moment, they were one still form. I kept my back close to the door as I waited for my heart's audible thumping to slow.

"Get me towels and water. Now." I rushed out of the bedroom — the foreign hallways churned as I stumbled through them, eventually getting to the kitchen and turning on a teakettle. While the water boiled, I flung open cabinet doors until a stack of towels at eye level greeted me in the linen closet. A scream through the closed door stilled the entire house.

"Miriam!" Mrs. Cade yelled when the screaming subsided. Her voice shook.

When I got back, the light was on. The

room smelled damp — like copper and sweat — and the lump that I had seen before showed itself to be a woman who Mrs. Cade must have helped onto the bed. A sticky puddle stained the sheets, but I hadn't heard Mrs. Cade telling her to push. I clutched the towels to my chest and walked closer to them — in Mrs. Cade's cupped hands was something small and blue.

"Is she breathing?" the woman screamed.

Mrs. Cade placed a bulb in the baby's mouth and squeezed before pulling it out. Thick, gummy strings came out with the bulb, but the baby remained silent. Mrs. Cade swiped at her bag and pulled out an oxygen mask that she placed over the baby's mouth. The baby's stomach rose and collapsed violently each time Mrs. Cade pumped the mask, but her eyes stayed closed.

I dropped to my knees in a warm pool of fluid next to the bed. With two trembling fingers, I reached out to touch the baby's clammy forehead and closed my eyes, shutting out the mother's primal screams and shaking away the images of Isaiah's face. My secret would be out once I did it, but I couldn't watch this baby die. I would just have to suffer whatever Mrs. Cade had to

264

say to me — what sins she said I had committed — when it was all over. There would be no going back.

"Lord, touch and heal this child of Yours. Bring air into her lungs and breathe life into her body. In the name of the Lord Jesus Christ, you are healed."

As I traced a sign of the cross on the baby's head, the room fell away in pieces. It was just me and the baby as pain radiated from my hand and curled behind my eyes. As the air was being sucked from my lungs, the baby's forehead scalded my hand, and I pulled it away, falling to the floor with my body throbbing and tiny gasps of air coming out of my mouth. I felt every splinter of the hardwood floor beneath me, the rough loops of the rug's fiber, then nothing.

Bright blue walls and the sound of a siren in the distance. I closed my eyes and kept my cheek in a pool of sweat on the floor, even as the screaming ambulance split my head open. When I couldn't stand it any longer, I pushed myself to a seated position.

"How are you feeling?" Mrs. Cade's voice was a yell, and the mug of tea that she held in front of my face swam in my watery eyes. I wanted to respond, wanted to ask her about the mother and her baby, but my throat was sandpaper. Mrs. Cade balled the linens on the empty bed and tossed them into the corner of the room.

"What happened?" The words burned.

"The ambulance just took them away. The baby started breathing on her own right before you passed out. They say she will be fine."

Mrs. Cade's eyes were wide with recognition as she squatted in front of me and placed the mug to my parched lips. The liquid scorched my throat, but I stared into the mug with each sip, unable to glance at Mrs. Cade, who had taken a seat next to me. When I finally looked over, her gnarled hand was a tree root on my thigh.

"How long?"

"Didn't you hear me in the car? The past several months, since Bethel." Each word took more wind out, and I paused for a few breaths.

"I'm not talking about your father anymore. I'm talking about you. This wasn't your first healing. How long have you been doing it?"

Mrs. Cade slid from my side and crouched in front of me, her hands, still warm from the mug of tea, pressed against the sides of my face the way they always did on Sunday mornings. I tried to look away, knowing that whatever I said now couldn't be unsaid. And even though Mrs. Cade was on my side, had always been, Papa had ways of finding anything out.

"Not long enough." The flecks of tea in the bottom of the mug rearranged themselves into shapes — a tree, a cloud, a star — that I stared at to keep the tears at bay.

"What do you mean by that?"

"Why couldn't I do it last time?"

"Last time when?"

"With Isaiah."

At the mention of his name, my hand shot to my mouth. We were forbidden from saying it at home, as though not saying it meant that we would forget about him. Mrs. Cade reached out a hand.

"Let me take you home. But we're going to talk on the way back."

In the car, I told her about Micah, Dawn, Nadia, and Suzette. She kept her eyes on the road the entire time as the words flowed out of me. Words that she promised not to repeat to anyone. The blinker flickered in the darkness as we drifted off the highway and decelerated; my words vanished the closer we got to the house, and the car filled with silence.

"Do you mind if we take a detour?" Mrs. Cade asked.

Before I could answer, she made a left in the darkness when we should have made a right toward the house. She drove the car onto an unlit street, and we crawled beneath a wrought-iron sign overhead that read EDGEWOOD MEMORIAL GARDENS — where Isaiah was buried. We drove up the hill into the company of stone angels, their shadows dancing even in the darkness, morphing into obscure shapes that looked nothing like wings or praying hands. Mrs. Cade stopped the car, got out, and made her way down the path to Isaiah's grave. She walked directly to it, like she had memorized the route to his small granite grave marker pressed into the earth.

I knew what it said: *Isaiah Samuel Horton — Children are a gift from God.* There were no dates to display to the world how long he lived, and the grave marker was bigger than he had been. Mrs. Cade dropped to her knees and dug her hands in the manicured grass. I got out of the car and fell beside her, fingering the roughly etched letters that made up Isaiah's name in the smooth granite. Tears raged out of my eyes, plinking on the grave marker before soaking into the surrounding grass.

"There was no way to heal him, Miriam," she said as she sat next to me. "There are some things that we aren't meant to do, some people who God doesn't intend to heal."

I fell into her chest, heard her words echo into my ear as she repeated them, her hand carving designs into my scalp.

"I'm so sorry," I said over and over again, my words falling in the direction where Isaiah lay. She rocked me back and forth until her dress was wet and my sobs quieted. It was hard to tell exactly how long we had been there. She pulled away from my embrace.

"When you're ready, I'll be in the car." Her footsteps plodded away. My hand lingered on the granite for a few more minutes, even as Mrs. Cade's headlights washed away the darkness. I unrolled my legs from underneath me and walked to the car.

TWELVE

The Sunday after Isaac's birth, Papa and Caleb, both red-eyed with exhaustion, left at 6:00 a.m. for Sunday service. A bit later, I walked a wailing Isaac in circles on the kitchen tile to quiet him down. While stroking his damp curls, I stared into his almond-shaped brown eyes and breathed his baby-skin smell of lotion and shampoo. Every day he looked more like Papa than Ma, especially as his skin darkened. Papa had tasked me with taking care of him while Ma recovered from the delivery; I reveled in each gurgle and cry that entered our house. When I traced the cleft in his chin that led to his tiny pink lips, he opened his mouth as though to cry. I shushed him, shifting my weight from one foot to the other.

There was a knock on the door — too early to be Papa and Caleb, since they had just left a couple of hours ago. I could hear Hannah stirring upstairs, her bellowing making its way to the first floor. I peered through the peephole at a magnified version of Mrs. Cade, her bag by her side. She liked to brag that she hadn't missed a Sunday service for ten years — the longest streak in our church — and yet here she was. I cracked the door, and only when I smelled the fresh air outside — the scent of yesterday's rain — did I realize how close and stale it was in the house. Except for my trip with Mrs. Cade, I hadn't been out in the two days since Isaac's birth.

"Morning, Miriam. Let me see that baby."

I passed her Isaac, whose whimpers had graduated into a full-fledged wail. And though I loved the sounds of his cries, any noise jangled Ma's nerves lately. She seemed to be constantly on edge, so I did everything I could to quiet him — even in the middle of the night.

As Mrs. Cade stepped into the hallway, she must have seen the stack of pizza boxes piled by the trash can and the tower of dishes next to the sink. When Isaac was safely in her arms, I ran upstairs to get Hannah. At the top of the stairs, I looked to the left at Ma's closed bedroom door. I knocked once, then twice, but there were no signs of life. Hannah bellowed again down the hall and I rushed to her side, releasing the rail at the edge of her bed and placing my face close to hers.

"I'm sorry, I'm sorry. I'm here." I rested my hand on her forehead and traced my fingers through her hair the way she liked. With the sleeve of my nightgown, I wiped the sticky puddle of saliva from her lips and chin before raising her upright in bed and sliding her braces and crutches on. As we moved past Ma's door, I pressed my finger to my lips and Hannah mimicked me. Downstairs, water ran into the sink on full blast as plates clanked together.

"So this little guy looks perfectly healthy. How's your mom?"

"She's upstairs recovering."

"Can I go see her too?"

I nodded — Papa didn't want anyone to come inside, much less go upstairs, but I didn't need to keep the secrets of this house from Mrs. Cade anymore. She finished the dishes with one hand while snuggling Isaac in the other; then she dried her hands on the dingy dish towel. Resting Isaac on her shoulder, she walked up the stairs.

She was up there for at least fifteen minutes — long enough for me to make Hannah breakfast. "How does she look?" I asked when she came back downstairs.

"Physically she's okay. She just needs

more time to rest. And the bruises are healing — there are no new ones either. She should be fine." As she said the final sentence, she looked around at the kitchen instead of at me. I looked around at the kitchen too, at the dishes that Mrs. Cade had washed, at how quickly my house had descended into entropy.

"It seems like my work here is done." She paused between each word, still scanning the kitchen, figuring out what else she could do to help. She must have seen a pang of regret on my face — she stopped on her path to the door and waded deeper into the kitchen instead. She set down her hat and white gloves near where Hannah had made a mess of her oatmeal; then she scooped a heap of dark grounds onto a paper filter in the coffee maker. A few moments after she pressed a button, black rivers of liquid fell steadily into the glass pot below.

"Can I pour you a cup?"

I shook my head. "Ma doesn't let me drink it."

She looked up at the ceiling where Ma's bed was and winked. "It will be our secret."

She poured two mugs and brought them to the kitchen table. She set one on the table in front of her and pushed the other in my direction. As I stared into the still, black pool, the wisps of bitter steam tickled my nose. One acrid sip swirled around in my mouth before I forced it down. I grimaced just as Mrs. Cade looked up and smiled.

"I visited the baby in the hospital yesterday. Her name is Hope. They're going to release her tomorrow. You can add her to your list."

Hope. I'd been wondering what happened to her but had been too afraid to ask.

"You certainly have the gift, young lady."

Her words mixed with the strong smell of coffee as the front lock clicked — I closed my eyes to steel myself as Caleb and Papa barged into the kitchen. Mrs. Cade drank the rest of her coffee quickly and finished the mug that I'd shoved back in front of her.

"We missed you in church today, Gladys." Papa's words toed the line between concern and a reprimand.

"It was the only time I could check on your wife and son." She matched his tone of barely veiled anger. "And since you're so concerned, Isaac is doing well. And Joanne is —"

"Thanks for coming by, Gladys," he cut her off.

She got up, washed her mug, and placed it on the drying rack. I walked her to the door and received her kiss on the forehead.

"Take care of her." Her lips vibrated against my hairline. "And keep doing what you're doing."

When winter break ended in January, Ma still hadn't gotten out of bed. At nights, with Ma and Papa shut behind their bedroom door, I heard him grow increasingly frustrated with her. He'd been gentle immediately after Isaac's birth — whether due to the birth itself or his guilt at what had happened the night before — but I could tell his patience was wearing thin.

"Take care of Isaac while your mother gets back on her feet," Papa said to me, his voice unconcerned.

"What's wrong with her? Why hasn't she gotten out of bed?"

He didn't answer my questions. He and I both knew she hadn't even been like this when Isaiah had died; instead, she had worked silently and methodically, scrubbing the house and sewing for days.

I watched from the front door as Caleb and Hannah walked to Mrs. Nesbitt's house every morning to attend homeschool with the other students who'd been displaced from our basement. With each step of freedom that they took away from the house, my tethers tightened. Each afternoon when Caleb came home, he brought me snippets of the outside world like bread crumbs that I pretended not to want, that I resented him for getting instead of me. But I still listened to the ways that kids in home-school speculated about what had happened to me and Ma — I hated that they were talking about her without me being there to defend her.

The closest I got to going outside after Isaac's birth were the times I'd open the door to some of the bolder church members who showed up without asking, ringing the doorbell and trying to peek through the locked screen door. Papa told me and Caleb to tell them that Ma was under the weather and that she would call when she was feeling better. Then we were supposed to accept their gifts and close the door politely without letting them in. But I watched their eyes as they scanned behind us — at the kitchen table piled high with dishes, the laundry heaping out of over-stuffed hampers, spilling excess pajamas, socks, and underwear onto the hallway tile. I tried to hurry them through their questions, answering yes abruptly so that the door could finish its arc into the jamb.

"Look, Ma," I said when I had festooned

her bedroom with the gifted bouquets of lavender and coral and fuchsia. I expected her to lift her head from the pillow, to open her eyes and take in the vivid colors. But she was asleep, her breathing heavy, her hair plastered to her forehead. I tucked the dampened strands behind her ears and let my arms fall to her shoulders.

"Get up, Ma." My voice was angrier than it had been the previous times. Her body was heavy under my nudging, her limbs limp at her sides. The sheet moved in tandem with her body, pulling taut on her stomach. Her snore grew deep and heavy, her eyelids still.

"Open your eyes!" I lifted the paper-thin skin of her eyelids and raised them toward her brow bone. Beneath her lids, veiny eyeballs focused on me without a whisper of recognition.

"It's me!" I yelled again before dropping her lids. Even though they stayed closed, there was a stirring behind them, as though she wanted to open them and look at me. But after a few minutes, they stilled as she sank back into sleep.

Second Sunday — Baptism Sunday — used to be a cause for celebration, but Papa had decided that the second Sunday in January would be Isaac's dedication back to the Lord. The date, one month after Isaac's birth and circled on the calendar in red, felt menacing. Ma had never missed a baptism service, and for weeks I'd been praying that her sadness would break, like clouds dissipating after a storm, but by the time second Sunday arrived, I knew that her mood was more than just sadness. Papa must have known it too because his answers about her were getting more clipped. But there was no way Papa would call a doctor for help — I knew that like I knew the sun would rise in the morning. *Sickness in the mind is a manifestation of weak faith,* Papa always said. *To get better, you have to pray and ask to be healed.* We were praying. We were asking.

I pulled one of my white dresses from the closet and shimmied into it. Its hem stopped just below my knees, and the seams — tiny, orderly rows of silken white thread — ran down the sides in perfect darts. Ma had made us matching dresses from a beautiful piece of fabric that she had found on the revival circuit this past summer. I imagined the hours that Ma spent with the pattern at the sewing machine, her hands pushing the fabric through the dipping needle. It hung loose around the waist, and I felt her arms gripping my shoulders and spinning me around — admiring her handiwork and saying I looked beautiful.

"Miriam," Papa called from downstairs.

I walked down the hallway and paused by Ma's closed door. My hand lingered on the doorknob, and I twisted it a bit before releasing it. I didn't know what I would say to her, but I wanted her to spring out of bed, to stand beside Papa as Isaac was given back to the Lord. To participate in the ceremony that Isaiah had been denied. I rapped once, then twice, but there was no response from the other side.

"Miriam," Papa called again, his voice louder.

When we arrived at the lake, six minutes late, a few regulars were already there, but attendance at baptism services, like all other services, had been declining. People were clustered in the shade of the few trees that dotted the brown grass. All eyes were on us as we arrived with Isaac in tow for his first church outing. As we brought him down the hill, the bolder people murmured their loud speculations about where Ma could be. *Maybe she needed a break. It hasn't been easy on her since the other baby died. It's no wonder she's having a hard time.* I bit my bottom lip until the skin split and I tasted

279

coppery blood.

The chords of the baptismal hymn plinked out of the speakers that were staked in the dirt. Papa hurried into the shallow part of the lake to baptize the people who had been waiting for him. The youngest children were the first in line — elementary school students who gave their lives to the Lord — followed by older people. Papa baptized them in the same water because he said all souls were identical to God.

Even though I'd gone to baptisms for years, there had always been new things to notice, from the way Papa's robe floated on the surface of the water like a cloud to how his voice echoed back to shore, asking the congregation to support people in their newly reborn lives. I used to hold my breath as he dipped people underwater, knowing that they would be brand-new creatures when he lifted their sodden bodies from the lake. And when they stood under their own power, I was already on my feet, cheering them into the kingdom. This time, however, my body felt empty, and I could barely lift my hands to clap when it was time.

After the baptisms were complete, Papa stepped back onto dry land for Isaac's dedication. He changed out of his wet robe and beckoned Caleb, Hannah, and me to join him by the edge of the lake. Papa held Isaac in front of the congregation in his long white gown that caught the breeze; all who were gathered at the lake repeated the oath promising to keep Isaac on the path of righteousness. The words that used to feel like fire in my mouth were now just a string of meaningless sounds as I said them about my own brother.

When we got home, Papa went upstairs, but instead of holing himself up in the study, he turned left toward the bedroom. The door slammed, and we all froze on the main floor in the unsettling quiet that followed. After a few moments of silence, I left Caleb and Hannah on the first floor and walked up the stairs.

The bedroom door was open a crack, not quite wide enough for me to see through as Papa's voice barely reached outside. I squeezed my nose into the space and almost gagged from the nauseating stench of Ma's unshowered body combined with Papa's overpowering musk. He was standing at the side of the bed facing where Ma lay, his back to the door. His arms gesticulated wildly overhead before they came to rest on her arm. A minute passed, and Papa hung his head low and raised his arms again. His

281

voice was louder this time, the words echoing in the stagnant air before reaching the door.

"In the name of the Father . . ."

It wouldn't work — he and I both knew it — and I couldn't watch him fail with her. I wanted to back away and leave them be, but my feet wouldn't budge. He leaned closer. When he rose again, she was still an unmoving form wrapped in sheets. He collapsed to his knees. This was supposed to be the time when he would recite a prayer asking God to heal her, but a guttural sob escaped from his open mouth instead. He held Ma as her limp limbs dragged on the bed, rocking her back and forth. He'd pretended with so many people; why wasn't he trying harder with her?

The sobs swelled, reaching a crescendo not unlike in his sermons, and just at the point when I thought his voice would break the way it did when he talked about the trials of Job or how Shadrach, Meshach, and Abednego escaped King Nebuchadnezzar's fiery furnace, there was nothing. No sobs, just a dry-heaving noise. Ma was lifeless on the bed, and now Papa was prone beside her, his arms stretched over her.

Every inch of the house ached with Ma's

absence. A presence was easy to feel, but an absence was much more acute: the empty chair at the kitchen table, silence greeting you instead of the voice that you were so used to hearing. The house also felt more dangerous with her gone: there were fewer places to hide. I stood up straighter when I heard Papa behind me in the kitchen. When he yelled Ma's name through the house, I shivered because I was the one to answer him. His hands wouldn't stay quiet long — especially since I overheard him telling the deacons that offerings weren't enough to pay the church's mortgage anymore. Caleb and Hannah would be safe, but someone had to replace Ma in the house.

Even though Hannah couldn't say it aloud, I knew she felt the absence the way Caleb and I did. She crawled up the steps in the direction of Ma's room, only to be snatched up by older arms before she could reach the door. Sometimes she let herself be comforted, but more often than not, she would wail inconsolably.

"Ma will be back soon," I told her in a steady voice. And as I repeated it, I started to believe it myself.

Isaac was fussy as January marched on. He enjoyed playing with a dingy zebra that had been Hannah's favorite toy at his age. At night, when I brought Ma plates of food that she barely ate, I told her about each milestone and rested Isaac against her chest, but she didn't move to hold him.

A few days later, right after Isaac smiled at me for the first time, there was a knock on my bedroom door.

"Please get her dressed," Papa barked.

I knew better than to ask questions. He was gone when I walked down the hallway to Ma's bedroom door. The wadded sheets didn't look like anyone was there, but then the slightest movement came from the middle of the bed. I stepped over the nursing pads and clean diapers on the floor and made my way to her. I slid my body behind Ma's, wrapping myself around her solidness and folding my arms around the loose flesh where her pregnant belly used to be. She didn't even move — didn't nestle into me — the only sign of life was her chest rising and falling at regular intervals. I pressed my nose into her hair, which smelled dank and had no hints of the coconut oil that she loved. I sank into the warmth of the sheets, trying to get as close to her as possible.

"Hi, Ma," I said, snuggling closer. With my index finger, I separated some of the matted tendrils and smoothed them into something that resembled a style. Ma's heavy head didn't move from the pillow. I lifted myself on an elbow and looked at her face, expecting to find her eyes closed. But when I glanced over the curve of her jaw and found the arc of her chin, tracing it up to the contour of her cheekbone, her eyes were wide open. I shook her shoulder, but she didn't blink.

"Ma!" I shouted into her ear. Still no response. I yanked back the covers. She was wearing an old gray nightgown that used to be white. Large oblong stains darkened the part of her nightgown that covered her breasts. The familiar sour-sweet scent of milk that used to come from her body was long gone; since she hadn't nursed Isaac in a month, her milk had dried up weeks ago.

I crept out of the bed and into the bathroom. The washcloth that rested over the basin was stiff with soap, but it wasn't from touching Ma's skin. I wrung it out in a stream of warm water and brought it back to the bed.

"I'm going to wash you off now, okay?" I asked in the same voice I usually used with Hannah. My hands trembled — I'd only really seen Ma's body when she gave birth. Her flaccid breasts flopped to each side of her body as I lifted her left arm carefully over her head and rested it against the pillow like a bird's wing. I half expected her to swat the washcloth out of my hands and tell me that she could wash herself, but she just lay there in her sour-smelling nightgown.

I peeled up Ma's nightgown, inch by inch, slowing down when I got to her stomach. My eye caught some faded blue stains that seeped into her skin — old bruises. A knot of rage rose in the back of my throat when I palpated the evidence of the hollow thumps that Caleb and I'd heard last month. I swallowed it and moved the washcloth, my strokes gentle on the loose skin of her stomach — the rivulets of water sliding over her body and onto the fitted sheet like tears.

The washcloth moved to white rings — like the ones that dated trees — that lined her middle. Caleb's lines were the faintest; the slightest press of my fingertips moved inward to mine, then Hannah's and Isaiah's. The new ones from Isaac were stark white against her darker skin, and my finger lingered there a little while longer before rolling the nightgown up to her breasts. My eyes stayed on the sheets around her as the washcloth traveled over her swollen nipples. Pulling the filthy nightgown over her head, I cast it into the growing pile of dirty laundry in the corner of the room. I slid her underwear from beneath her body, exposing a triangular thatch of hair where her legs were pressed together. A clean pair of underwear was folded in her drawer — one of the last vestiges of her careful housekeeping — and I shimmied it up her legs. In her closet, a long gray dress that used to be snug now made her look tiny.

I took a few steps away from the bed, and Ma looked just like she did when I arrived — still and small. I couldn't look away from her, but a minute later, Papa walked in, breaking my stare. He scooped Ma from the bed and adjusted her weight in his arms; her limp hand dangled behind his back as though she had just dropped something.

It was dark when they arrived back home from wherever they had been. Papa didn't make any pronouncements at the kitchen table; he just took her upstairs. There was no victory in his arms sagging beneath her weight, his creaky knees halting every step to take a breath.

There were no conversations that night or the next as we went back to business as usual. Papa preached that Sunday about faith and sickness to a crowd of about a hundred people huddled into the first few rows.

"When we are sick, brothers and sisters, we need to rely on our faith to heal us. If we remain sick, we need to ask ourselves: *How strong is my faith?*" I stiffened in the pew as he spoke lies into a microphone whose feedback intermittently interrupted his halfhearted climaxes. He was going off-script, departing from biblical teachings that he had subscribed to for years, teachings that were the basis for his ministry. And for what? As the words echoed through my skull, I heard the undercurrents of a veiled message about Ma. That her weak faith was keeping her sick, even though her faith had buoyed the family during the darkest times like Isaiah's death. He'd said as much to her.

As he asked us to rise for the final prayer, everything he'd said echoed back to me. He was saying that he wasn't getting her any help — he was saying that what had happened to her was her fault, ignoring the fact that he'd tried to heal her and failed. That he had tried to heal other people and failed. So now, rather than admit that he couldn't heal, he was casting the blame on anyone but himself. He was sacrificing Ma to the altar of his pride in order to hold on to his convictions.

By the time the crowd had dispersed after

the sermon, Papa had left me with no choice. He wasn't going to heal Ma. If I could do it for Micah, Nadia, Dawn, Suzette, and Hope, I owed it to Ma to at least try.

THIRTEEN

Wind came through the open window of Ma's room, snatching the door from my grip and slamming it behind me. Next to her rumpled bedsheets, lavender gossamer curtains caught the breeze and billowed inward. The stale smell was now gone, replaced by distant chimney smoke and the night-blooming jasmine plant that Mrs. Cade had brought over last week.

"Ma." I announced myself as I approached, my voice rushed. There wasn't much time: Caleb and Hannah would be back from homeschool in twenty minutes, and Papa's church meetings would be over in about an hour. I pulled the sheet away from her foot, exposing the prickly hairs on her ankle and calf. Lifting her leg from the bed released a pungent stench of urine and exposed the damp sheet beneath her. The bottle of holy oil jutted out of the pocket of my pajama pants. I sat it on the nightstand next to the remnants of the morning's uneaten breakfast.

I pushed her left shoulder, and the rest of her body followed until she was flat on her back, her arms at her sides. Her eyes fluttered, but they didn't open. I shook her again, but she didn't stir. I needed to hurry it along, but I couldn't deviate from the routine — from asking questions that I knew she couldn't answer.

"Ma, what ails you?" I paused a few beats, imagining the lilt of her voice in the silence. A loud noise sent me to the window, but Papa's car was still gone. I rushed back to Ma's side.

"Do you believe that I have the power to heal you?"

A twitch of her leg responded. She had clearly heard me, proof that she was still with us through the clouds and fog, which meant that she might be aware of what I was doing. It was a risk, but I had to take it. If anyone understood having two lives, it was Ma.

I emptied double the amount of holy oil on my palm and traced the sign of the cross on her clammy forehead, pressing my hand there to seal the healing. "Joanne Renée Horton, in the name of the Lord Jesus Christ, you are healed."

The place where our skin touched felt electrified — a mixture of heat and tingling that intensified the longer I kept my hand there — but I couldn't pull it away. It had fused there, skin against skin. As a gust of air swept into the room, the curtain surged in and its corners, unmoored, snapped in midair. I kept my hand on Ma's head, the tingle becoming warmer by the moment, and closed my eyes.

My hand went limp, but it stayed on Ma's head. The pain that flashed from her body to mine drove me to my knees by the side of the bed. The room thrummed, a taut guitar string that pulsated with each breath. Screams curdled in the air and pressed against the walls. I assumed they were Ma's, but her mouth was still closed, so they must have been mine. Her eyes had opened, though, but my lips couldn't move to ask her if she was okay. I slid onto the carpet by her bedside as the room went black.

When I opened my eyes after what could have only been a few minutes, my head felt like it had been slammed into a block of concrete. I pushed myself onto my hands and knees, arching my back where a dull ache had settled at the base of my spine. Gripping the side of the bed, the mattress coils gave under the weight of my hands, and I pulled myself up on shaky legs. As soon as I got to my feet, pain flashed behind my eyes, and I cowered on the carpet. I tried to push myself up again but fell to the ground. The open bottle of holy oil was lying on the floor by the bedside table, spilling its contents onto the beige carpet. My eyes scraped against my eyelids as I tried to open them, and spots speckled the room where shapes had previously appeared.

"Ma," I said gently, touching the bed where her shoulder should have been.

She slowly turned her head toward me, and her eyes took me in.

"Hi, Ma," I whispered. I'd hoped that something more profound would come out after all this time: how much I'd missed her, how the house hadn't been the same without her. But my head throbbed, and it was getting harder to stay on my feet. I leaned against the side of her bed to keep from falling. The room came back into focus: the family picture on the bureau, the hope chest by the foot of the bed.

Ma slid to the edge of the mattress and put her feet on the carpet, inching ever closer to me. She tried to stand up, but her legs, wobbly from disuse, buckled under her weight. As she slumped back on the bed, the sodden sheets that had been covering her fell away, revealing bony legs and a shoulder blade that jutted out beneath a thin scrap of skin. Eventually, I crossed the inches it took to sit beside her.

In her lap, she turned her hands from their palms to the backs and then over again; she blinked with each slight motion, as though snatches of memory were replaying themselves on the insides of her eyelids. Every few seconds, her head shook like she was reliving Papa's fist coming at her, knocking her to the ground — next to Isaac's birth, it was probably the last thing she remembered before she'd gotten sick.

"Ma?" I touched her shoulder.

She jumped as though only now realizing that I was sitting next to her. Her disoriented eyes landed on my face, squinting like someone who was adjusting to the light after being in a dark room.

"Miriam?" Her voice was gravelly and worn. "What did you do?"

Papa's partial smile and hooded eyes stared back at me from the other side of a dusty family picture on the dresser. I couldn't say it under his gaze, hadn't said it to anyone except Mrs. Cade. Ma looked down at the carpet by her feet, at the plastic bottle and the slick of holy oil.

"Miriam." She spoke again — an answer to her own question. She reached down and grabbed the holy oil — her balance pitching her too far forward before she caught herself and straightened. She pinched the flattened bottle and brought it close to her face like it was something foreign, even though we had filled them together for years. I stiffened next to her in anticipation of her anger at my sin and closed my eyes to shield myself against her yells. Her breath quickened as her shoulders rose and fell next to my stillness.

"I know I wasn't supposed to, but he wasn't going to do anything to help you. He was just going to let you stay sick." I spat out the words without pausing to take a breath.

Ma was about to answer when I heard a car pull up in the driveway. A minute later, the front door flew open — Papa's meeting must have ended early. I heard him calling my name on the first floor as Isaac started to cry. Loud footsteps bounded up the stairs two at a time — in an instant, Papa appeared in the doorway.

I winced and pushed myself to a standing position from the tangle of Ma's limbs and sheets. I held his gaze, even as his eyes bounced around the cluttered room before finally landing on Ma and me. Me, standing a little too tall, my posture overcompensating for the fact that Ma was still seated. She had turned her face to meet Papa's, her neck at an unnatural angle, her eyes a hunted animal's.

"What's going on here?"

He rushed over to her before I could answer — his loud voice ringing in my ears — but he stopped short of sitting next to her. His looming presence blocked the light as he crouched by her face and touched her head with a gesture that wasn't tender at all. As his hand lay against her forehead, he stared in her eyes, but it didn't look like he was trying to see if she was better — it seemed like he was gauging the limits of her memory. He'd had over a month to rehearse an apology — it should have been out of his mouth when he got to the door and saw that she was sitting up in bed for the first time since Isaac's birth. But I could count Papa's apologies on one hand, and by the time he stood up again and dropped his palm from her forehead, I knew that this wouldn't be one of them.

"What's going on?" he asked again.

Ma tried to stammer an excuse as she scooted away from him and toward the headboard. He looked from her to me. The holy oil bottle had disappeared from her hand somehow.

"What's going on, Miriam?"

Papa's words tightened the fist at the pit of my stomach. *I healed her.* I pushed the words to the roof of my mouth and pressed them in place with my tongue. I was ready to force out the truth, but I caught Ma's eyes on the way back to Papa's. She shook her head slightly, almost imperceptibly.

"Nothing. She just woke up this morning when I brought breakfast. Said she felt better." My words came through clenched teeth. I couldn't even look on the bed to see whether Ma was nodding her approval.

"It must have been something that you did, Samuel. I kept hearing your voice praying for me like it was coming through a tunnel." She finally looked up at Papa, fear quivering right beneath the surface of her words. "You prayed over me, saying healing words. And I followed your voice out. Thank you."

I dragged my eyes off the ground to look at her, but her gaze shifted as she lied. Anger blurred the sight of the two of them. Papa looked to me and back at Ma, needing to believe what she was saying, but clearly confused by the rumpled comforter and the darkened oil spot on the carpet near his toe.

"I healed you?" His incredulous voice rose on the final word. But with each repetition — *I healed you; I healed you* — he grew more convinced of something he hadn't done.

"Praise the Lord!" Papa dropped to his knees next to her.

The part of me that was supposed to summon anger for him had been lopped off with a dull blade — in its place, all I felt was numbness. But Ma's betrayal was a new, fresh wound.

"May I be exc— ?" I asked the carpet.

"Yes," Ma said before I could finish the question. I wanted to inch away, wanted her to ache with each eternal second it took me to walk to the door. But my body jolted out of the room, and my hand made a glistening trail of oily sweat on the wallpaper as I hobbled down the hallway. When I reached my bedroom door, out of breath, Ma's voice rode the hallway air — breaking into spaces where I'd yearned to hear it for weeks. I'd wanted to hear it whispering my name when she kissed me in the morning or the inflection in it when she asked me to reread sections of books to her. When I closed my eyes and drank it in, I could pretend that her words — *thank you* — were directed at me rather than at Papa. If I hadn't done anything, she'd still be in bed where I found her. As I climbed under the covers in the middle of the day, shivering under my prayer quilt, I wished I'd left her there. As soon as the thought was out, my stomach seized. I was taking credit for something that was in God's hands — not mine. It was the same thing Papa had done.

On the bookshelf, a family picture from three years ago stared back at me: I still felt the heat from Caleb's right hand touching my shoulder, remembered the scratchy feel of my tights as I crossed my legs in the chair. Ma sat next to me in a long dark blue dress that she'd sewn for the occasion. "Act naturally," the photographer had told us before asking me to tilt my chin in the most unnatural way. The braces on Caleb's teeth sparkled, and Papa's golden cross hung suspended from his neck, catching the light from the flashbulb. Hannah, smaller then, hadn't yet graduated to leg braces and crutches, but she sat in a wheelchair, baby teeth on display for the camera.

I walked over to the picture; as I swiped arcs into the dusty glass, memories came back. My cheeks were chubbier then, my teeth glinting silver with braces. My long skirt hid the raised scabs on my knees from a fall that I'd suffered on my bike. The scab had sloughed off long ago — in its place, a slick pink hunk of new skin had sprouted.

I lifted the picture in its lacquered frame and released it like a Frisbee — it flew across the room with more force than I intended, crashing into the opposite wall where my homeschool books were squeezed together on the top shelf. Cracked spiderwebs radiated outward from the deepest hole near Papa's mouth, and a jagged line split his face diagonally. Several pieces of glass came loose, and I pulled on the largest shard in the center. With a small amount of force, it broke off in my hand. I pressed the pointed end into my fingertip; the skin reddened and then split with no protest. This pain was sharp and acute as a line of blood the width of a hair made its slow path down my index finger, stopping briefly at the knuckle before meandering to my palm. My teeth pressed together as I lifted the shard and moved it toward my upper thigh with a shaky hand. It plunged into my flesh — excruciating relief sent my head lolling backward as though I was drunk with too much communion wine. A wavy line above my right kneecap pooled with blood that dripped to the carpet below. The bloody husk of glass fell from my hand with a thud.

The pain subsided for a moment when I

removed the glass, and I needed it to hurt more, to displace the anger that swelled inside, but the sight of all the blood made the room swirl. I sidestepped the splatters of red on the carpet as I walked to the bathroom, past the open door where Papa's stilted voice told Ma everything she had missed. In the bright bathroom light, the cuts gaped until I swiped them with gauze and covered them with Band-Aids.

Back in my room, I stumbled to the window, yanking open the curtains, then sliding the glass up. Cold air buffeted my face as I took one breath and then another, but there still wasn't enough air in here. There would never be enough. One small push and the plastic frame popped out. I slid out of the bedroom window and landed on the peaked roof before swinging from the gutter and letting go.

A gravitational pull had always drawn me to Micah's house — after a fight with Caleb or upon returning from revival season, I sank into her beanbag chair while she stared at me with her chin cradled in her hand. My bike tires jerked to the right like they were on autopilot, whizzing past homes whose backyards had housed my best forts and whose treehouses bore my carved initials. Micah's house rose at the end of a cul-de-sac, and even though we hadn't really spoken in months, I could feel her fingers on my cuts, her reassuring voice asking me if they hurt.

Bright light from inside her family room leaked onto the driveway as I parked my bike by her steps. I tossed a pebble at her window and listened to its hollow ping against the glass. Closing my eyes, I pictured her bedroom that I knew by heart — when I opened them, Micah's face was angled down to where I was standing. Her face had slimmed, and she looked older, but she didn't look like she saw me. I waved my arms, and her eyes finally met mine. But there was no glimmer of recognition, not even a wave. Then the room darkened as she shut her blinds and disappeared.

I swiped at my tears once and then again as I wrenched my bike out of the thicket of bushes and climbed on, unsure of where to go next. A few downward pushes of my pedals dragged me out of her orbit. I couldn't go home to participate in their lie, so I turned down Mrs. Cade's street, speeding under the shadow of elms before turning into her driveway.

"I healed her," I confessed into her blouse when she answered the door.

■ ■ ■ ■

The next morning, there was a knock on my bedroom door; it opened before I had a chance to tell whoever it was to come in.

"Morning, Miriam." Ma closed the door behind her, trapping us in the room together for the first time since the day before. I winced from the cuts as I sat up in bed; she seemed not to notice as she plopped next to my blanketed feet, still ostensibly unaccustomed to moving her body. Her skin was dewy from the shower, and her wet hair was set in pink foam rollers that sprouted all over her head. Her nightgown was freshly washed, and her eyes were clear and wide as she looked over where Hannah was still sleeping. All remnants of the Ma who had been haunting our house since Isaac's birth were gone: everything except the skin that still hung from her bones like a dress that was too loose.

"We need to talk about yesterday." On top of the comforter, she moved her hand up my leg, inching ever closer to the deepest cuts. She took several deep breaths before letting them out slowly, methodically. I could imagine her counting as she exhaled the way she always did to calm herself down

— one, two. Her expression was inscrutable.

"What have you done?" she finally asked, breaking the silence that had grown thick around us. She'd asked the question of me and Caleb so many times that it almost seemed rhetorical. She would stand in the kitchen with her hands on her hips when the evidence of our mischief — a broken window or a singed tablecloth — was irrefutable. This time, however, her tone demanded an answer.

What does she want me to say? She'd seen the empty bottle of holy oil yesterday. She knew that I'd done what Papa couldn't.

I shrugged, knowing that wasn't really an answer. She removed her hand from my leg as her anger rose.

"Miriam. You know what a sin it is. If your father knew . . ."

"He did know! He saw you in bed all that time and didn't do anything. What was I supposed to do? Leave you like that forever?"

"Lower your voice." The words slid between her teeth. Her scared eyes bounced to the closed door and then to Hannah, who hadn't moved.

"Why are you so worried about him hearing us? Yes, I know what I did was a sin. But it also seems like a sin to know someone

304

is sick and do nothing when you can heal them."

"Women can't —"

"Clearly they can, Ma. And maybe Papa's been telling us that all along to make himself feel better about —"

She held a flattened hand out to me. "Don't finish that sentence."

"Just because I don't say it doesn't mean it isn't true. You know as well as I do that he hasn't been healing people."

The faces of the other people that I had healed jumbled in front of my eyes, with Ma's face now joining the group. I didn't want to tell her about the rest of them, to have her pollute everything I'd done by calling it sin. I swallowed their names.

"And now he thinks he healed you. Why did you make me lie to him?"

"He's been having a hard time." Her angry gaze softened as she looked at her lap. "He needs some good news." She pinched the daisies on her flannel nightgown as though she were trying to pluck them from soft earth.

"You've been having a hard time too, Ma." I remembered the way she had tried not to wake us when she came downstairs with her suitcase, the resigned look that settled on her face as she stepped back into the house, the way that she couldn't even look at the street as her sister drove away. "I want to show you something."

She looked up at me with eyes that were softer than they had been when she came inside. I slid out from beneath the comforter, careful not to jostle her, and took stiff steps to the closet door. My cuts oozed and reopened with each movement, and I focused on my breathing to ignore the pain. The closet doors bowed toward me, and I hefted her suitcase from where I'd stowed it in December. It felt heavier now than it did then. Ma watched me as I brought it to the bed and set it at our feet like a time capsule. The zipper snagged on something as though reluctant to expose what was inside. When it finally lay open in front of us, piles of folded clothes seemed like they were castoffs from a different life. Jeans I didn't even know Ma owned with tank tops that she'd never be allowed to wear — all of them with tags attached. Nothing was strewn inside or packed in a hurry — the bag had been packed for a while.

Ma crouched in front of the suitcase and sorted through the clothes with jerky movements, as though with every bend of her joints she was reminding her limbs how to move. She sifted through the orderly piles

— holding each garment to her nose and breathing it in. In the middle of the clothing was a photo of me and Caleb kneeling on either side of Hannah's wheelchair with our arms tossed around one another's shoulders. She had opted for that photo of the three of us instead of the many others that had Papa in them.

"Were you really going to do it?"

She sorted through clothes and objects, running her fingers around the circular edges of buttons; I thought she didn't hear me and was about to ask my question again when she looked up at me and nodded.

"I am so sorry."

"What about us? About me? You were going to leave me here?"

"I know that makes me the worst mother in the world, but I couldn't take it anymore. It was selfish, I know that, and I should have taken you with me. You and Hannah. But all I could think was that I had to get out."

"And I made you stay."

Instead of an answer, she turned her attention to refolding the clothes and placing them back in the suitcase.

"Can I leave it in here?" she asked.

"Sure. You know where it is in case —"

She pressed her index finger against my lips, silencing the rest of my answer. "If there is a next time, I'll take you with me. I promise. I'll never leave you behind . . ."

As her voice trailed, I thought about what it would feel like to get in the back seat of her sister's car and leave this house behind. Ma was motionless beside me, a pile of unfolded clothes on her lap. I wondered if she was thinking the same thing.

Papa called to us from downstairs that breakfast was ready. His voice jolted us, and Ma lost her balance as she tried to stand up too quickly. Clothes spilled off her lap as she reached down to steady herself, and I grabbed her hand that was planted on the carpet.

"What are you going to tell him? About the healing." I'd never thought I could say it so freely to her, but now I had something on her too.

"I can't tell him anything."

"You can't tell him that I healed you?"

"Honey." She cupped my face, and I let it go heavy in her hand. She was still the same Ma, albeit a little weaker, with sunken cheeks and dark bags underneath sadder eyes. "You know I can't."

"You can do whatever you want."

"I know you think that I can, Miriam, but I can't. That's not what you want to hear, that your mom is a disappointment, but it's the truth." She exhaled a deep sigh that made her cough.

"You're not a disappointment, Ma. I promise." But she was right. I hoped she couldn't see the way her heavy words were collapsing my shoulders. But that thought was followed by the memory of the bruises I saw when I washed her: the price she had already paid for standing up to him.

"I knew you'd understand," she said, kissing my cheek. "Now let's get to breakfast."

She was so quick to shift — to become the woman Papa needed her to be rather than the mother I so desperately craved. For once I wanted her to choose my needs over his.

"I'll get Hannah up and meet you downstairs," I said. As she walked to the door, I hefted the suitcase back onto the shelf. When the closet was finally closed, hiding any evidence that she'd ever tried to leave, I woke up Hannah and carried her downstairs.

"Look who's awake!" Papa gestured in my direction with a spatula when Hannah and I rounded the corner into the kitchen. He was wearing Ma's apron, the one that she always let me wear when I helped with dinner.

I dug my nails into the underside of the

table until they bent as Papa delivered the breakfast of scrambled eggs, wavy strips of crisp bacon, and miniature stacks of pancakes on two outstretched arms. Papa served himself last and took a seat at the head of the table.

"Let us pray," he announced.

With red arcs forming in my nail beds, I reached for Hannah's smooth fist.

"Lord, I want to thank You for delivering Your child Joanne from demons and darkness. Let her continue to grow in strength in the coming days and weeks. Thank You for Your faithfulness to this family. Thank You for the healing powers that You continue to renew within me. Let me remain an instrument of Your holy will. Amen."

He had been pretending for so long that he had convinced himself he had actually done it. Or maybe he thought her healing had restored something he had lost long ago. He had to know that it wasn't him. It hadn't been him for a long time. Saying the thing I'd wanted to tell him since Bethel meant that I would betray Ma, and I couldn't sacrifice her like that. I couldn't bear to know that the hollow thumps on her body later would be my fault. But wasn't the fact that she was sitting with us, letting him think that he healed her, betraying me?

"Amen," I grumbled.

My stomach was an aching maw, yet I couldn't bring myself to eat. As I watched him from across the table, his posture already taller, I didn't know if I could keep the lie anymore, even though I had just promised Ma that I would. I didn't want to break her trust, but wasn't she the one who always said that secrets were only heavy until you released them? Maybe she could forgive me when it was all said and done. When she could see how different life could be when he knew the truth. I tried to make eye contact with her, to give her a hint of what I didn't want to do — to her and to me — but what I had to do to save us.

"Papa? What makes you so sure?"

"Sure about what?"

"That you were the one to heal her."

"I don't know what you mean." He started cutting his pancakes; he had one triangle raised to his open mouth as a sticky line of syrup hung over the plate. My heart quickened at his dismissal, and at how much I wanted to tell him about what I'd said to Ma upstairs. If I could find the right combination of words, the consequences wouldn't be on her. The sin had been mine, so the punishment would be mine too. Maybe I could make Papa see that.

Next to Papa, Ma pretended to be focused on the food. Papa had done a good job conditioning her all these years. She was compliant. Subservient. But as much as it pained me to think about, Ma had almost worked up the courage to leave him. I could be brave, too. And I couldn't see how things at home could get much worse. So I closed my eyes and focused on breathing before letting the words spill out of me.

"You didn't heal her. Like the guy in Bethel."

A chair pushed back across from me — Papa's chair. "What did you just say to me?" Somehow he'd moved from the other side of the table, and now he was standing over me. Spittle shot onto my plate as the words flew out of his mouth. "What did you just say? Who do you think you are?"

The same vein that bulged in his neck in Bethel was jumping beneath his skin, and as he repeated his questions — "What did you say? Who do you think you are?" — Caleb appeared by his side. Caleb's hands pulled at Papa's fists that were raised above me, and Papa strained against Caleb's strength. The edges of the room turned black, but everything in front of me — the brown table and the eggshell walls and the gleaming silver of the refrigerator — came into sharper focus. Hannah's shouting was the high note above everything else, and her rocking back and forth next to me in the chaos made the room materialize again: the hard floor under my feet, the table beneath my hands, my knees knocking against the table even though I didn't remember getting up.

"How dare you? Of course I healed her."

"Calm down, Samuel." Ma was standing next to him with her hands on his shoulders, gently guiding him back to his chair.

"What are you doing?" Caleb mouthed at me.

I shook my head — my body was acting before my mind caught up. The man we were all terrified of looked so small in the chair.

"So if I didn't heal her, who did?" he scoffed.

Ma looked at me, her eyes pleading for me not to open my mouth. *This will be better,* I wanted to tell her. *I promise.*

"I did."

A loud cough sent flecks of chewed pancake across the table. "Don't be silly," Papa said after he resumed breathing normally. He exaggerated every movement of taking a bite: opening his mouth wider than normal, inching the fork closer to the gap between his teeth, clamping down hard on the fork's tines.

"She's not the only one. I've healed other people too."

I hadn't planned to tell him about the others; saying it out loud poisoned the sacred bond of those private healings, defiled the trust they had placed in me. Papa's expression morphed from feigned nonchalance to disbelief and then anger before landing on scorn. With pinched fingers, he removed his glasses from the bridge of his nose and laid them in front of his plate.

"You've done what?"

"Before Ma, I healed a few other people. Mostly people in the church, but some others too." My heart rose to my throat as soon as I said it, but I straightened as the words tumbled out louder and faster, gaining strength like a storm.

Papa's head was between his hands, his fingers pressing against his temples. No one else moved.

"Go to your room," Papa's voice seethed.

I left my breakfast untouched and stormed out of the kitchen and up the stairs before flopping onto my bed. Why did Papa insist that this spiritual gift that was no longer his could never be mine? The thoughts faded as I heard his feet on the steps — before I could brace myself, he was in my bedroom.

He stood in the doorway and unbuckled his belt — then he wrapped it into a fat coil around the middle of his hand, the silver buckle lost somewhere in his palm. Errant pieces of thread poked from the seams as he gripped the loose end of the belt until the taut leather strap snapped the air between his hands.

"You are no healer, Miriam." Another snap of the belt in the middle of his words made me shudder. He wanted me to agree with him, but I couldn't. With his socked left heel, he kicked the door closed behind him. The belt swung backward on an arc as Papa said it again. "You are no healer, Miriam."

I knew I couldn't say what I so desperately wanted to: *You are no healer either,* so I settled on shaking my head instead.

"You have one last chance to save yourself."

At this point, I normally would have said anything to avoid the spanking. He had told me that he wouldn't hurt me when we were in Bethel, and even though there had been discipline sessions since then, he had always used his hands; he had never used a belt to hit me before.

"Fine. Bend over."

I started to bend over the bed on my forearms, but I stayed upright instead. If he was going to do this, he wouldn't get the satisfaction of my whimper or the anonymity of my back; he would have to look at me the whole time.

"I'll take it like this."

"Have it your way."

He let go of the long end of the belt; it whizzed through the air before zinging my shin. I winced as the strap bit into my flesh, but I kept the tears at bay and fixed my gaze on the storm that brewed behind his eyes as he raised his right arm higher than last time. He grasped my forearm tighter to hold me in place, and the belt sliced into the skin at the tops of my thighs, reopening some of the cuts that the pajama pants covered. It felt like I was naked as the belt shredded into me. My knees buckled, driving me onto the floor in front of where Papa stood, his belt swinging overhead like a sickle.

"You are no healer, Miriam." Globules of sweat formed at his hairline and slid down his puffed-up cheeks as he delivered the proclamation again. My legs screamed as I placed my hands on the carpet and rose, returning to face him even as my body ached to stay in the fetal position. I heard the slap of another blow as it landed on my right thigh — a sharp pain radiated outward to parts of my body that he hadn't even hit, driving me back to the divot in the carpet that I had just left. My muscles burned as I pressed my lips closed, inhaling deeply and releasing short puffs. I shook everywhere as I stared at him from feet below, unable to stand anymore. I gritted my teeth as the belt's edge sliced my legs several more times.

Above me, he slid his hands onto his knees — his belly heaved in and out with his panting, straining the buttons on his dress shirt until they almost broke. The belt flopped against the floor, an accusing tongue. Small details came into focus — the position of Papa's watch hands at nine and four, the diagonal rays of light that hit his chrome belt buckle and made a glinting pattern against the wall, the slight dark-red nick on his neck that must have come from shaving. And then he was gone.

Silence. Stillness. It was over. Cries finally emptied from my stomach and spilled out of my mouth onto the carpet. I kept my eyes closed — somehow it seemed to lessen the pain just a little bit. I lay on the floor, writhing and squirming as minutes turned into hours. Eventually, I pulled myself onto the bed.

Hours later, my head was under the pillow, unable to block out all the light that flooded into the room in the middle of the afternoon. The bedroom door opened. Finally, Ma had come. I wanted her to tenderly lift the legs of my pajama pants and apply ointment to my welts, silently, methodically. Wanted her to cradle each foot in her palm and inspect my legs — Mary Magdalene at Jesus's feet — working her way up to my knees. I wanted her to apologize for staying downstairs, wondered if the same horror that had passed through me when I'd heard him hitting her had passed through her as well. If her fear had immobilized her the way mine had.

"Here." It wasn't Ma's voice; it was Caleb's. I opened my eyes and moved from underneath the pillow to see him standing by the door. He was holding a flattened tube of ointment and a bag of cotton balls and looked almost scared to get too close to me. Every inch of my skin throbbed as I tried to sit up.

"Don't move." He took tentative steps closer to the bed, placing his offering near my hands.

"Thanks." His good deed complete, I

318

expected him to turn around, but he stood there and examined my legs.

I squeezed a line of ointment onto the cotton ball. My hand trembled, unable to get more than an inch away from the welt.

"Let me." Caleb took the cotton ball away and pinched it between his thumb and forefinger. I couldn't look at him, ashamed of the deep cuts furrowing my legs that would no longer be my secret. When the cotton ball finally grazed my skin, I closed my eyes, focusing my energy on keeping still.

"It's okay. I think that was the worst one." Caleb inspected his handiwork and the rest of my legs. He didn't ask about the jagged, gaping gashes that had nothing to do with Papa's belt.

"I think that's it." He screwed the cap back onto the tube. "You hungry?"

I thought about the breakfast I'd left untouched on the table, the lunch that Ma must have also served between now and then, and nodded.

"I'll be right back."

I didn't want him to leave, not even for a second, as he slipped through the door and closed it behind him. It felt like he was gone for hours when he returned with a plate — a hastily made sandwich comprised of two end pieces of bread, some slices of turkey slipped in the middle, and mustard oozing from the edges. He shrugged as he handed it to me, as though he was embarrassed about his offering.

"Thanks." I held his sandwich to my chapped lips. He stood in the doorway, shifting his weight from one foot to the other while I took one bite and then a second. On the third bite, the sandwich was gone, and only crumbs remained on the plate.

"Do you need anything else?"

I tried to think of something to ask him to do, something that would keep him in my bedroom. But my mind was blank. I shook my head. He waved and turned to go, pulling the door closed.

"Caleb," I called before the door shut all the way. He put his head back inside.

"Can you stay?"

He stood at the door for so long that I thought he didn't hear me. But then the door swung open all the way; he came over and sat on the bed.

We didn't say anything, but it was enough to feel his weight on the mattress, to hear the slow cadence of his breathing next to mine. He didn't ask the questions that I expected him to: *Why did you do it? What were you trying to prove?* He didn't say anything at all; he just laid his heavy hand on my head. It wasn't Ma's soft caress, but it would do for the moment.

The next morning, an unfamiliar weight made one side of my bed sag. I opened my eyes and saw Caleb, splayed on his back next to the wall. He must have fallen asleep there the night before. We hadn't shared a bed since revival years ago, before Hannah was born. I slid closer to the edge of the bed, careful not to wake him. A slight snore, a little louder than a breath, escaped his mouth. On Sunday morning, he would once again be in the pulpit behind Papa, but for now, he was in my room, among my yellow walls and daffodil sheets. I pulled my prayer quilt from undermeath his heavy legs and spread it over him, leaving him to sleep.

FOURTEEN

Over the next few days, Papa and I were like two billiard balls — never actually touching or interacting. I entered a room, and he left it. In the places where he couldn't avoid me — like church — I knew how to stay out of his path. I lingered in the back of the sanctuary until he was done shaking hands with the few families who were left. When he finished and went into his office, I came to the front of the sanctuary to clean up after communion — the task that Micah and I once had down to a science took twice as long alone. But I could only complain to Hannah, who played behind me as I watched the blood of Christ seep down the drain.

It should have been freeing to be in church without supervision, but even though Papa had been avoiding me, I could feel his judgment and sense him staring me down when he thought I wasn't looking. It was hard to understand how he could simultaneously ignore me and watch me like a hawk, but somehow he managed. In the hallways, I received more notes asking for healing, but I felt Papa's eyes on me and knew it would be too risky to try.

In homeschool, the pain of Micah's absence was still acute, even though things had ostensibly returned to normal. Ma circulated through our sections — tapping my shoulder when I got a math problem right, whispering *good job* in my ear, and I knew that her gentleness was her way of showing me that Papa's distance from me hadn't spread to her. I watched Isaac grow and learn the nuances of Ma's face while strapped to her chest; the ache in my lower back was still present from all the days when he had been strapped to mine.

There were no more dances or visits to my room at night to read library books — Ma seemed to want to make up for the weeks she'd missed with Isaac. She reveled in each announcement of a new milestone: *Isaac just smiled for the first time. He's holding his head up.* The fact wasn't lost on either of us that just because those milestones were new to her didn't mean they were new at all.

Nothing lasted in our house for too long

— even my anger at Papa ebbed as winter released its hold to spring, but it never fully went away. As warm air crept into the open spaces and buds formed on dormant trees, Easter came with its renewed promise of resurrection. Ma and I stood side by side in the kitchen the Saturday before Easter, a table with meager groceries in front of us. All of the preparations for Papa's service had already been made — he was going all out this year in a thinly veiled attempt to lure more people to the church. The dwindling tithes barely covered enough for supplies, but the Sunday school classes had created a life-size cross out of plywood beams and a rock out of papier-mâché that the deacon playing the angel of the Lord would roll away. For the dramatic moment when it was revealed that there was nothing in the tomb, Papa and the deacons had rigged the pulleys behind the pulpit that would lift him into the air, mimicking Jesus's ascent into heaven on the third day. The only thing left to do was prepare the Easter feast that we would eat as a family when all the festivities were over.

Ma opened bags next to me, pulling out onions and celery for the dressing, a can of pineapple, and a ham wrapped in white plastic. Her stilted words recited the recipe that we'd been using for years, but I wasn't listening to her at all. Above the sound of a rolling boil on the stove, Papa's last-minute stumblings through the rehearsal of what should have been his best sermon of the year floated down to the first floor. I tried to summon a feeling of pity, but I couldn't muster it. As Ma whistled to fill the space, I grabbed the onion and placed it on the cutting board, slicing through the middle with the gleaming blade, remembering the sweet release as the shard of glass plunged into my flesh months ago. As I hacked through the white orb again and again, I fought the urge to turn the knife on my arms.

My hands went through the motions of cooking. And even though they had given life and health back to people, they were expected to go back to the muscle-memory motions of chopping, bathing, and stirring, like a rubber band returning to its original shape. It was like falling from a mighty height and crashing back into what was familiar — the fall was supposed to kill you before the landing, but in this case, the landing seemed even worse.

After dinner was prepped and stored in plastic containers in the refrigerator, I ran a bath and dipped Hannah into the water — a baptism of sorts. She let her body go limp

— her trusting head was heavy in my hands as I cupped water onto her scalp and massaged a dollop of shampoo into a lather. I leaned Hannah's head back to rinse out the thick suds. Her mouth hung open; her small pink tongue peeked through the space at the bottom of her mouth where a tiny shard of a permanent tooth was growing in.

Then a thought crawled across the front of my brain, mocking me with its simplicity. *Hannah.* Ma and Papa said that God had made her this way on purpose — that she was meant to be stricken with cerebral palsy, that she was whole just as she was. But that had only been what they said after Papa had tried to heal her and failed. On the nights when her seizures lasted too long, when she choked on her thick saliva, when we had to rush her to the emergency room, it was hard to think that God would bestow that upon anyone. I cupped Hannah's chubby face in my hands — her warm, damp skin was slippery in my palms.

"I'm going to heal you."

She stared back at me, her eyes a few shades deeper than almond, her mouth still open. She jerked her head backward in a violent motion. I leaned forward and grabbed her stiff body, pulling her toward me. Her back arched away, resistant to being hugged. She stayed there for a few moments until a bleat came from the back of her throat. As I grabbed the washcloth and wrung out the excess water, I ran the warm cloth over her back. I straightened her left arm as much as possible and cleaned the thin, tender skin of her armpit and elbow. Then on to her left leg — her knobby knee joint, her thin calf with little muscle tone, her foot that was angled inward. I imagined Hannah with arms that fell to her sides without bending, feet that pointed forward, legs strong enough to hold all of her weight without buckling.

After she was dried and lotioned, after her wet hair had been oiled and sectioned and braided, I pinned her arms to her sides and wrapped her in her favorite blanket. I climbed in bed behind her and breathed her in. *Would she be the same person when she was healed? Would she still let me snuggle with her, or would she resist?* I waited for the magic moment of sleep when her body grew heavy against mine in bed, when the water from her hair soaked through my shirt. Slipping my arms from around her shoulders and sliding to the wall behind her bed, I walked to the headboard and raised the side rail. Her face was so peaceful in sleep. No tremors or spasms. No seizures for now. And soon, no seizures again.

"Good night, Hannah." I leaned over and kissed her forehead.

Although I wanted to see him stumble, Papa's Easter sermon went off without a hitch. But even so, no one lined up to be saved. I knew we were all realizing that if Papa — a man who had saved souls in regular clothes in a storefront church with a dozen folding chairs — couldn't get people to line up for him on Easter Sunday, that meant ordinary Sunday services were all but doomed.

Papa's spirits had been briefly lifted in the weeks after he thought he'd healed Ma, but Easter Sunday brought them right back down. It didn't seem possible for him to seem more defeated than he had been in the dark days after Deacon Johnson left, but as he trudged to the van after the service with the empty garment bag draped over his arm, it seemed like he'd been hollowed out.

When we got home from church, Papa called us down to the kitchen still wearing the white Easter suit that now looked dingy in the dim kitchen light. "I want to an-nounce this year's revival season circuit," he said when we were all seated, facing him at the head of the table. As he spread out a map, layers of pen markings stared back at us, chronicling our revivals for the past thirteen years. There were tiny *X*'s, red pen circles, and scrawled dates — hieroglyphs denoting the cities where we'd been and when we'd been there. This was always an exciting moment, when our upcoming summer was spelled out for us. As Papa spoke, though, there was none of the typical fanfare in his voice — just a monotone reciting cities as though they were groceries on a shopping list.

"We are beginning at Grateful Life Temple of Holiness in Sweet Home, Arkansas."

Papa continued his announcement, naming a city in Tennessee where we'd never been before and a town in North Carolina. No one acknowledged the fact that the incessant invitations to churches for revival seasons of years past had just about stopped. Over the last few weeks, I'd heard him through the wall that my bedroom shared with the study as he made countless calls, introducing himself as the Faith Healer of East Mansfield. The people on the other end must have sounded incredulous because his words would quicken as he generated calculations about how many souls he had saved and people he had healed over the years, seemingly trying to finish his spiel before they could hang up. I wondered what else he had to promise these preachers in exchange for permission to visit their churches on his redemption tour.

Papa's words trailed off, and my brain snapped back to my idea of healing Hannah, how her healing would be somewhere far away from home, wherever God led me to do it.

"We're kicking off a new tradition this year as well. We're going to start with three places and let the Lord lead us where he would like us to continue. This revival will be about trusting the Lord to provide for us and dictate the course of revival season."

Three revivals instead of eleven. It would have been too much for him to tell us that no one wanted him in their churches, too much to admit that the long shadow cast during last summer's revival season loomed over this one too.

"That's a great idea, Samuel. It allows us to be open to the Lord's guidance." Ma's voice was as distant as her eyes. Caleb, normally Papa's staunch defender, didn't chime in. While Papa searched my face for assent, I got up from the table and felt his gaze creeping on the back of my neck as I pulled out plates for Easter dinner.

Later, after everyone else had scattered upstairs to their separate corners, I sat at the kitchen table among the post-meal detritus: plates scraped clean with utensils crisscrossed on their surface, a carcass of glazed ham with pineapple rings barely hanging on, and stained cloth napkins tossed haphazardly on plates. In the darkness, I ran water in the sink and slipped the plates inside until all of Easter disappeared under a thick layer of soap bubbles. Next to me, moonlight danced off the stainless-steel refrigerator and illuminated Hannah's crayon drawings.

"I will heal Hannah," I said when all the dishes were done and the kitchen was clean, but I still couldn't make myself go upstairs. Cracking the front door and stepping into the black, I wandered away from the house until I reached the sidewalk. *"I will heal Hannah."* I repeated it in the warming night air to the stars that twinkled overhead. I turned around to walk back toward the house, jumping when I saw Caleb on the porch outside.

"What are you doing out here?"

"I needed someplace to think."

I walked up the driveway and sat down next to Caleb on the top step of the porch. His gangly legs were folded beneath him in cartoon character pajama pants that were far too short. The distant buzz of a plane flying overhead interrupted the silence. Caleb and I looked up to see the blinking light moving slowly across the sky. I closed my eyes and imagined myself gliding tens of thousands of feet above this place, turning the houses into specks and the people into grains of dust. I'd never actually been in a plane, but I'd imagined flying many times, especially when we were on the revival circuit, feeling every bump of the road underneath the van.

"Where would you go?" Caleb asked after the plane droned away and left a trail of vapor in its wake.

I'd only ever really thought about the places where we'd driven — Arkansas, Tennessee, Georgia, Louisiana, South Carolina. So I surprised myself when I said Alaska.

Caleb laughed. "Why Alaska?"

Mostly because it was bigger than Texas. But also because it was far away, even though I knew I couldn't tell Caleb that part. "Not sure. It would be nice to see the northern lights. What about you?"

Caleb's teeth glinted as he smiled. "Arizona." He didn't even pause before he spoke — he'd clearly been thinking about it for a long time.

"Why?"

"The Grand Canyon."

Ma had taught us about the Grand Canyon during geography lessons several years ago — Caleb's eyes widened as he heard about a 277-mile-long canyon that was a mile deep, as though he couldn't fathom anything that large.

"What would you do there?"

I imagined him telling me that he would build a church out in the desert, or that he would use it as his main base while traveling the country to preach the Gospel like Papa.

"I'd be a park ranger at the Grand Canyon."

My neck swiveled over to him. "Really?"

"Yup. I'd help people hike down there. But mostly I'd get to stand there and look at it every day."

I hugged my knees to my chest as a chill settled in. The flickering filaments of fireflies sparked and extinguished just as quickly, briefly lighting a path to nowhere.

"What's it like?"

"What's what like?"

"Healing people."

I whipped around to look at him, to see if he was really saying that he believed me. But he was still looking at the sky. My shoulders relaxed from where they had been by my ears, and the first real smile in months cracked my face. I took a deep breath and let my body return to each of the healings — from the stuffiness of the annex when I'd healed Micah to the claustrophobic bathroom with Nadia. "Kind of weird. This tingly feeling travels through me when it happens — kind of like a tiny electric shock. Then everything hurts as though I've taken some of their disease into my body."

Another long pause.

"When did it start?"

"With Micah, I guess. It was an accident. It happened right after we came back from revival season. And it didn't work all the way. That was the first time I felt something though." I caught a glimpse of his profile, his strong jaw moving, like he was chewing all the taste out of the words he couldn't bring himself to say. His eyes widened for a moment with a slight twinge of jealousy before they returned to normal.

"Did you really heal Ma?"

I nodded, but he didn't look over. Maybe he sensed the disturbance in the air, the subtle wind from my swaying head.

"How many have there been?" His voice was tight.

"If you count Micah, six."

I wanted to tell him more, about how Hannah would be my seventh this summer, but I knew I shouldn't — not yet. The moon shone above us overhead, and next to it, the unmistakable pan and long handle of the Big Dipper. Even though I was older than Caleb, he had been the one to teach me about constellations. When he was nine and I was ten, he gloated as he took me by the hand and led me in the backyard one night. I had followed where his finger pointed as he told me how to identify Cassiopeia, the Big Dipper, and the Little Dipper. But that day felt like ages ago as we sat there for a few minutes in our older skins, looking at a canvas of dark sky that stretched above us, dusted with stars.

Spring drew to a close, and the house fluttered with activity as we prepared for the upcoming revival season. And finally, without much ceremony, the day had arrived. While Ma and Papa finished packing, Caleb, Hannah, and I spent the last few minutes in the front yard. Caleb fake chased Hannah on the grass, exaggerating the slow-motion speed of his arms and legs. Hannah squealed and sidled away from him, looking back over her shoulder to see if he was still on her trail. When he finally grabbed her waist, she looked happy to be caught. *Click.* I froze the moment in time when Caleb's hands were on Hannah's waist, her head leaning into his chest. *Click.* I froze Hannah in Caleb's sure arms, clapping in delight.

Mrs. Cade's car pulled up and stopped at the end of the driveway, leaving some space behind where Papa was loading boxes into the trunk. She always came to say goodbye to us before we left for revival season. As soon as I saw her, I rushed to her car, almost dropping the box in my arms.

"Mrs. Cade!" I fell into her embrace. My nose pressed into the crepe skin of her chest as her hug squeezed me too tightly to speak.

"I wish everyone greeted me like that," she said into my scalp. She walked over and tousled Caleb's hair before kneeling down to hug Hannah. When she walked back into the driveway, her eyes searched my face. She scowled as though she had seen something in the way my cheeks puffed with air or my eyebrows were raised.

"Take a walk with me." She grabbed my wrist, leading me into the humid late-spring air that had already pulled my hair out of the careful curls that Ma had made that morning. We walked past where Papa was standing in the driveway.

"Can I borrow her for a moment, Pastor? I promise I'll bring her right back."

Papa waved his hand in assent. I slowed my steps at the corner to match Mrs. Cade's lumbering gait, her shoes' thick soles clomping on the sidewalk squares. She threaded her arm in mine.

"Something's weighing on you. I can see it."

My head dropped to see my feet straddling a sidewalk crack.

"You can tell me anything."

We stopped four houses away; over my shoulder, Papa was hefting one box and then another into the trunk. At the edge of the street, electricity poles towered above us and swooping power lines crackled in the silence; I was one of those wires, with so much surging inside that I didn't know how to keep it all contained.

"I'm going to heal Hannah," I whispered.

She closed her eyes and nodded as though I was telling her something that she already knew. A sound ricocheted from down the street, and our necks snapped in unison to see Papa wrestling with a box that had fallen on the driveway.

"Does he know?"

"Not yet."

"Are you going to tell him?"

337

"He wouldn't believe me even if I did."

She inhaled and closed her eyes again, tilting her head as though summoning wisdom from the breeze. "I know you think you're doing the right thing, but this is bigger than you."

"I thought you believed in me. You were the first one. The only one for a while. You *saw* what I did for Hope." I took a step back as though the widening expanse of concrete between us would take away the sting of her words.

"Just because you may be able to heal Hannah doesn't mean that you should."

"*May* be able to heal? I can heal her like I healed Ma. Besides, I thought you were on my side." My voice was rising.

"I am on your side, Miriam. But this isn't a game. You're treading in serious water." Her voice dropped as her tone turned grave. With a shuffle of her feet, she collapsed the distance between us. I tried to get away, but she grabbed my elbow and pulled me into her. I kept my arm slack by my side.

"Just think and pray more about whether what you're doing is in God's plan." Her lips buzzed right beside my ear. "If it is, then do it. That's all I'm saying. I know you'll do the right thing."

She squeezed me once more and then

started to walk back to her car. Papa eyed her as she approached the driveway, but his forehead was flat, placid — he hadn't heard anything. He kept his eyes on her as she pulled down the driveway, waving out of her window as she drove away.

I walked back inside and surveyed the partially empty living room. I had been waiting for this moment for weeks, but as it got closer, Mrs. Cade's words filled the room's emptiness. She was right — God still hadn't spoken to me, hadn't confirmed that this healing was in His plan. The excited jitters I'd felt the first few days after Easter seemed more like nausea every time I thought about what I was going to do.

I walked over to the dwindling stack of boxes by the door, bent down to pick one up, and brought it out to the driveway. Papa stood a few feet away from the trunk, surveying his handiwork. I stepped closer to him, one unsteady foot in front of the other.

"Papa," I began. He turned to look at me with one arm resting on the open trunk; barely veiled disdain scored his forehead and his bottom lip hung open as though he'd eaten something putrid. Through his glasses, I saw the outline of my face, my slumped shoulders, the quaking box between us. From his side of the lenses, what did he see? He had already told me I wasn't a healer, but there had to be more than that — more than annoyance and shame when he saw me. He must have also remembered all the other times — the times when he carried me to bed, his biceps sturdy beneath me, my head against his clavicle. Or when he led me by the hand into his study and lifted me into his tufted leather chair as my feet dangled. He had loved me once — that love couldn't have just disappeared. And I had loved him once too.

"Here's one more."

"Miriam, this isn't going to fit," he snapped. "The trunk is already full. This box will have to go in the back seat with you."

My shock at the sharpness of his raised voice sent the box out of my arms and onto the driveway. Hannah's toys flew out as the cardboard flap opened. Tiger, a rag doll, and other colorful plastic baubles that kept her quiet at night rolled down the driveway. I rushed after them, snatching Tiger from the fate of the waiting sewer grate. I stuffed all the toys back into the box, Tiger's floppy head drooping from the side in his own silent protest, before I shoved the box in the back seat.

As we settled in the car, Ma said the

obligatory parting prayer: "Lord, watch over these, Your children. Use us to do Your will. Amen." Papa looked over his shoulder as he eased the minivan down the driveway and rumbled onto the road. I never liked to watch the house receding in the rearview mirror — to know that when we came back in three months, the structure, though physically the same, would feel different. But the house hadn't provided me with the comfort it usually did this past year, so maybe different would be okay.

Normally, families lined the side of our street to wave goodbye to us. The littlest kids from homeschool would hold poster-board signs that they'd decorated in the last few days before summer break — rudimentary crayon letters formed barely legible words that Ma had dictated while standing over their shoulders. Papa would put down his window and we would hear the shouting of our last name — *Horton, Horton* — accompanied by applause. We would wave like celebrities until reaching the stop sign, when the crowd died down. Today, the sidewalks were empty and silent as Papa drove slowly down the street. With each glance out of the window, he waited for someone to realize we were leaving and come outside, but no one did. Ma sang to Isaac to quiet his cries as we got onto the highway — her lilting lyrics about climbing Jacob's ladder modulated into higher octaves and drowned out the music from the radio. The rest of the minivan joined in with her at the chorus: "Soldiers of the cross."

FIFTEEN

Shelby Church of the New Covenant — the third and final stop on this new iteration of revival season — was at the end of a dirt road, miles away from the highway and anything else that resembled civilization. It sprang from the dust that surrounded it like a mirage — wavy at first, and then the sharp perpendicularity of white towers, gold turrets, and a sloped cathedral started to take shape. Ma and Papa always warned against places like this, places that worshipped vanity more than God, yet there we were, pulling into the biggest parking lot that I had ever seen, turning off the engine, and piling out of the car.

I stretched my legs, looked up at the cloudless sky, and closed my eyes. *A miracle will happen here.* A light breeze ruffled the trees and blew across my face, confirming the conviction that had just settled in my soul. *I will heal Hannah here.* Despite my

343

fervent prayers every night, the conviction hadn't come among the modest crowds during the previous weeks in Tennessee or Arkansas — crowds that Papa had stood in front of, staring at me as he proclaimed that he'd healed members of his church from diabetes and heart disease. But now time was running out — the miracle had to happen in Shelby if it was going to happen at all.

Caleb pushed open the heavy gold doors that led inside, offering a partial glimpse of the sanctuary. The carpet looked like no one had set foot on it before. I wanted to take my shoes off to feel the plushness beneath my toes.

"Reverend Dixon?" Papa asked into the empty room. The words echoed off the dozens of rows of gleaming white pews.

"Reverend Horton, welcome!" A short man with thick gold chains around his neck came out from behind the pulpit where he must have been crouched. All along I'd been trying to imagine what the man who pastored this church would look like. As he descended the stairs to get on our level, he was smaller than I imagined — a couple of inches shorter than Caleb. A white short-sleeved dress shirt contrasted his deep-brown skin and revealed a thick layer of coarse hair on his arms. The clink of gold bracelets resonated through the empty sanctuary as he reached out and shook Papa's hand that enveloped his like a catcher's mitt. Papa forced a smile as he introduced us.

"Anyone in the mood to go to the revival space?"

I wanted to settle into the place that would be our house for the week, but my opinion meant nothing as Papa told Reverend Dixon that he'd be happy to. As we followed Reverend Dixon's gold luxury SUV along a winding North Carolina road to the revival location, I pressed my face against the warm window and watched the trees pass by at a rapid pace. Reverend Dixon turned a corner, and the familiar outline of a tent took shape: with its swirling yellows and blues, it could have been mistaken for a circus tent.

We stepped out of the car. Papa jumped out first and walked around the perimeter, examining the tent's stakes that had been driven deep into the ground. While he traced his forefinger on the tent's vinyl walls, he was seemingly trying to measure how many souls he could deliver and heal in one night's time. Caleb hung back for a minute after Papa went into the tent — his reluctant support of Papa had become more obvious this revival season. Hannah and I stayed with Ma and Isaac in the back of the tent while Papa walked up and down the aisles. His fingers grazed the wooden folding chairs at the end of each row; from my estimate, there were about six hundred of them. Way bigger than most of the revivals that Papa had conducted — twice the size of the previous ones this season in Tennessee and Arkansas.

I watched Papa like a hawk as he hoisted himself up onto the stage, his microphoneless voice barely audible in the emptiness. I needed to memorize every foot of this space without him knowing what I was doing. Trying to look as nonchalant as possible, I stayed close to Ma and clutched Hannah's arm. All the while, I mimicked Papa's steps from the back of the tent — my sandals shuffling on grass rather than up on the stage where he was. I made my hand into an O to practice holding the microphone when the time came. I knew so many of Papa's motions by heart already, but since this would be bigger than any healing I'd ever attempted before, it needed to be exactly right.

When everyone was in bed that night, thoughts lapped the edges of my brain. *Is this the right thing to do? Is this what God*

346

wants? I had felt so sure when we arrived here, but after seeing the tent and watching Papa make his final preparations, the conviction that had settled so firmly in my heart dissipated. I looked across the room at sleeping Hannah, nestled under the covers. This was all supposed to be for her, but maybe Mrs. Cade was right — maybe this was too big a thing to attempt.

I climbed out of bed and walked over to Hannah. Three months since the last seizure — a new record. I sank to my knees in front of her, my arms stretching to where her jutting shoulder blades were exposed under the thin sheet. I closed my eyes, and a prayer formed on my lips. "Dear God, if it is Your will for Your child to be healed, give me the strength, the ability, and the power to heal her. If it is not in Your will, reveal Your will to me. Amen."

I expected to feel lighter when I rose from the edge of her bed, but I didn't feel much different. It felt like God, who had always been near — the breeze behind me, the heat on my face when I prayed — was receding like the sun behind a cloud. As I was getting closer to my miracle, God's will for me was getting more obscure.

Monday morning's sunrise teased the hori-

347

zon before breaking into full-fledged splendor. When God had previously revealed Himself to me, it always happened like this. Radiant sunrises, torrential downpours, rainbows — anything that we couldn't control was a reminder of His power. It was God promising me that Hannah would be healed in Shelby. Tonight.

Thank you, Lord.

Hours after Papa and Caleb left with Reverend Dixon, I slid into a dress and zipped it in one motion. Then I lifted a stolen bottle of holy oil from the front of my suitcase and put it in the pocket of my dress. When we marched into the tent later that evening, my posture was a little straighter than normal as we took our seats in the fourth row.

"Can I sit on the aisle tonight, Ma?"

Ma nodded as I placed my hand over the protruding bottle of holy oil so no one would notice its outline through the thin layer of cotton. Hannah settled into her spot next to me, and I laid her crutches onto the ground in front of us. After I healed her, she wouldn't need them.

The bulbs in the tent made an electric crackle overhead that was only matched by the low din of people's voices as they filtered inside. I could barely sit still as people filed into the tent, whispering polite hellos to one another, asking about children, and fanning themselves with programs before finding their seats. The humid air breathed sweltering puffs into the spaces where the revival tent didn't close.

The lights dimmed and people shuffled into their seats. The choir began with "Amazing Grace," one of Papa's favorites, as they marched into the tent in a single-file line. Papa, wearing a new gray suit he'd bought the week before, walked up: his slow, sure steps lingered several paces behind the black-clad choir as they swayed down the aisle. He lifted his hand to greet people, smiling as flashes from the congregation's cameras and cell phones flickered. He walked up to the stage and took his seat. From high up, he must have noticed that this was the biggest crowd of the season so far.

When Papa stood up to begin the sermon, he looked confident. He loosened his tie and asked the congregation to turn with him to Matthew 24. My tongue went limp in the bottom of my dry mouth as I flipped to the chapter about the end of days. This was a brand-new sermon that he hadn't preached in the past two cities, and he never deviated from the sermon order during revivals. This must have been what he'd been so busy coming up with since I'd told him I healed Ma.

"The message for today is about the end of days — the signs that God has given us to show that the end is near. The Scripture talks about wars, famines, and earthquakes. These are all things that will precede His triumphant return. But He also warns us about something more insidious — a threat from within the church."

Papa paused and drummed his fingers on the podium as the congregation gasped — the reaction that he must have been waiting for. People nodded as he lifted a water bottle and placed it to his lips, earlier in the sermon than he normally did. *Why is he doing this tonight? What does he know?* My heartbeat got louder, drowning out his echoing words. Maybe this was a sign that I should abandon my plan. It wasn't too late to call it off. No one would have to know. But I shook the thought away as quickly as it entered. I had to do this. Papa was a consummate performer — he didn't know anything at all. I dried my sweaty palms on my skirt and inhaled as he continued preaching.

"Another sign of the end of days is that false prophets will appear and deceive many

350

people. Ladies and gentlemen, I am here to tell you not to accept the false prophecy of infidels who claim to have gifts of the Holy Spirit. Don't believe them! They are not sent from God." His eyes searched the congregation and zeroed in on me in the fourth row.

My cheeks bristled under his gaze as cheers and applause trickled through the tent. I pressed my hands on my legs to stop them from moving. Would the same cheers come for me when I healed Hannah before their eyes? I leaned into Hannah's warmth as Papa walked from one side of the stage to the other, his voice rising and falling as he preached about staying firm in the word of the Lord during the end times. Hannah swung her legs in the chair like she was propelling herself in a swing, and my eyes traveled down to the braces that must have pinched her exposed skin. Ma looked over — Hannah's moving chair had started to become a distraction. I placed my hand on Hannah's kneecap; as she turned her face to me, her legs calmed.

Papa was on the ground among the audience — a sign that the sermon was winding down. My pulse quickened at the thought of what would happen in just a couple of moments. I leaned toward Hannah, and she inched closer to me.

"I'm going to heal you," I whispered for the first time since the day months earlier in the tub. Back then, it had seemed like the time would never come, but as Papa brought his sermon to a close, we were minutes away.

"The end of days is coming, brothers and sisters. We are in the midst of wars and famines, of natural disasters and people turning their backs on the Lord in record numbers. Get right with the Lord. The first way to do that is to give your life to Him — a God whose back is never turned to us."

Amen.

"A God who is with us during every trial. A God who is standing next to you when you bury a spouse or a child. A God who is with you during unemployment, during unimaginable heartbreak."

Amen.

"He will never leave you or forsake you, even in the midst of your test. That God is faithful and just to cleanse you of sin and forgive you of all unrighteousness. Be strong in your faith, brothers and sisters."

While the congregation whooped and stood, I closed my eyes and wrapped myself in the promise of those words. I had been taught to believe each verse in the Bible —

Ma and Papa liked to joke that the first words out of my mouth had been Scripture. I remembered sitting at the kitchen table when I was eight, the typeface and glossy images of my children's illustrated Bible swimming in my brain as I had tried to commit Joshua 1:5 to memory. *As I was with Moses, so I will be with you; I will never leave you nor forsake you.* As the last words had escaped my lips in the empty room, a prickly sensation shot down my spine. I turned around, prepared to yell at Caleb for trying to scare me, but no one was standing behind me. Looking to distract myself from the fear, I repeated the verse, and, as the words left my lips, my fear seemed to leave with them. God's presence filled the space around me — it was the paradox of faith that Papa talked about — we go through this world alone, but God is always with us. Suddenly, I knew that the same God who had been with me when I was eight and every day afterward was looking down on me in the tent right now.

"Can everyone please rise? Christ is the door to eternal life, brothers and sisters. He is standing at the door to your heart, knocking. Let Him in and allow Him to change your life. The doors of the church are open."

For several moments, no one moved. I

wanted this section to speed up, for Papa to move on to the healing so that it could be my turn. Maybe no one was going to come forward today for deliverance, but that was unlikely. A moment later, one woman from the back of the church — her arms folded over large breasts — walked slowly to the front. Then more people stood up, and soon, around thirty people followed her up to the front of the tent to give their lives to God. After Papa welcomed them into the kingdom, it was time for healing.

"Brothers and sisters, are you ready to be healed?" Before he finished the sentence, lines of men and women gathered in the aisle. Papa moved through the line, his confidence building with each healing. I patted my pocket with the holy oil in it before closing my eyes and whispering a prayer. "Lord, let me be an instrument of Your will. Amen."

Forty-five minutes after the healing part of service had started, the line had dwindled to two people — a man who towered over Papa, and a woman Ma's age who cradled a wailing infant. After Papa's healing words, the tall man sank to the ground like a felled tree in an exaggerated flourish. Papa got to the end of the line and traced a tiny cross on the baby's forehead.

"People of God, all have been healed." He walked back up the steps to the makeshift pulpit. The keyboardist started the closing anthem. The crowd stood and cheered for the people whose ailments, visible and invisible, they thought Papa had cured. I stood too, but not to cheer.

It was time.

Ma's eyes were closed, her chin tilted toward the ceiling with Isaac asleep in her lap. I stepped into the aisle and reached my hands out to Hannah. She grabbed hold, and I pulled her to a standing position. When she was on her feet, she braced her body. She knew something was wrong — no one was walking down the aisle now. Ma opened her eyes and lunged for us in the aisle, but she was too late: her closing fist clutched air.

"C'mon, Hannah," I chided. "It's time." People around us cheered as Hannah and I took slow steps toward the front. With my arm around her back, I supported most of her weight. She kept her eyes on me, pleading for an explanation. I looked away from her and toward the pulpit where Papa's eyes narrowed behind the thin barrier of his glasses. He sucked air into his cheeks as his chest heaved. The keyboardist stopped mid-chord, and the cheering that had just been deafening faded into silence.

Without music, my feet shuffled down the aisle in time with Hannah's. Neither of us had ever been this close during one of his services; the whole production looked so large from where we were standing. The speakers onstage, now silent, seemed to pulse — maybe it was the remnants of percussion or maybe it was the rushing of blood between my ears as Papa made his way over to us.

I had rehearsed this moment over and over — I had to grab the microphone and tell the congregation that I was going to heal Hannah. A moment of silence hung in the air. Papa's eyes tried to read my intentions while Hannah stood between us, her legs becoming less steady with every second. I reached for the microphone from Papa's hand, and it hit the ground as I grabbed it. All the excitement and strength that I felt back in the audience was fading, like a star exploding — bright against the dark sky at first and then diminishing to nothing. Fumbling in my dress pocket for the elusive bottle of holy oil, my fingers finally landed on the rounded plastic. It tumbled out of my hand in slow motion, hurtling through the air, and the top came off as it landed. A pool of viscous vegetable oil leaked from the open spout and glistened on the grass, inching ever closer to Papa's shiny shoe.

Papa fumbled in the grass for the microphone. Time lengthened as he stayed crouched; when he rose, he massaged both clean-shaven cheeks with a trembling left hand. But it wasn't just his hands that were shaking: everything on him shook as he exhaled heavy, amplified breaths into the tent.

"Brethren, it appears that we have a special healing this evening. My daughter Hannah." Papa cleared his throat. He took one step closer to Hannah. "How many of you are ready for one more miracle?"

The congregation erupted in thunderous applause.

"When Hannah was born, the doctors told us that she was stricken with cerebral palsy and would never walk without crutches."

Though I knew this about Hannah, no one had ever said it out loud, much less over a booming microphone to a group of strangers. I pulled her closer to me, and she resisted.

"But, saints of God, do we believe that report?" Papa continued.

"No," the congregation asserted in unison.

"Saints of God, do we believe that report?" Papa asked again.

"No." The congregation was much louder this time, their voices threatening to send the roof of the tent careening into the sky.

Papa dropped to his knees next to Hannah, encircling her arched back with his arm. Hannah relaxed her neck onto his shoulder, and he pressed his lips against her forehead. Then he whispered something into her ear that I couldn't hear. Maybe he told her that he loved her, or that he was sorry that he couldn't heal her when she was a baby. Or a mixture of the two.

Papa carried Hannah onto the stage like she was a rag doll. *No heavier than a sack of sugar,* Ma always said whenever she lifted Hannah. I watched from the ground below as, like magic, a bottle of holy oil appeared in his hand.

"Hannah, I believe that the Lord can heal your body. Do you believe?"

Hannah's body grew rigid in Papa's arms as she nodded in response to his question. With her head cocked back, Papa traced a sign of the cross on her forehead. He laid her on the ground with her weight resting on her forearms. She looked around, confused, at the people in the congregation who were staring at her. Her right eye probably saw them in crisp colors and shapes while her left eye saw them in grades of shadow and light. Then she turned to me on the ground below, powerless to rescue her.

"Rise up and walk, my child." Everyone was Papa's child when he did a healing, but his words felt more tender now, like this was the first time he meant them. Hannah balanced herself on her forearms and pulled herself forward, the way she did when she played with Tiger. She had moved about an inch, but a Red Sea of turf separated her from Papa. She should have been on her feet by now, or at least trying to get there. Her scissoring legs cut the fake plastic grass, but she didn't rise.

"Rise up and walk, my child." Sweat dropped from Papa's forehead as he leaned closer to her, as if the words themselves would be sufficient to bring her to her feet. Hannah continued her slow crawl, closer and closer to him.

"Congregation, I need your help. The devil is working here. I need you to pray."

Moans and wails rose from behind us as people stretched out their hands to Papa. The keyboardist plinked the opening chords to another song. Papa flailed his arms like he was losing his balance even though he was on solid ground. It startled Hannah, and she started to cry, burying her face into the ground.

I sprang to the stage, crouching by Hannah's side. It was against the rules for women to be in the pulpit — I knew that — but I wasn't asking for permission anymore. I placed my hand on Hannah's back and rubbed it in circular motions to calm her down. This is where I had wanted to be all along, with my hands on Hannah, healing her. Hannah's body heaved, curling in on itself and then straightening again like the beginning of a seizure. I rubbed my hands on her legs, kneading the slack muscles below her braces, the places where her legs felt too wiry, unable to hold her weight. A few moments later, Papa, spent, rested his hands on his knees. He hadn't healed Hannah. Again.

"There are some people whom God does not heal, whom it's not in His will to heal. These are tests that God sends to each of us. Children we can't heal, wives who miscarry, stillbirths . . ." His frantic sentences rose at the end as he rushed to the ground and tried to reassure the crowd who had just watched him fail. Over the microphone he told them that they were witnessing a mystery of faith.

Hannah rolled over onto her back and looked up at me. She writhed on the scratchy turf, desperate for rescue, her hands reaching toward me to help her. I was the one who had put her in this position and made a spectacle of her in front of the whole tent. Tears budded in the corners of my eyes as I pulled her body toward me. I wanted to snatch her from the ground and take her far away from here. But I knew I had to carry this through. I wanted to tell her that it would all be worth it.

She had started to howl, her voice chasing the keyboard's loud chords into the tent's eaves. I stared into her eyes, and it seemed like even the left one focused on me. It was just me and Hannah — there was no stage, no congregation. I slipped my legs from underneath her prone body, my knees wobbly like hers. In the long shadow of the cross, I helped Hannah to her feet. My lungs burned as heat rose through my legs. When the tingling started and my body pulsated like a beating heart, it was time.

The back of the crowd was dim and shadowy, but the rows closer up came into focus. Ma was standing, frozen on the balls of her feet as though she wanted to run up to the stage but couldn't. Her body was shaking so violently that it looked like Isaac would fall out of her cradled arms. Caleb was standing on the ground near Papa, blinking as though he couldn't believe what was happening only feet away, as though the brief darkness each time he shut his eyes would reveal a new picture to him that didn't involve his sisters on the stage in a revival tent. Papa's hands were raised to the congregation — his words running together in some incoherent mash of syllables about God and trial — when he turned back to see me. He thrashed his head from side to side as he hurtled toward us in what seemed like slow motion.

"Hannah Faith Horton. Do you trust that I can heal you?" I spoke in a normal tone — shouting would scare her. I pretended like it was just the two of us on the altar. She moved her hands at her sides in what I needed to believe was the sign for yes. There was no more oil, but I didn't need any. The power wasn't in the oil but in the Spirit, and I could suddenly feel the Spirit rushing through me. I raised my left arm above Hannah's head before bringing it down slowly, inching ever closer to her face.

"In the name of the Lord Jesus Christ, you are healed."

My fingertips landed on her forehead. A flash of heat entered my hand and coursed through my arm and the rest of my body. I kept my hand on her head to seal the healing, but the spot of skin had become a scalding burner. I opened my mouth wide and exhaled as an escape valve for the pain, but the hot breath that came out of me didn't make the rest of the heat dissipate.

The room drained itself of color — the walls became gray and the turf melted away beneath my feet. Silence descended. I closed my eyes and focused on my breathing. Soon, words to a prayer to heal Hannah were stones in my mouth — with my hands pressed against her, I asked God to take away her pain. I tried to remove my arm from the small of her back, but her legs still felt limp. I eased my hand away from her a little bit at a time, but her legs started to buckle as I squatted close to the ground and eased her onto it. She fell into a heap by my feet — all I could do was stare at her on the ground, my eyelids scorching each time I blinked. She writhed in front of me, but I couldn't move to help her.

"Hannah Faith Horton, rise up and walk." I squeezed the methodical words out of a throat that was closing. Weights were attached to the ends of my arms, but I raised them in a V the way I had practiced. A kaleidoscope of Nadia's face morphing into Suzette's and Micah's and Hope's turned in my brain — I shook them away and stared at Hannah, still lying at my feet. She curled herself into a ball — the position that she always assumed before she tried to get to her feet. It was working, slowly, but it was working.

I kept my arms raised, afraid to move and disrupt the miracle even though every muscle raged. Hannah scooted her butt into the air, her forehead against the turf like she was praying. She inched her knees ever closer to her hands, until her knees and her hands were finally touching. All she had to do was get her balance and stand.

Lord, make Hannah walk so they can witness Your power. Please. It was more of a plea than a prayer, but I didn't care. The voice inside my head was fearful, even though I knew that fear was the enemy of faith. The miracle definitely wouldn't work if I was afraid of failing.

"Hannah Faith Horton, rise up and walk." I always thought that Papa repeated things to hear his voice echo through the tent — to remind himself of his power. Maybe he repeated things when he started to doubt himself.

Hannah crawled along on the turf with limp legs behind her. She lifted her weight on her forearms and collapsed on her face. With one cheek pressed to the turf, she turned her neck and looked up at me with weary confusion. Her arched eyebrows pleaded with me to make it all stop. It had been too long.

She wasn't going to walk. She was never going to walk. I lowered my hands slowly, and the room came back into focus — first colors, then shapes, then details — angry eyes, the glint of glasses, open mouths. Sounds trickled up from the ground — whispers that erupted into yells, words that weren't discernable over the loud jeers.

Papa towered over us onstage — then he crouched to my level. His hands were close to my face, and it looked like he was wringing water out of them. I searched his expression for a kernel of tenderness or love or mercy, but there was none. The full force of his open palm struck my right cheek, his wedding band landing square on my cheekbone.

I fell to my knees on the thin layer of turf that covered the stage. I crawled away, blind, feeling my way toward the steps. My hands felt the lip of the stairs, and I slid down the three steps that brought me back to the level of the congregation. I opened my eyes when I got back in the aisle and stumbled down the narrow path that I had come down, stopping briefly by the fourth row, next to the two empty chairs where

Hannah and I had been sitting. Ma wouldn't turn to look at me, even as the eyes of the rest of the congregation seared my flesh. Her jaw was clenched as she looked up at Papa and Hannah. When I peered into the shocked faces of the crowd, I expected them to be pointing at Papa, yelling in his direction for the violence he'd just inflicted against me. But their fingers were pointing at me — their round mouths were yelling at me. My feet took me all the way outside as the tent released me into the darkness.

Overhead, the thin crescent moon was barely visible in a sky that hid it like a secret. I ran out of the parking lot, away from the noise of the tent. Away from everything. Darkness obscured the road. My feet struck the uneven gravel, sinking in divots and moving up inclines. The throaty croak of frogs and the hiss of crickets drowned out the ragged, panting breaths that couldn't get into my lungs quickly enough, escaping just as fast as they came.

It was too dark to tell if these were roads we'd driven down earlier. All the landmarks that I had memorized — the swooping power lines that threaded between leaning wooden poles, the fork in the road — had vanished in a disorienting night sky so black and thick that I had no idea where I was going. I just knew I had to keep moving.

A crack of branches. I spun around, but there was nothing to see behind me. I twirled all the way in a circle, dizzy as I looked up at what I imagined was a dense overhang of trees knit together. Maybe a bird had landed on a branch. Or some kids had even wandered out here to play a prank. But there was no flutter of wings, no birdsong, no laughter. My heart quickened.

Another crack — louder than the first one, louder even than my thumping heart.

"Hello?" I called out, my voice barely audible among the chirps and susurrus. Nothing. I took one step back and then another, my heel striking the ground before I was ready, buckling my knees until I had fallen backward. Before I could stand back up, I heard a rustle in the leaves.

"Who is it?" My voice was wavering and thready. I dug my palms into the gravel and scampered backward as my eyes adjusted. My right hand struck a tree root, and I gripped its shriveled heft to push myself to my feet. In the distance I heard a quickening of footsteps. It sounded like someone was speaking to me, calling my name, but only my relentless heartbeat and my arrhythmic breathing echoed in my ears. Fear surged through my body as I flew into thicker, denser patches of inky dark woods. My body seemed to separate from itself. Part of me hovered above the woods while the rest of me ducked the few tree branches that I could see while getting swatted in the face by others. I jerked to the left, into a copse farther away from the road. I kept running, and soon I heard nothing at all — no footsteps quickening to catch up with me. When I slumped against a tree to catch my breath, the distant sound of footsteps came back — running this time — even though I couldn't tell where they were.

I knew I had to keep moving. Gathering up the little remaining energy I had, I stood up and took off again. But, as soon as I did, my toe struck something hard, and I soared through blackness, my arms swirling out of time with my legs until I landed on a steep incline. The ground slid away as I tumbled down a hill, gaining speed as my head struck tree roots, and my face sliced through dense webs of branches. A hard fragment came loose and floated in my closed mouth; blood filled the spaces between my teeth.

I finally stopped moving in a small space of gravel, but my head bounced like I was still tumbling down the hill. As I tried to push myself up, rocks bit into the soft flesh of my palms. My throat wanted to cry out, but it felt like hands were pressing on my chest each time I drew a breath. A sharp pain started in my knee and shot all the way up the rest of my leg. I lay on my back as the stars reeled and a new sheet of darkness fell over my eyes.

SIXTEEN

I heard someone breathing next to me as I peeled the left side of my face from a sticky pool and placed my forearms in the gravel, trying to turn my body to see who had found me. As I moved, the blinding pain that pulsed through my chest and my leg made me curl back into a ball.

"Why were you running from me? You're okay now. Don't move." Caleb. Was he the person who had been chasing me? I watched his fingers pressing my forearm as a way to reassure me, but I couldn't feel the touch. Then the muted sound of dialing on his cell phone, the sharp rise of fear in his words as he tried to describe generic landmarks around us — a hill, a lake, a dense patch of woods. He stayed on the phone, his left hand on my arm, until a distant siren interrupted him and got closer. Soon a red light pulsated, punctuated by flashes of blue.

"She's down here." His dress shoes ran

away from me, and I tried to get him to stay, but I couldn't speak or move. When he came back, someone was with him, inching closer to me, but I still couldn't move my head to see a face.

I floated away from the scene until the paramedic pulled me back into my body by strapping me to a gurney that clattered into the back of the ambulance. I didn't let Caleb's hand go — or maybe it was him not letting mine go — even as they loaded me inside. Throughout the whole ride, Caleb held tight, his forehead pressed against the spiderweb pattern of dried blood on my hand. I wanted to play the squeezing game — one squeeze firmer than the previous one until someone relented. I squeezed once, but he didn't squeeze back. When the ambulance bumped to a stop, his voice — no louder than a whisper — was praying. I slid into darkness again.

Beep beep beep. The sounds snaked their way into my ears that felt like they had been stuffed with cotton. My right leg was immobilized in a splint, and I tried to wiggle my toes, but my brain didn't seem to connect to the rest of my body, and my legs stayed still above the thin sheets.

In the din of noise, the glass doors

wheezed open to the nurse's station, visible through the gap in the curtain next to my bed. A frazzled Ma, still wearing the same dress from revival the previous night, rushed over to the desk. I could hear her frantic voice but couldn't make out her words. A few seconds later, she entered my room holding Isaac in one arm, with Hannah and Caleb a few steps behind. No Papa.

I lurched in bed at the sight of Hannah, wanting to rush to her side and take her into my arms — to kiss her face and tell her that I was sorry about the night before, that I was sorry for thinking that she wasn't whole, that she needed fixing. But before I could say anything, Papa rushed into the room. He had assumed all types of expressions in the pulpit — anger, rage, joy — but never the unvarnished fear that I saw now.

Soon they were all next to my bed in a cluster — Ma looked frail as she stood above me, the belt of her dress hanging loosely from her waist like an afterthought. She spit out questions rapid-fire: "What were you doing? Where did you go? Where does it hurt? What happened last night?" They came out so quickly that when I tried to answer one, the next one replaced it. I gave up speaking. She touched every inch of my face and looked at me as though she were seeing my features — the moles on my cheeks that I'd inherited from her, the steep arch of my bushy eyebrows, my stubby eyelashes — for the first time. She was extra gentle on the scratches and bruises, as though her touch could magically put me back together. Then she kissed everywhere that she touched, finishing with my cheek. Hannah didn't move — her eyes were fixed on my leg. I patted the mattress next to me and told her it was okay, but she stayed put, even as Caleb nudged her forward.

"Are you Mr. and Mrs. Horton?" The doctor who had been bobbing around the periphery of my room came back and stood next to my bed. "I'm Dr. Reynolds, the ER attending." He held out his hand to shake, then he looked around at my siblings before taking Ma and Papa outside to talk. Through the partition, I heard Dr. Reynolds say that I had a cracked rib that would heal on its own, but that I needed surgery to repair a fractured leg. As I sighed into the pillow and blankets, pain radiated to every part of my body.

When they came back inside, Papa stayed on the outskirts of my family's semicircle — he looked me over once, as if he were verifying that I was alive — but he didn't say anything to me as the orderlies dressed in blue came to wheel me to the operating room. Everyone else stayed in the room except for Ma. She walked down the hallway with me — her left hand holding mine. Her hand tightened as we rounded one corner and then another. The bed stopped by a final set of double doors.

"This is the end of the line, Mrs. Horton. You can wait in the waiting room with the rest of your family, and we'll let you know as soon as she's out of surgery."

As I looked at her fingers wrapped around mine, I knew that she had loved me the best way she knew how — the only way she knew how.

"I'm sorry, Ma," I managed. As I spoke those three words, it felt like something was stabbing me from the inside.

She came into my field of vision and pressed her finger against my parched lips. "Don't speak, Miriam. You know how much I love you. I've never told you that I don't know what I would do without you. But I don't." Her voice cracked as she spoke, and tears leaked out of puffy eyes. I wanted to reach up and hug her, but even the smallest movement was excruciating.

She didn't say goodbye, but her hand slowly lost its grip on mine. I couldn't turn around, could barely move my neck, as we pushed our way through the double doors. She couldn't hear me whisper *I love you* as the doors closed.

I opened my eyes to a soft, hazy light — what I imagined heaven might look like. But I wasn't dead, even though part of me wanted to be. My chest rose and fell beneath a smooth sheet as tubes that I couldn't feel snaked into my veins. I could only keep my eyes open for seconds at a time: could see brief glimpses of my family as they passed in front of my eyes. Ma paced with sleeping Isaac cradled in her arms; Caleb and Hannah ate metallic bags of chips as crumbs fell onto Hannah's dress; Hannah leaned on Caleb's shoulder as he pointed to pictures in a book. Memories, piecemeal shards, came back — the warmth from Hannah's head on my shoulder the night before, her look of fear as she stared up at me from the floor of the pulpit as I begged her to walk.

The next evening, Ma, Caleb, and Hannah wheeled me outside to the minivan, and we drove back to the compound. I hadn't seen Papa since he left the hospital the day before and imagined him, miles away, repairing the damage in the revival tent — damage that I'd caused. Back inside the Dixons' house, our boxes and bags had already been packed. Sometime while I was in the hospital, Papa must have also gotten the news that his service this revival season had come to an end. *We no longer need you,* I imagined Reverend Dixon saying.

"We're home, Samuel," Ma announced when we stepped inside.

Suddenly Papa was downstairs and standing inches from my face. His lips wobbled from rage or fear or relief — I wasn't sure which. He took a step closer, and I closed my eyes in preparation for the rebuke. But there was no contact, no heat on my cheekbone, no lingering feeling of fingertips on my face. When I opened my eyes again, he was still standing in front of me, his hands at his sides.

"Look at you." Now I could see that his expression was one of fury. He scanned my broken body — my slumped posture on crutches — before landing back on my face. "Are you proud of yourself? Are you proud of what you've done to this family? You've ruined us." It was easier to focus on his Adam's apple bobbing out of time with his words than on the words themselves.

"Enough, Samuel," Ma said, pulling him back from my face. "Can't you see she's been through enough?"

"She needs to say something for herself, Joanne. God has already punished her sin, but I want to hear her say she's sorry. God got His due, now I need mine."

The rubber bottoms of my crutches straddled perpendicular grout lines in the tile. Nothing in the room moved. He was not going to relent. What I wanted to say was, *You've ruined us. I was trying to save us. To save you.* But my windpipe felt like it had been snapped along with the other broken bones, and no words escaped.

He was still inches from my face, ignoring Ma's pleas to leave me alone. I looked down at his hands. Knew the harm that they'd done two nights ago. Knew what else they'd been capable of.

"I don't know what you want from me, Papa. I can't apologize for something God gave me."

"God didn't give you the ability to heal," he seethed.

"What if He did? Have you ever thought about that?"

"No, I've never thought that because it's ridiculous." His laughter jangled among the boxes and bags.

"Is it? I've read the same Bible you have, Papa. Show me where it says that women can't heal."

"I'm not going to argue Scripture with you, Miriam. If you could heal, why didn't you heal Hannah?" He was getting impatient — I could see it in the way the vein in his neck bulged. But I couldn't explain what happened with Hannah beyond what Papa said — that some people weren't meant to be healed. That she was whole as she was. I had tried so hard to make him see that I could heal that I'd tried to heal someone who didn't need it.

"You didn't heal her either. Twice. Maybe because she doesn't need healing. But you didn't heal Ma — I did. And you didn't heal the man from Bethel; you beat him when he questioned you."

Ma and Caleb gasped — a reminder that they were still in the room. Papa straightened his hand, and I flinched — a reflex. But instead of hitting me, he took a few steps back and focused his anger on a nearby packing box, which he turned over in a rage. He did the same with two other boxes, spilling and kicking their contents like a spoiled toddler. We all watched, silently, none of us stooping to clean up after him.

The grandfather clock dinged eleven in the living room. As if something deep within him was spurred by the clock's reminder of the time, Papa stopped. He sat down on the floor — his shoulders slumped and heaving — and slowly, methodically, began to repack the overturned boxes. I felt frozen in place, but watching this diminished version of Papa was painful. It must have been excruciating for Caleb and Ma, too, because we all turned around and continued loading the car in silence. This time, there would be no map with directions to the next revival site, no prayer for a record number of souls saved or healed. We slipped away before the Dixons arrived home — the gold gate clanging shut and permanently separating us from a world we would never inhabit again.

The minivan skittered across the double yellow line that divided us from the semis speeding in the opposite direction, their horns blaring staccato rhythms before droning off as they passed. Papa, gripping the wheel as though it would fly away if he let go, swerved the minivan back onto our side of the yellow paint. The road was hypnotic as it rose in front of us, lulling me to sleep in the seat behind where Caleb and Hannah were huddled, her head under the fold of his arm instead of mine, the cast on my right leg propped up on pillows on the empty seat beside me where she should have been.

When I woke up, a bright, bold sunrise shone through the windows of our car that was no longer moving. Papa had stopped by the side of the road, and a slight breeze entered through the open doors. I looked out and saw Papa step onto a narrow path, lifting a few branches before moving onto an expanse of sand that led to a surface so glassy blue that sunlight bounced off it and refracted in multiple directions. The Atlantic Ocean. He had never taken us to the ocean before — I'd only seen it from the road, my forehead fused to the warm window as a seat belt pinned me in place.

I stepped out on crutches as Papa inched toward the ocean, his heavy dress shoes sinking into the sand. Caleb carried Hannah into the blinding early-morning sunshine while Ma, a few steps behind Caleb, held Isaac. Dwarfed by the ocean, Papa dropped to his knees in the sand; his head and hands fell forward as though he were being tugged by a different gravitational pull. Ma reflexively rushed to his side and stopped a few feet away as his forehead reached the sand and his arms stretched out in front of him. His voice rose from the sand, quiet at first, but shouting before long. His prayers were angry, his chest heaving.

"Why — why — why?" Each word sputtered out like he couldn't muster enough steam for the whole sentence. He took a breath and composed himself. "Why me? You are the God of Abraham, Isaac, and Jacob; You keep Your promises. I have been Your faithful servant, and You have turned Your back on me. What have I done but serve You? What have I done but try to be like You and do Your will?"

I thrust my crutches into the sand and took a few steps back, even as Ma stepped closer to him. We were intruding on something private.

"My God, my God, why have You forsaken me?" His voice reached an angry crescendo as he cried out the same helpless words that Jesus did when He was dying on the cross, when He felt abandoned by God. Papa repeated the question louder and louder as the tide washed in and receded, erasing the tracks that his fingers had traced.

Before Bethel, the trip back to Texas had always been full of reminiscences. We'd laugh as we shared different versions of *Remember when Papa did this?* This time, we waited silently in the minivan as Papa walked back from the beach. Ma and Caleb had come back to the car after Papa's words had broken into sobs, after he'd been lying prostrate on the sand for minutes that dragged on.

Papa didn't say anything either as he climbed in, jerked the car into gear, and pulled away from the ocean. In radio static and silence, we sped down streets that pressed in on us and turned down a highway that unfolded into more monotony. An hour ticked away without anyone uttering a word — although the words from Papa's prayer on the beach seemed to echo through the upholstery. Papa was never a man to admit when he was wrong — he fought against facts about the order of presidents or the population of the towns we visited for revival season. *Well, just because that book says it's true doesn't mean it really is.* It was his standard response to avoid saying that he'd made a mistake. But he couldn't rely on that excuse now. He had finally broken — I had been the one to break him — but there was no joy in the admission.

Papa stopped for gas at a station about six hours away from the ocean. The rest of us exhaled when he left the van, but we didn't say anything to fill the vacuum of silence. Ma made eye contact with me in the rear-view mirror, nodding her head toward the mini-mart. I took my cue to scuttle inside and use the restroom. I'd barely climbed back into the car before Papa accelerated and peeled away. The dull pain in my ribs became sharp as I knocked into the door. Papa was watching me as I winced, but his eyes revealed no sympathy.

We drove nonstop in the reverse direction — west instead of east — weaving in front of semis without signaling, going above the speed limit even when night fell. When Ma would have normally told him to stop at a hotel for the night, she let him continue driving.

A large sign loomed overhead: WELCOME TO TEXAS. There was no glory in going home — it felt like surrender as we passed drugstores and playgrounds and even the darkened steeple of Papa's church. A red light stopped us by the wrought-iron arches leading to the cemetery where Isaiah was buried. I wondered if Ma and Papa would turn to look in the direction of his grave, but their heads stayed glued to the traffic light. I craned my neck toward the right window and touched the glass, remembering the feel of the hard earth around his grave marker when I'd gone there with Mrs. Cade. When the light turned, Papa gunned the engine.

We arrived back at the house two and a half weeks after we left. Papa placed the minivan in park and killed the engine. We sat in the driveway; no one dared to make the first move. I waited for Ma to say the prayer that thanked God for bringing us safely home, but her mouth was sewn shut.

In the rearview mirror, Papa was looking back at me with a weary expression — the first time he'd held my gaze for more than just a few seconds on the drive home. One blink. Two.

"There will be no more of that," he finally said. "Right?" His voice had all the accumulated heft and weight of everything he'd wanted to say to me. *No more of that. That.* He had reduced everything I'd done to one word; he couldn't even get himself to say the word *healing.*

I held his gaze. The simplest thing would have been to tell him what he needed to hear, to pretend like my confession and absolution would restore him to the preacher and healer that he had once been. As though my healing was a sin that required absolution.

"Answer me, Miriam. Yes or no."

As though on a movie reel, I saw the future that he wanted for me — the future that he needed me to want. Like a shutter, my eyes closed — I felt the hands that would stay in the pockets of my homemade

384

starchy skirts without touching another forehead, the truths that I'd have to hold deep inside while I pretended Papa could still heal and I never could.

When the shutter opened again, my eyes bounced around the minivan — to Caleb whose eyes darted in their sockets, to Ma whose chin was resting on one palm, at sleeping Isaac, whose body was curled in on itself in the car seat like a comma, and finally to Hannah, who still managed to smile at me even after what had happened in Shelby. I saw her again, bleating on the ground, her eyes begging me to help her. Tipping forward in the seat, I swallowed the white heat and pain that came from my ribs and touched her clammy cheek — she leaned into my hand. I prayed this meant she was forgiving me.

I looked to the porch of the house, remembering the days I played on the front steps, writing my name in sidewalk chalk with ashy pastel hands, the epic games of hide-and-seek when I always beat Caleb, only coming back inside the house when Ma called my name. I had crossed a line, unmarked and unseen, and now those memories were on the other side. The Miriam I had been before had died in Shelby — saying no meant I would no longer sit on the porch after revival with Ma, feeling the numbness on my tongue after dipping it into an ice-cream cone. Would never again stand ankle-deep in lukewarm water playing baptism in an inflatable pool with Caleb, my skirt hitched up to my knees.

"Well?"

A *yes* would bring me out of exile, back into the fold, while a *no* would cast me into the wilderness, into the land of Ma's family and the nonbelievers that we prayed for. Then other memories came flooding back to me: the sweat above Micah's lip as she lay lifeless in front of me; the convulsion in Nadia's body as she pressed against the sink's ceramic basin, the trust in her eyes when she'd believed that I could take away her pain; the puff of Hope's first breath in my mouth and the tiniest rise in her chest as her skin turned pink; and then Ma, her forehead smooth when I touched it, slick with holy oil as the sign of the cross lingered on her skin long after my hand was gone. And there could be so many others.

"Miriam?"

I dipped my chin to my chest and closed my eyes, pressing the ice pack into my aching ribs. I whispered a prayer to God. Wind wafted into the minivan through the open windows, making goose bumps sprout on my skin, and I knew He was here with me. I opened my eyes, my gaze a laser on Papa's, and felt the answer tickling the edges of my mouth.

I took a deep breath and parted my lips to speak.

ACKNOWLEDGMENTS

Duvall Osteen, you believed in this book even when I had my doubts, and you have been its champion all the way through. Thank you for your ideas, enthusiasm, patience, support, and warmth; I can't imagine anyone else guiding me through this process. Carina Guiterman, your enthusiasm for this story came through during that first call, and your clear, precise vision and edits have shaped the novel into what it has become. Every moment that I've been able to work on this book with you has been a gift. Lashanda Anakwah, you have been a lifeline during this process, and I'm grateful for your quick responses and guiding hand throughout this journey. To Cat Boyd and Elise Ringo, thank you for all of your hard work on behalf of this book. Tristan Offit, thank you for designing a stunning cover that was better than I even imagined it could be. To the rest of the team at Aragi

389

Inc. and Simon & Schuster, thank you for the tireless work that you've done on behalf of my book.

To Julia Fierro, thank you for nurturing my early writing at Sackett Street and giving me confidence in my voice. In addition, before *Revival Season* was a book, it was a chapter and an incomplete idea, and there were a few people who saw it during its infancy and helped shape it into what it has become. Peter Ho Davies, you workshopped the first chapter in Napa and encouraged me to think about getting my MFA. The trajectory of my life changed after that week, and I'm forever indebted to you for your critical feedback, careful reading, and generosity through the years. In July 2014, my week in Taos as a Kimbilio Fellow came at a time when I needed solitude and community to turn this book into something more tangible. David Haynes, your vision for this community, along with your keen insight and wisdom during that week and beyond, helped this book in immeasurable ways. Sam Chang, before I attended Iowa, I was in your workshop at Napa in 2014. I was grateful for your insightful feedback and wise mentorship then, and I am even more grateful now after having had the opportunity to spend two years at Iowa with you.

Thank you for the ways that you have changed this book and my life.

I was the beneficiary of incredible teaching at the Iowa Writers' Workshop. Paul Harding, you were the first person to read an early draft of *Revival Season.* From that moment forward, you have believed in the possibilities of this book and in my ability to write it. Thank you for your belief in me and in the story I had to tell. Margot Livesey, you are the most generous and gracious person I have ever met. You have loved and believed in Miriam, always pushing me to make changes to the story to make her come alive. Miriam is better because of you — this book is better because of you — and I am better for having known you. Allan Gurganus, when you came to Iowa in the fall of 2016 and workshopped the first chapter of *Revival Season,* I couldn't believe my good fortune. Thank you for your generous guidance and wise feedback about those early pages that stayed with me through each revision of the book. Ayana Mathis, you have been an inspiration from the first moment that I was in your seminar, and I am so grateful that I ended my two years in Iowa with you at the helm of my workshop. Your lessons about the "aboutness" of my fiction and your urging to make my characters "be mean to one another" still resonate with me and make me a better writer. Finally, my time at Iowa would not have been nearly as enriching without Connie Brothers, Deb West, and Jan Zenisek. You are the heartbeat of the Workshop; thank you for making my time there so fruitful.

In addition to being taught by incredible writers, I was also fortunate enough to find my people in Iowa — people who were my social lifeline in Iowa City as well as wonderful readers for my fiction. Jade Jones, De'Shawn Charles Winslow, Will Shih, Regina Porter, Grayson Morley, Dawnie Walton, Afabwaje Kurian, Melissa Mogollon, Tameka Cage Conley, Derek Nnuro, Christina Cooke, and Jamel Brinkley: I am grateful for your friendship, support, and inspiration. You are amazing writers and incredible people; I'm honored to know you.

Thank you to the Rona Jaffe Foundation for giving me the financial support to focus on this novel while at the Iowa Writers' Workshop. Thank you also to Hedgebrook for giving me the time, space, and community to write in Whidbey Island.

Novels are conceived and written in seclusion, but they are nurtured in community; I have had the best communities surrounding me during the nine years that I've been writing *Revival Season.* Gabi Ryan, I'll never forget the conversation in your backyard when you pushed me to pursue my MFA. I am beyond grateful for your friendship and the way you have celebrated me all along the way. Bill Ryan, thank you for your friendship and for your time explaining all of my contracts. LaKimbre Brown, my travel buddy and amazing friend, this book has been with you in so many places across the globe. Thank you for always supporting my dream to become a novelist.

I am grateful for the love and support of my former school community at the Park School of Baltimore. In addition, to my past and present colleagues in the English department and at the rest of Lick-Wilmerding High School, I am so proud of your amazing work and am grateful to change lives with you every day. Thank you for your support of me and the book. I have also had the opportunity to find an amazing community of people who started out as colleagues and later became close friends. To Linnea Ogden and Josie Halpern-Finnerty, thank you for the firsts: you were two of the first readers of this book, and you were also the first to celebrate with me when I sold it. To Jennifer Selvin and Eric Guthertz, thank you for giving me feedback on draft after draft, and thank you for celebrating each milestone with me along the way. This journey has been sweeter because I've been able to share it with you. Finally, I can't believe that I was fortunate enough to find amazing friends where I worked: Jackie Spivey, Christine Godinez Jackson, Melissa Nagar, Cristal Ogletree, Rebecca Hong, Oscar King, Nate Lundy, and Michecia Jones — thank you for your support and love during this journey.

Over sixteen years of teaching in Phoenix, Baltimore, Iowa City, and San Francisco, I have had the opportunity to spend life with over a thousand young people who inspire me every single day. Although I was technically your teacher, you have taught me more life lessons than I could have ever imparted to you. It has been the biggest privilege of my life to be called your teacher.

To my family at the Movement, I have felt completely known and loved here; thank you for supporting me, giving me a safe place to be known, and helping me grow deeper in my faith. To my Wednesday women: Alicia Jay, Briana Clarke, Junia Kim, Debra White, Nadia Tsado, Divine and Praise Adesida, Chika Egbe, Lydia Clinton, and Patrice Reynolds, thank you for loving me, supporting me, and doing life with me.

The word "friend" doesn't even begin to approach what these three women have been to me. Marlissa Hudson, Tynesia Boyea-Robinson, and Demetria Elmore, you are my sisters — my chosen family. I don't know what I did to earn your unconditional love and support, but I never want a day to go by when I don't thank you for being incredible, amazing women who know me better than I know myself and push me to be the best version of that self. I can't wait to celebrate this book release with you!

I come from a big extended family of grandparents, aunts, great aunts, uncles, great uncles, and cousins who have loved me from the beginning and been instrumental in making me who I am. A piece of all of you is in me, and this novel is a testament to your enduring influence in my life.

To Angela Malone — my big sister — you were the first audience for many of my stories. I always hear your voice in my ear spurring me on and telling me that you believe in me, and that has made all the difference. I love you so very much. To Ava, Evan, and Lauren Malone, I am honored that I get to be your Auntie Monica. It has been one of the biggest joys of my life to watch you grow into the brave, smart, fearless, and kind young people that you are becoming.

Last, but definitely not least, to my mom and dad, Edna and Henry West. You read to me when I was little and helped me imagine worlds that existed in books. You fed my imagination, supported my creativity, nurtured my wild dreams, answered my incessant questions, and loved me unconditionally. Even when you haven't agreed with my decisions, you supported them. I have never known a love like the love you both have for me. Every word in every book that I will ever write belongs to you.

ABOUT THE AUTHOR

Monica West was born and raised in Cleveland, Ohio. She received her MFA from the Iowa Writers' Workshop in 2017, where she was a Rona Jaffe Graduate Fellow. She currently resides in Oakland, California.